What the critics are saying...

THREADS OF FAITH

"*Threads of Faith* is a sweet yet erotic love story of a man who is the perfect match to a very special woman. *Ms. Hill* has written a story that will linger in your heart long after the story is over." ~ *Sensual Romance Reviews*

MAKE HER DREAMS COME TRUE

Reviewer's Choice Award "*Make Her Dreams Come True* is like a multi-layer cake created by a master baker, with intriguing variety, sections of almost unbearable sweetness, the occasional tart layer, a few surprise ingredients, and a firm, solid foundation. It's erotic romance that touches the heart and mind as well as the libido." ~ *Scribes World*

4 ½ stars "*Make Her Dreams Come True* is an exceptionally moving and powerful story which I cannot praise highly enough. This is an incredibly hot and sensual story, but it is the emotional intensity *Ms. Hill* brings to the tale that touches the soul." ~ *Romance Studio*

BEHIND THE MASK

Board Resolution

5 Cups "…a collection of three stories from some of the best writers of women's romantic BDSM. While *Board Resolution* is a shocking story, it is a wonderful example of the relationship that can develop in a Dominant and submissive partnership, and how liberating it can be to surrender to another person, especially with someone who loves you passionately…" ~ *Coffee Time Romance*

Faith

and
Dreams

Joey W. Hill

ELLORA'S CAVE
ROMANTICA PUBLISHING

An Ellora's Cave Romantica Publication

www.ellorascave.com

FAITH AND DREAMS

ISBN # 1419953206
ALL RIGHTS RESERVED.
Threads of Faith Copyright© 2004 Joey W. Hill
Make Her Dreams Come True Copyright© 2002 Joey W. Hill

Cover art by Syneca

Trade paperback Publication March 2006

Excerpt from *Natural Law* Copyright © Joey W. Hill, 2004

Warning:

The following material contains graphic sexual content meant for mature readers. *Faith and Dreams* has been rated *E-rotic* by a minimum of three independent reviewers.

Ellora's Cave Publishing offers three levels of Romantica™ reading entertainment: S (S-ensuous), E (E-rotic), and X (X-treme).

S-*ensuous* love scenes are explicit and leave nothing to the imagination.

E-*rotic* love scenes are explicit, leave nothing to the imagination, and are high in volume per the overall word count. In addition, some E-rated titles might contain fantasy material that some readers find objectionable, such as bondage, submission, same sex encounters, forced seductions, etc. E-rated titles are the most graphic titles we carry; it is common, for instance, for an author to use words such as "fucking", "cock", "pussy", etc., within their work of literature.

X-*treme* titles differ from E-rated titles only in plot premise and storyline execution. Unlike E-rated titles, stories designated with the letter X tend to contain controversial subject matter not for the faint of heart.

Also by Joey W. Hill

ഔ

Contents

Threads of Faith

Make Her Dreams Come True

Threads of Faith

ഌ

Threads of Faith

∞

"I know you're there," the old woman murmured. She inched forward on her knees and pulled a handful of weeds from the tangle at the base of the rose bushes. The heavy clusters of blooms arched over her head, tickling her nape with their silk petals and her nose with their heavy fragrance.

"Ow!" She laughed and made a grab at the black paw that shot out from the cover of the hedge to bat at her hand. The claws had been sheathed. It was her instinctive jerk that caused her pain, knocking her hand into the thorns.

"Beezle, you are a menace. One of these days I'm going to have cat stew for dinner."

A whisper of breeze, a rustle, and she realized she had let down her guard. She spun around, a hand up, and the stone struck her forehead, propelling her frail body back into the bushes, thorns pricking through her light cotton dress like a bed of nails. She heard Beezle scramble away, frightened. She was frightened, too, because her head was spinning and she couldn't marshal her wits to raise a defense.

The laughter of teenagers was reassuring, their act of unkindness likely a fleeting gesture of bored cruelty as they pressed on to mischief deeper into the woods.

She was wrong. Another stone struck the bridge of her nose and she cried out, averting her face. The pain drove her to one knee.

"Ain't no one around to help you, you old witch." The jeer came from the trees. "You're all alone, and we're gonna get you!"

11

Cackling laughter. She struggled to right herself. If she could just focus, get her sense of balance together…

"Jesus fucking Christ!" A frightened yelp and a crash, as if someone had been tossed out of a tree. Was that a snarl?

Marisa staggered toward her door and stumbled over her garden tools. The world was blurry, and something warm and wet trickled down her forehead into her left eye and mouth. Metal and salt, substance of earth, of herself.

"Wards of earth, fire, water and wind, may your powers rise and blend. Take this home out of evil's view, Lord and Lady allow no harm to break through," she rasped, seeking to connect to the power. The concussion made the connection tenuous, and the wards flickered weakly, even where she could discern them on the clearing's edge. Fear clutched her low in her stomach. She'd not been this vulnerable in a long time.

A pair of feet came toward her. She crawled across the ground and clasped a rock, perhaps the same rock that had struck her. She could see the fragility of her blue-veined hand, the skin shimmering beneath her gaze. No, surely she was not that weak. The illusion spell had a life of its own. She had made sure it existed separate from her consciousness.

The feet, sizeable ones in hiking boots, were attached to long calves and a pair of muscular thighs. Her attacker had the physique of a lineman for the school football team. She tried to scramble away, but he caught her in one stride.

She squalled like Beezle and turned on him, the rock gripped in her fist. Even wounded, she was quick, but he was more so, and caught her wrist in a strong grip.

"Be easy, miss. They're gone. I ran them off. It's all right."

His voice stroked her frantic emotions, soothed them down, even as his hands gentled her physically. She felt his fingers stroke her hair. Not the brittle and sparse strands of an aging woman, but the raven, waist-length locks of her true form.

"No," she whispered. The only thing that could dissolve the spell was a more powerful witch, or a person who possessed True Sight.

"It's all right," he repeated, and gathered her to him. He lifted her off the ground easily, as if she were a child, and gave her the words of universal comfort, as empty as they might be. "I won't let anything happen to you."

Her heavy head wobbled onto his shoulder. His fingers tangled in her hair at her shoulder, his other hand curled around her thigh beneath her plain calico smock dress.

Men did not touch her. Most women did not. It was shocking, this easy familiarity of a man's hands upon her. People were afraid to touch a witch, even if they claimed not to believe she was one. They stood at her door with averted eyes and insisted they were there on a dare, or a lark. The way he held her was possessive, intimate, as if they knew one another far better than they did.

He stepped across the open threshold to her three-room home. "Where's your bed, miss?"

She shook her head. "Just put me down in the kitchen chair," she said. "Sitting up will help me get my wits about me."

"If you had your wits about you, you wouldn't be living out here in the middle of nowhere with no one to protect you."

She aimed a frosty glare at him, and collided with a sexual heat that startled her. It threatened to melt her ire before it could be vented.

He had eyes like Beezle's, a yellow-green, but more blended, a vibrant hazel. His hair was the brown of rich, dark earth, almost black. Brows like slivers of fine dark silk, and firm lips that looked somewhat angry at the moment, but once she saw him clearly, she wasn't afraid. His face had the strength of character immortalized by old film. Jimmy Stewart, Gary Cooper, Gregory Peck. The face of a white knight, a hero, the man who would never think to leave women and children behind, who would guard the back of a friend no matter the cost, who would face up to his mistakes with the same unflinching courage. He possessed the True Sight. To her trained gaze, it was as obvious as the fact he was a man. He would see through any spell, any deception, the smallest white lie.

He wore a brown soft twill shirt, and blue jeans. Not tight, but snug in the way that men of good physique wore them. He smelled like sweat and soap, and a light aftershave.

"My name is Conlon," he said, with a nod. "Conlon Maguire."

"Marisa," she responded automatically. "I'm fine now. I appreciate your kindness, but I don't need—"

"I was coming to see you."

"Oh." That startled her into silence. People only came to her door for one reason, and she found that reason hard to reconcile with the handsome, confident man standing in her kitchen.

He found a cloth in her sink, a basin of water she drew from the deep creek behind her home. "Here." He touched at the blood on the bridge of her nose, catching her chin to hold her still. He ignored the hand she latched onto his powerful wrist to tug his touch away.

"I can do it."

"I'm sure you can, but I want to do it, so be still, kitten, and stop squirming."

His shirt was open at the neck, so the fabric gapped with the forward cant of his body. She saw the smooth curve of a pectoral and a soft pelt of chest hair, narrowing down to a line over a flat, muscular stomach. After that it was shadows, as the shirt tucked into his waistband. She pulled her gaze away, back to his face, which was intent on hers, washing away the blood with small gentle pressures on her forehead, her nose, her lips. He cradled the side of her face as he moved downward. What would it be like to feel his fingers delve into her hair, tug her head back so that he could place those firm lips over hers?

The unexpected thought surprised her. Men did not interest her. This was her quiet world, the world she had created for herself with great effort and painful sacrifice. Her wits were just beyond her fingertips, waiting for her to reach out and reclaim control of them, and the situation.

He pushed back the hair over her left ear and the damp cloth slid there, touching in those tiny crevices. The trickle of blood and dirt down her neck went next as he moved his touch there. His thumb rubbed her jugular, his fingers curved around the side of her throat. Her wits moved a deliberate step out of reach as she discovered how sensitive her throat was to a man's caress.

Her cats rubbed against her in affection and slept close to her at night for companionship, but this man's hands made her think of wild, unsettling actions, far beyond affection. With little effort, she could imagine his body heat and strength curled around her as well as her cats, keeping them all safe while they dreamed.

Marisa surged out of the chair and clambered over his knee awkwardly to get into the more open space of the kitchen. He rose, and the kitchen shrank.

"How…how did you get here?"

"They told me it wasn't accessible by car, so I hiked in. I thought it odd, an elderly woman living so far from civilization. They didn't mention you." His gaze coursed down her body in a way that flustered her.

"You're teasing me, sir," she said coolly. "You and I both know you can see through the illusion I maintain. Further, I doubt someone who looks like you needs a potion to attract a woman. So perhaps you should tell me why you're really here."

He reached out, and the table behind her blocked her retreat. He caught his fingers in her hair, wrapped it once around his knuckles so she was tethered to him. He pulled her a step toward him.

"Based upon the illusion you maintain, Marisa, I'd say you already know that looks don't bring you everything you desire. Sometimes it brings things you don't want at all."

Like big, unsettling men in her kitchen. His body and hers were only a deep breath apart, and she felt their auras touching, exploring the shape of one another. Her fingers were itching to do the same, to tug his shirt from his waistband, feel the hard line of those muscles. She wanted to let her fingers glide through the soft hairs on his stomach and chest and get to know the hot skin and muscle beneath.

Despite the table, she did take a step back, and the legs scraped their complaint on the wood floor. There was a strange feeling in her chest, and it was moving lower. It grew more noticeable each time she drew in his scent and met those steady, hazel eyes.

Potion. He was here for a potion. What was the matter with her? Perhaps that rock had done her genuine harm. Perhaps she should consider a trip into town to the doctor.

"Even if I weren't here for a potion," he added, "you're stuck with me for awhile. I'm not leaving until I'm sure you're okay."

"You can't stay on my property if I tell you to leave," she said. "That's trespassing."

"Call a cop," he responded. "Oh, that's right. No phone." He glanced around. "No electricity." His fingers curled around the back of her neck, and she snapped her glance up to him, uneasy. "No way to call for help if you were injured, or needed help."

"You seem overly obsessed with my protection, Mr. Maguire," she managed. "If it makes you feel better, I have a two-way radio for emergencies, and I keep transportation in my shed, if I need it."

"A broom?"

She narrowed her eyes and jerked free. "I'm beginning to see why you need a potion."

When he smiled, she saw a dimple at the left corner of his mouth. "So you think you can help me, then?"

"The potion makes that decision. I just mix it. Belief is important to its success. If you're here as a joke, or on a dare, then the potion will be useless to you."

"What's the cost?"

"The potion also sets the price. The magic that fuels it speaks to me and tells me what it demands in exchange."

"That's convenient."

"That's how I acquired my mansion and Ferrari, Mr. Maguire," she said dryly, circling around the table to her cabinets. "It usually requires acts of service," she added. "Not donations to me. I am bound by its will, as much as the recipient. The seed of love must be there, and the person must be willing in their hearts to accept the potion's will. You can have a seat if you like. This will take a few minutes."

"Can I get things together for you?" He frowned, studying her unsteady movements, the cut on her head. "I told you, I'm not leaving until I'm sure you're all right. You can take your time."

"I'm fine, really. I'm getting my bearings back."

The sooner she made what he wanted and assured him of her health, the sooner he would go, him and his disturbing presence. So she opened the doors of the large oak cabinet on the wall, revealing a larder full of bottles and jars with a rainbow of liquid and plant contents.

"I need to focus for a few moments in silence," she said, her back to him.

"All right," he murmured, and the tone of his voice told her he was watching her, with a penetrating intensity that sank into her skin and bones like the warmth of the sun. She drew a deep breath. Despite her personal preferences, she did not block him. No matter Conlon Maguire's arrogance, at the moment he was part of the Web that bound them all, the body of the Lord and Lady, one of the many cells of the blood that ran through Their Veins. She accepted his presence, his life force, into the circle of her own. She let the magic feel his shape and form, his worthiness, purpose and desires.

The exercise always gave her a necessary sense of a person. Usually it was a fleeting touch, like the brushed kiss of acquaintances. In this instance, the soul of Conlon Maguire reached out and surrounded hers, and pulled her into him. She felt the man from the inside out.

He was a man of True Sight, as she had already sensed. A man who would always protect those weaker than himself. A man generous in opening his heart, but who had never given his heart away to a woman. A man who liked to laugh, a physical man, a man who would not be denied what he wanted. Heat washed through her, and for a moment she was in the body of the woman he sought. His chest pressed against the softness of her breasts. His hands clasped her waist, his palms sliding down to cup the cheeks of her backside, holding her against his rigid desire. She felt it move against the quickening flesh between her thighs. His tongue claimed hers. The name of the woman hovered on his lips. Marisa struggled to hear that name, though she had never before asked or tried to discover the name of a person for whom a potion was mixed.

She started out of the vision, her pulse pounding.

"Are you all right?"

Marisa nodded, a quick jerk, and held up her finger to keep him back. "The magic has agreed to mix a potion for you."

With unsteady hands, she withdrew three of the four ingredients she would need and set them on the sideboard.

The potion didn't often call for the fourth ingredient, and so she turned to drag her chair over to use it as a stepping stool. She bumped into him. He stood behind her, considering all her bottles and jars. Conlon looked down at her. "Which one, kitten?"

She frowned, and pointed. He reached up and over her, and took down the large jar with one hand, putting it into both of her waiting ones.

Something curled in her stomach, unsettling but not unpleasant, roused by the unfamiliar sensation of being able to count on someone's help, someone's strengths balancing out her needs.

She nodded courteously and skirted around him, going to where the other ingredients waited. Spreading out a clean linen cloth, she laid the herbs she had chosen on it. Marisa took up her athame, a curved and sharp blade of stainless steel she had fired and stamped herself, and cut the proper measure. She dropped the plants into a mortar and pestle carved of white stone.

He had turned from his study of her stores to a study of her, and she felt a need to fill the silence that seemed too comfortable to be having with a stranger.

"So, why will this woman not have you?"

While she did not ask names, she did sometimes ask other things, to help the potion along by giving the seeker an additional dose of common sense. In this case, she suspected her motives were not quite so selfless.

"I think she will, but she's very unique. I need a special approach, something to help me get my foot in the door."

Marisa nodded. She ground the herbs with deliberate turns of the pestle, infusing them with the power of the Lord and Lady and of the four elements. When she was satisfied, she scooped the herbs out and dropped them into the small cauldron of water she had simmering on a gas burner. Curious, she dipped a spoon into it to get a sense of what color the steeped mixture would take.

This time it was going to be Marisa's favorite, a sparkling amethyst, but the sight of the hue startled her. Amethyst was the color of strongest intent. This man's request was closely aligned with the Lord and Lady's Will, and great good would emanate along the strands of the Web from its success. It was almost a certainty that, with or without the potion, his suit for his chosen lady would prevail.

Why should she be surprised? Only those of pure hearts, coupled with great courage and integrity, were blessed with the True Sight. Perhaps that was one of the reasons she felt so disturbed around him. There was nothing she could hide from him, and yet he was not a man from whom one *needed* to hide.

She took the small cauldron from the burner and set it on a quilted square potholder on the sideboard. The linen cloth went over the top to protect it from debris in the air while it steeped, and to block the steam from scorching her face as she leaned over it. Marisa placed her palms flat on either side of the cauldron, cleared her mind, opened her energy centers, and drew in the aroma, waiting for the magic to tell her the price of the potion.

The answer was immediate, a rush of information and images that were clear and impossible to misunderstand. Regardless, Marisa asked again. The same answer came, just as clearly. Emphatically.

She took her hands away and stepped back. She was a servant of the Craft, a priestess, and she was obedient to the Will of the Light. She understood that Its ways might be beyond her understanding, but that they were what was meant to be. This was the first time she had ever thought the Lord and Lady might have fried a circuit.

"Problem?"

Conlon had taken a seat on the other side of the table to watch her finish the preparations, and now her desperate eyes flitted to him. He should have looked out of place in her kitchen, but he didn't. In fact, she could well imagine him being there everyday, watching her with those intent hazel eyes that became gilded verdigris in the shadowed light inside her home.

She continued to stare at him, speechless, her face drained of color. Frowning, he rose and came around the table. It drew her attention to the broadness of his shoulders, the lean strength of his thighs, the fine structure and power of the man beneath the clothes. He reached forward, as if to lift the cloth and see what had caused her such consternation.

"Don't." The word snapped out of her like a whip. "You can't touch it until you hear its cost."

"All right." He settled back, his hips propped against her table. He crossed his arms across his chest and hooked his fingers under his armpits. She was distracted by the firm, unsmiling curve of his lips. For some reason, she wanted to reach out, trace them with her fingertips, feel their texture.

"Tell me," he prompted, lifting a brow at her startled jerk.

Just say it, and it will be over. He can refuse, and it will be nothing to you.

That was a lie and she knew it. The color of this potion said his intent would serve the highest good. The love he pursued, if consummated and brought to be, would enhance the Pattern and the Will of the Lord and Lady. How could she refuse? How could she possibly find the courage to convince him if *he* refused?

"You must lie with me by full moonrise tonight. That is the potion's price."

Surprise crossed his features, but not the pigment-draining shock she had experienced. He straightened, freeing his arms, drawing her eye to the way his fingers slid across his own skin. "You're sure."

"The voice is clear enough." She rubbed her temple. "You know I don't lie. You have the right to refuse, and the potion becomes powerless. The Lord and Lady's Will is focused through the potion, but it's a tool. You may find your desires will prevail without it, if They support your cause."

There, that was fair. Hadn't she thought much the same thing when she first explored his soul? "If you believe in honesty, the woman you desire may be displeased with the price you paid to win her heart, regardless," she added, a bit tartly.

Conlon gave her an even look and stepped forward. Marisa did not move, her body frozen like an anxious doe. Her head tilted back as he got closer so she could still meet his gaze. She had her hand over the linen cloth, and could feel the heat of the cauldron's lip beneath it. He laid his hand over hers, covering her fingers and bringing his own in shared contact with the potion's vessel.

"What about you, Marisa?" He reached out, touched her chin with a fingertip. "You don't have to accept the potion's price. I want the love of this woman, but I won't have it at the price of forcing your affections."

While his words did not ease the quaking in her belly, it reminded her that he was an honorable man. An honorable man deserved a truthful response.

"I serve the Light, Conlon, and if it says this is the price of your potion, and the love you seek serves Their Will, then I will obey it. I know it serves a greater purpose than my own fears."

"Fears?" His brow furrowed, and his touch became a firm hold on her delicate jaw. "Tell me what you fear."

"I just…" She couldn't avert her face, but she did shift her gaze to the wall, feeling heat wash over her skin under his fingertips. "I've never done this, Conlon." She crossed her arms over her body, a protective gesture she knew suggested vulnerability, but she couldn't stop herself from making the gesture of self-comfort. "I'll be fine," she said, more firmly. "I just need a little time to get used to the idea."

He studied her, and his hand gentled, stroking her cheek, so she looked at him. "You *will* be fine. I won't hurt you, Marisa. I'll make sure you feel only pleasure, no pain."

His easy acquiescence startled her. "Are you sure? What of this woman? Won't she…"

"The people in town hold your power and your potions in very high regard, Marisa. You've told me my cause is true, and that the potion has named a price. I want this woman for my own."

She nodded, a quick dip of her head. "Then you must say you accept the potion's price, out loud." She put her hand back on the cauldron, over his this time. The firm skin, the light layer of hair on his knuckles, felt different to her, intriguing.

"I accept this potion's price," he said formally, his gaze never leaving hers. "Because the woman I wish to claim is the total of my desires. I knew the moment I heard her name that she is mine. I knew, when I first saw her, that she is the one. The only."

He was wrong. He would cause her pain, a shrieking banshee within the hollow emptiness of her chest. To have someone want her like he wanted, that was beyond anything Marisa could hope for in her reality. From the time she was born, isolation had been required for her survival. Now she must bear to have such a man in her arms for nearly a full day, knowing he was only there for another, and let it shatter her, as she knew it must.

She slid her hand off of his. "The potion is now charged. When you leave me, I will put it in a flask, and you will share it with this woman, and the Lord and Lady's Will be done." She found her palms nervously damp, and wiped them on her skirt.

"Marisa." Conlon bent his knees to catch her eye, a reassuring look on his face. He took her hands in both of his. "I assume the potion doesn't require us to hop on each other like rabbits. We can take some time to get to know each other. Enjoy each other. The sun's still high in the sky."

Enjoy a taste of something she might never have again. But every day was like that, wasn't it? Today might be the last day she got to watch dew melt off a flower, or see Beezle chase a butterfly across the yard. If today was all she had, how could she spend any part of it regretting what she might not have tomorrow?

She took a deep breath, nodded her head.

Quirking his brow to give her some warning, Conlon exerted a gradual but inexorable pressure on their linked fingers, bringing her closer to him, until she leaned into his body. He folded one of her palms low on his waist, over his hipbone. She felt his warmth, the softness of the shirt, and the firmness of him under her touch.

"Your willingness is a precious gift to me," he said. His voice dropped, got rougher in a way she liked, though she didn't know why. "Every man hopes to be a woman's first lover, to experience her innocence."

"To take it."

"To open and pleasure it, together." His face drew closer to her upturned one, and his arm slid around her waist, gathering her up against him.

He did not let her other hand go when he brought her to him. As his arm came behind her, he took her hand with it, turning her wrist so her elbow bent and her arm folded up behind her back. The position pushed her breasts up and forward, displaying them on the hard platform of his chest. Increasing the pressure, he pushed her up onto her toes, his fingers laced through hers at the small of her back. The ends of his fingers curled into the skirt and dug into the thin elastic band beneath, so she felt a tug on her panties against the sensitive cheeks of her bottom.

"I'm afraid," was all she managed. His lips touched hers at the moment she formed the words, so his tongue eased between her parted lips, and his mouth closed over hers, sealing in the heat.

She had been kissed once years ago by a boy who had been dared to kiss her. That swipe of clammy lips was so far from Conlon's kiss that she forever discarded the idea of even calling it a kiss.

Surely the bones had melted in her body, because all of a sudden she couldn't stand on her own. She lifted her hand from his hip and gripped his shirt at his ribs for balance. He caught the back of her head in his large palm, his fingers in her hair, and deepened the thrust of his tongue. He ran it along the edges of her teeth, the inside of her cheek, learning her, and stroked the quivering surface of her tongue with his when he was done with that.

His body was all a new experience to her, the hard muscle, the musk of sweat from hiking through the woods, male. No doubt of the last, as the strength of his hold against the small of her back pressed her against a hard ridge growing larger under straining denim. It rubbed against her belly, and her hips rocked forward in an instinctive reaction to it. The place between her legs contracted with a startling sensation that flooded her body.

A key turned, tumbling open a locked room of her subconscious. It was as if she were a person who had wandered in a desert for so long that she did not know she was thirsty, until someone offered her a glass of ice water. Her thirst was abrupt, all-consuming, but she found herself staring at that glass, lacking the knowledge of how to reach out and bring it to her lips.

It was disturbing to have to depend on him. She was helpless to do anything but let him lead. Academically, Marisa knew the urges of the human body, but she had divorced herself from her own. With one kiss, he was reconciling her with them.

His middle finger straightened and pressed against the thin gauze fabric of her skirt, even as his other fingers remained intertwined with hers at her lower back. Insinuating the fabric of the skirt, along with his finger, under the waistband of her panties, he rubbed a small vertical stroke in the dip at the top of her buttocks. Marisa gasped into his mouth. She wiggled against the touch, against his strength, increasing the friction. He tightened his grip and her feet left the floor. When he settled the apex of her thighs directly over that hard ridge in his jeans, she moaned at the pressure. Panic filtered in, as she floundered in the wash of unfamiliar sensations.

"Stop," she managed against his mouth. "Please, let go… Let me down." She turned her head so her cheek was pressed hard against his jaw, hiding her face. His fingers stilled, his unsteady breaths moving the loosened strands of her hair against her skin. Slowly the grasp of his fingers in her scalp eased off and became a caressing stroke. His chest expanded beneath her breasts, a slow, deep breath, and he let her down, one inch at a time. She had to bite her lip as that hard part of him dragged along her vibrating tissues.

He did not let her feet touch the ground. As she slid down those excruciating inches, his thigh came forward, parting her legs. She came to a halt seated on that column of muscle that shifted against her throbbing center.

"Holy Mother, you could make a man lose his mind with one kiss, Marisa. No wonder they call you a witch."

"I suspect that's not the reason," she whispered. His eyes were now pure gold, because heat had melted the green, like the summer sun burnishing everything in a meadow. His lips were moist from her mouth.

He held her fast as she made to wriggle free. "No, Marisa. If we're going to do this, I want you to be thinking about having me there, and keeping your mind on it. Do you know what this is?" He lifted his ankle, so he increased the pressure of his thigh between her legs.

"Of course." She tried to be casual, but knew her flushed wild expression and trembling body betrayed her. "I'm a virgin, Conlon, not ignorant."

"Tell me, then."

"It is…" She blew out a breath, shot him a glare that seemed to amuse him, "it's my vagina."

He smiled, passed a thumb over her lip. "You said that so primly, like my sex ed teacher, Mrs. Patterson."

"You never needed a sexual education teacher," she retorted. "Etiquette class wouldn't have been amiss, however."

"You also speak like you've spent more time reading than talking," he observed. "All formal. 'Amiss'. I haven't heard that word used in years." He increased his hold on the hand he still held pinned at the small of her back and began to rock his foot, heel to toe, counterbalancing it with the strength of his arm so he was rocking her back and forth on his long leg.

"How about this, Teacher?" His teeth nipped at her ear. "Pussy. Cunt. I like both of those. Cunt reminds me of a cave, deep underground, with a hot spring. The steam condensing and glistening on the slick inner walls, creating a smell of heat and earth, the way your cunt would smell if I buried my nose in it. Or pussy, like a pussy willow, soft under my fingertips, but round and firm too, the size of a finger pad, like your clit is." With a ripple of muscle, he stroked her in that exact spot, so no further English lesson was needed to identify it for her.

"I said I needed to go slow," she said desperately, clutching at his shoulder for balance as he worked his leg against her pussy.

"I plan to, Marisa. I won't try to claim your maidenhead until nightfall, and it's barely lunchtime now. I want you wet and aroused, so you won't be afraid."

"It's...you're making it hard for me to think," she said.

He smiled, though there was a tension around his mouth, and his eyes were a fire of desire that was almost as effective on her senses as his leg's movement. He began to bounce his leg gently. Since he kept her seated hard against him with that one relentless hand, each impact sent a ripple to her womb. Her breasts moved freely beneath the loose smock and his eyes followed their quivering movement.

"I...I need to know more about you," she managed, trying to fight off the spiral of sensations that screamed from that jarring focal point between her legs.

He let her go abruptly, and caught both hands in her hair. She fell against him, but froze at the ferocious need in his face. His mouth hovered just above hers, touching her with the heat of his breath as he spoke. "No man has ever had you, truly?"

"You know I speak the truth," she said, her body trembling against his.

"Yes," he said. "But your body responds like a woman born for sensual pleasure."

She pushed away, shaking her head, and he took her hand, holding it in a secure grip. She moved as far back as that link would allow and tried to keep her attention on his face, rather than the heat and need vibrating off that powerful body.

"Please, Conlon, I can't. This feels too fast. My body understands your desires and appears all too willing to capitulate, but I have to face myself in the mirror when you're gone. Whether it be the Lord and Lady's Will or no, I need to get my balance."

"All right." In a gesture that surprised her with its tenderness, he raised both her hands, brushed his lips across her knuckles. "So how do you want to do this?"

She pushed her hair off her forehead, a confused scrubbing motion. "What do you do for a living?"

He smiled, and something in her stomach tilted like the corners of his mouth. "Security. Professional bodyguard."

She blinked. "Like Secret Service?"

"Not anymore. I do private jobs. Businessmen traveling in countries with unstable governments, celebrities being stalked, witness protection work occasionally."

A protector, a white knight. Her initial vision had been more accurate than she expected.

"So you don't have much time to develop a relationship. The potion's a way to sidestep all that."

"Now see, that's why I didn't want to ease off," he said, tightening his grip on her fingers. "You want to retreat behind that serpent tongue of yours. It's a lot sweeter when it's occupied with something, like mine."

"I want to take a swim in the creek and get cleaned up." She backed away, keeping the tether of their arms taut. "I've been gardening all morning. I'm sweaty and dirty, and I've got blood drying in my hair."

"So you do." His gaze went back to the spot, and he released one hand to touch her there, gently, on the sore area, though the slightest pressure made her wince. "Okay, let's go do that."

"What? I meant—" Marisa had to swallow the rest of the statement because he was guiding her out the door. He stepped neatly over Beezle, now stretched across the sun-drenched threshold. The black cat seemed utterly unconcerned by the big man's presence in their home. Marisa tripped over him, and the cat gave her an aggrieved look.

"As familiars go, he's not tremendously intimidating," Conlon observed, dragging her along with him around the corner of the house, headed for the creek where she did her washing. He paused, glanced down at her. "There's not much to screen you here from Peeping Toms."

"I don't get many visitors, and those I do see an old woman. They're not interested in watching an eighty-year-old crone bathe."

"Maybe because they're looking at the flesh, not the woman. You'd be beautiful at any age, Marisa."

What was it about that steady gaze and set mouth that made her believe him? It raised that pain in her heart again, that futile wish for someone who would say such words to her, for her. Someone who wouldn't be afraid of her, who would be willing to stand by her as the inevitable changes of time altered her body, but not her mind. Not her need to be loved and cherished, not the need to be thought beautiful and worthy of love.

Such a person would be a quiet man. Perhaps a bookish sort with wire-rimmed glasses that liked to garden, like her. Certainly not a large, overbearing brute of a man with gentle, powerful hands and a mouth that turned her brain into a bowl of soup.

"How about I sit here while you bathe? Do you need a towel, soap?" At her look, he raised a shoulder. "If we've both accepted the potion's terms, I'm going to see you unclothed eventually. Wouldn't it be easier to get used to it, in a way like this, where you've got some distance from me?"

"Do you always take over?" she demanded.

He slid his hands into the back pockets of his jeans and cocked a hip, studying her. The posture only enhanced the size of his chest, the pull of the cloth against the impressive pectorals. "You said you wanted to take a bath," he pointed out, as if that were a reasonable response to her question, rather than an absolutely irrelevant point.

She turned her back on him to face the waters of the creek. The midday song of the cicadas vibrated patterns against the heavy summer air. She heard the far-off call of a hawk, and smelled the mint in her nearby herb garden.

Conlon let her be a moment, as she watched the current move. The shallows gurgled over slick rocks and dampened the sand on the banks. The deeper waters in the center moved in a tranquil but inexorable progress toward their destination, the Broken Sound River, a hundred miles to the south, which would eventually pour into the Atlantic.

Is this what she wanted? The potion had set the price, and she had never questioned it, but Conlon had asked her what *she* wanted. He had given her the choice. She was just scared. She had not been this close to another person, had not spent this much time with one, in a long time. Marisa now knew how to keep herself from shattering and letting in the images that could destroy her mind, as they had come close to doing too many times. Intimacy had the power to undermine her efforts, strip down her shields. Conlon already could see through her illusion magic. Could she protect herself and honor the potion?

She steadied herself with a mental shake. She had to trust the Lord and Lady knew what They were doing. She would have to trust Conlon.

As if he knew the conclusion she had reached, he moved. She heard him approach her, his hiking shoes moving deliberately over the ground. His hands, large and capable, settled on her shoulders, and rested there a moment. Gathering her hair in one hand, he pushed it over her left shoulder, revealing her nape and the fragile joining of her right shoulder to her neck.

She watched the water and trembled as his fingers unhooked the row of buttons down the back. The dress was loose and could easily lift over her head, but she did not stop him from working each button through its eyelet, his knuckles brushing the bumps of her spine and the shallow channel of it as he worked his way to her waist. When he pushed the sleeves down her unresisting arms, the bodice tumbled to her waist and pooled low on the flare of her hips, one button away from dropping the dress to her ankles.

The warm summer air and his breath mixed, touching her bare shoulder, and then his lips were there, tasting her flesh at that sensitive juncture. She had her head bowed, so she watched gooseflesh prickle up along the tops of her breasts. The shape and color of her nipples shifted, from a soft pale pink, like impatiens growing in the shade provided by an oak's canopy, to a deep, sun-kissed mauve bud.

She stayed very, very still. Being touched at all, let alone being touched like this, was new to her, and she wasn't sure if there was a right way to react. His lips felt good on her neck. They felt wonderful there.

His light kiss turned into a nibble, and her nipples grew fuller and longer, like stamens attracting the ministrations of the plush-backed bumblebee. Only in this case, the flower's response to heat attracted the stroke of Conlon's fingers. She tensed as his hands cupped her breasts, and the thumbs rubbed over the tips. She shuddered, her bare shoulder blades making contact with his shirt front, her bottom brushing the crotch of his jeans and tops of his thighs, causing those fingers to tighten.

"A further lesson in vocabulary, Teacher," he said against her ear. His hands lifted her breasts, brought them together before her eyes with the reverence of an offering to the gods. "These are the most beautiful tits I've ever seen. When I see your nipples tight like this, I want to suck on them until you come, just from the pull of my mouth."

When his palms slid down to the curve of her hips, it left her breasts aching. She felt the lingering imprint of his hands as if they were still there. With a flick, another button was free. The garment fell to her ankles, leaving her standing in her panties. His thumbs hooked in their elastic and slid them down her thighs. She had to turn and place a hand on his shoulder to balance herself as she stepped out of them. Rolling them into a neat ball, he folded them up in her dress, laying them to the side. His hand at her hip held her as he straightened. She stared down at her left bare breast, raised up higher than the right by the pressure of his body against it.

"Now." His voice was husky above her ear, his jawline brushing the crown of her head. "Go wash for me. I want to watch you."

Marisa swallowed. Took one step, then another, away from the shelter and imposition of his body. She focused on the creek, its laughing banks, its somber and thoughtful depths.

She kept a covered basket near the edge and she bent, her long hair falling forward and brushing her knees as she retrieved the soap and cloth there. His indrawn breath drew her gaze back to him. He stood stock still, his gaze coursing over her heart-shaped bottom and what her bent position revealed to him. Straightening quickly, flushing, she stepped into the water, the familiar warm mud sucking at her toes. Minnows brushed her calves as they scampered out of her path.

The water rose to her hips and then her waist. It was above her head from here, so she dropped below the surface to wet her hair. Swimming a few strokes, she rolled over beneath the water's surface, feeling in wonder the different texture of the water on her heated, aroused skin.

She knew about sex the way she knew how to mix vinegar and water to make a universal cleaner. She did not create the elements, did not truly understand how bringing them together achieved such a simple but effective purpose, but she knew how to make it happen. Her potions helped the process of sex indirectly, but it was never something she had understood as a participant. The unfocused yearnings of her body, particularly strong in the spring when so many animals came together around her in mating rituals, merely amused and puzzled her.

There was nothing amusing about her body's instant reaction to Conlon Maguire. Men had come often to the cottage seeking potions, some handsome, but she had never felt attraction, not even unvoiced admiration for a well-toned body. Of course, perhaps it was Conlon seeing her as she actually looked that roused her awareness of him as a man. Or perhaps it was the blasted potion placing such an unexpected condition on its price that had her focused on her up-until-now dormant libido.

She heard something. A voice, shouting? Marisa emerged in a turbulent wake caused by Conlon's splashing. He had come in to his waist, the water lapping at his hips, his face a worried mask as he called her name.

She paddled toward him, back to where she could stand, the soap in her hand. "It's all right," she said, a bit impatient with him. "I swim here everyday." She kept her knees bent as she moved into the shallows, so she wasn't exposed.

"I didn't realize it was that deep, and then you just vanished."

His expression softened her. His concern for her showed in his struggle to rein back his anxiety, and temper the edge of it in his voice.

"I'm all right," she said. Her gaze flickered to his wet jeans. A shy smile came through, despite her efforts to prevent it. "I didn't mean to make you jump in."

The corner of his mouth lifted in a wry gesture she liked. "My own fault. Occupational hazard. Always assume the worst."

He moved forward, lapping the water around her shoulders. Marisa watched him come to her, stared up at him as he put his hands on her upper arms and lifted her.

When she stood, she was in water that wavered at her hips, just above her pubic bone, and the dark hair there could be seen, just below the water's surface. The creek's soft tears slid down her breasts from the silken skeins of her hair resting on her shoulders.

One fingertip reached out, followed the track of a bead of water. It rolled down the outer curve of her breast, under it, over the ripple of her rib cage, and past her navel. His thumb brushed that shallow connection to her mother, and every mother of her lineage through her. The drop went into the water, but his hand stayed above the water line, tracing that indentation, the soft but defined rim, and caressed the tiny tight folds inside. Her stomach contracted under his hand.

"Conlon—"

"Give me the soap."

He took her handmade jasmine-and-orange-scented cake of soap from her hand to lather his hands. He passed the soap back into her palm, for he apparently wanted to have both of his hands upon her. Marisa couldn't dredge up a single protest to the idea.

The water they stood in was mid-thigh level on him. He had gotten the bottom of his shirt wet, so it clung to his abdomen. The wet jeans drew her eye to the way they stretched across his hips and sculpted out the groin area, the weight of his genitals.

His soapy hands started on her hair, working the scent of flowers into it. His touch made it hard to think, but she had spent twenty-three years learning that a person who could not be a part of society had to depend on herself. She had to pull her weight and contribute to the potion's success as much if not more than he did. If she was ignorant, she would have to learn, and learn quickly. There was nothing to be so apprehensive about. Animals, people, everyone did this. It would certainly be easier than learning how to make her own soap, plant a successful garden, or dig her own septic system.

"What do you call your..." She gestured vaguely toward his crotch. At his raised brow, she flushed.

"Well." She groped for his logic. "If I'm going to see it eventually, I should know what you call it. I mean, I know what it's called, but I know…from what you said inside, that you think of these things differently. Stop laughing at me."

He worked his expression from a grin into a suppressed smile.

"That's my cock, Marisa."

"Okay." She closed her eyes as his strong hands massaged the soap into her shoulders. Reaching out to him for balance was hard, but holding on wasn't. She caught her fingers in his shirt just above the waistband of his jeans and rested her wrists on his hipbones.

Sexual longing merged with pure pleasure as his hands worked magic on her shoulders and neck, and she arched, almost purring at the bliss of his soothing touch. Then his hands worked down over her breasts, soaping them, and she caught her lip between her teeth. She breathed through her mouth in shallow spurts as he massaged them, weighed and fondled them, squeezed them until her hold on his shirt became a tight clench.

"A man needs all the cold water he can get around you, Marisa," he muttered, but she didn't open her eyes to ask what he meant, surrendering all senses to his fingertips and what he could do with those hands. He seemed to be able to drive away her worries and rouse her body in this amazing way without disrupting her carefully managed protections. She hadn't known she would be allowed to feel this, not without the pain coming in as well. But a person of pure heart like Conlon didn't have any pain to drive into her.

Her eyes opened when his soapy fingers dipped beneath the water's surface and stroked through her curls, finding her…what did he call it? Pussy, or cunt. She liked the way he said both words. It made her imagine his mouth hovering just above that part of her, coming closer until his lips and tongue were upon the slick folds as he whispered the words. *Pussy.*

Cunt. She would open to him, as if those were the words of truth that would win him the right to take all that was there.

His fingers worked the soap over her clitoris, slid down over her opening. She gasped, and her grip moved to tough denim as his fingers worked her, not allowing her to close her legs against the rising, coiling need he stirred, his large hand not permitting her any escape.

"Conlon—"

"You're going to turn this into a hot spring, kitten. Gush your heat over my fingers."

Her toes strained upward, taking her higher out of the water, as if she was trying to get away from his touch, but she didn't want to get away. Something rushed over her, shooting up through her, faster than she could muster a defense against it.

He used her elevated position to get the hand further under her, move the heel of it against her clit. He massaged her in circles as his devilishly knowledgeable fingers played all around the outside of her pussy and dipped within, ticking the base of the clit from the inside.

"No,…I,…no…" Her hand flailed, splashing hard and awkward into the water. Her feet slipped out from under her, and his arm caught her around the waist, bringing her close and holding her up. The anchor allowed him to keep ruthlessly manipulating her, his fingers the pounding of raindrops beneath the water's surface. The wave of feeling crashed over her, arching her back in his arms. She cried out her passion, a wild lagoon bird, her pale body writhing like a flash of outstretched wings.

"Conlon, please…" She pushed against him and pulled him to her at once, as he worked the last spasms through her body. He bent and fastened his teeth on her exposed throat, a gentle, possessive pressure that made her mewl in yearning wonder. The emotional sensation rolled through her, spiraling and twisting together with the physical.

At length he raised his head. She was cradled in his arms, floating, her feet off the ground. His face was all that was in her vision and she couldn't look beyond him, did not want to do so.

"Let's get you rinsed, kitten," he said, his voice thick, almost violent in its need. "Close your eyes."

His mouth covered hers, and he took them both beneath the water's surface, his body wrapped around her, his fingers moving over her, caressing the soap from her skin, from the soft waving silk of her hair. Marisa held onto him. She'd lost the function of her muscles, including those of her vocal cords.

She didn't need any of them, though, for a moment later he was striding from the water, carrying her in his arms, the sun on her bare skin.

"I want to dry you, and then I want to dress you. I want to do everything for you, and to you. I want you to let me. Say yes."

Marisa closed her eyes and turned her face against the pulse beating in his throat rather than answering, making silence her acceptance. She didn't know if her shields were even in place. For the moment, she was dependent on him for protection, and she could only hope he would not be the key to the destruction of her mind she had always feared.

He set her down to dry her off, and she simply held on, unable to stand without his aid. He said nothing, but she felt his attention as if he were speaking a hundred thoughts in her head. She was mute, listening to the rush of whispered images that came through his touch on her body. He lifted her and she simply watched his face, feeling no need to say anything. She closed her eyes when he pressed a kiss to her forehead, and then there was a shadow as he crossed the threshold into her house.

He shouldered past the woven cloth dividing her bedroom from the living area, and found where she hung her clothes, behind a curtain she'd made of dried herbs and grasses, giving her clothes the fragrance that clung to her skin.

She didn't have many clothes, and most were sewn by her, simple shift dresses comfortable and appropriate for an old woman. Toward the back, however, was an outfit she had worn only once. It had been a gift from Laraset, the witch who had taught Marisa her craft as well as ways to protect herself. Laraset had been a tarot reader and seamstress on the Renaissance Fair tour before she fell in love with Kohana, a Sioux medicine man. Her gift to Marisa had been a gift of that time in her life, her "time of discovery", she had called it. It was this outfit Conlon lifted out now as Marisa sat naked on the bed watching him, her hair falling around her, covering her breasts and pooling in her lap.

When he turned to her, still clothed in wet jeans and shirt, and her completely naked, she felt even more vulnerable.

"I'd like you to wear this," he said. "I want to see you in a young woman's clothing."

There was a curious lassitude to her limbs and he seemed aware of it, for he laid the clothes on the bed and began to help her dress without asking. He threaded the linen shirt over her head and helped her find the sleeves. It was a peasant blouse with a wide scooped neck. When he slid the velvet skirt over her head and pulled it down to her hips, it tightened the fabric of the shirt over her upper torso. The untied drawstring allowed the neckline to dip so it was just above the line of her nipples. The fabric was transparent. Why that felt more provocative than sitting naked before him, she could not say, but before she could adjust it, he caught her hand.

"No, let me see them," he said. He lifted the last piece of the outfit, a corset to go over the blouse. He drew her to her feet and turned her so she faced the bed, and guided her hands through the armholes. The corset's neckline was even lower than the blouse, and it pulled the softer fabric down further, particularly as Conlon began to work the lacings through the eyelets and tighten the garment around her upper torso.

The binding of the corset felt curiously arousing. She was very conscious that it was his strong hands restricting her in this fashion, almost as if he were binding her to him.

She tried a deeper breath, and her eyes widened as she looked down and saw how close her breasts were to being revealed. The fit of the garment had restricted their space so they had been pressed together and up, as if they were on display for a man's eye. She could see the pale ring of color just above her nipples, and so could Conlon as he turned her around to adjust the points of the corset over her hips. He gazed down on her displayed bosom with full male appreciation.

"You were right to conceal your appearance, kitten," he said, his voice full of heat. "Any man who got a look at you wouldn't take no for an answer."

"Including you?" she asked, raising her chin.

He caught her about the waist and lifted her up above his head so her hair fell down around them, curtaining their faces in an isolated enclave. Marisa caught his shoulders, but more for her balance, for his strength was undeniable, not even a quiver in those arms that held her off the ground. He slowly lowered her, until her round breasts were there before his face. His tongue curled over the top of the right areola, tracing its arch, bringing the friction of her bodice and shirt into the blend of textures rubbing over it. He shifted his hold, circling one arm around her waist, the other around her hips. His large palm took a firm grip on her right buttock and he continued his delicate ministration on that one tiny spot of her body, just above a confined nipple that was erect and begging to be in his mouth. He did not heed it, instead tracing his tongue up and over the lifted mounds of both breasts, and working a warm, wet path into the dark crevice between them. Her grip slipped from his shoulders, bringing her more fully against his mouth, and she curled her nerveless fingers on his neck, in the dark short ends of his hair.

He raised his head at length, pulling her back from him enough to look at her flushed face. His eyes coursed over the excited heave of her breasts from her arousal and the tight fit of the corset.

"You won't ever say no to me, Marisa," he promised, and she could not argue at the moment, as painful as that possible truth was. Perhaps once her sexual experience quotient was much higher, like a rain gauge, she would be saturated and able to resist someone with Conlon Maguire's magnetism, but by then he would be long gone, wouldn't he?

Something warm and wet was trickling down her thigh and she shifted to press her thighs together. Conlon's brow lifted and he lowered her to her feet. He went down to one knee, which brought his head level with her breasts, and his large hand dipped, lifted the hem of her skirt. Marisa tried to stop him from moving aside the fabric to reveal the tiny drops of fluid that had splashed to the ground. He caught both her wrists in his and held them against her right leg, along with the gathered folds of skirt, as he studied the track of moisture that had run down her left thigh.

"I'm sorry. I need...let go, and I'll get a towel."

He lifted his gaze to her, and it was brilliant in its intensity. "No."

She sucked in a breath as he bent his head, brought his lip to the point of her knee where the moisture had dropped to the floor. Conlon followed its path back up her leg, using the warm pressure of his tongue and the brush of his soft hair against her bare thighs to loosen them, give him better access as he cleaned the moisture away up over her knee, up her thigh.

He stopped at mid-thigh and lifted his head to look at her flushed face and parted lips. "The flow of your honey tells me what I'm doing to you, Marisa. I like it. It's nothing to be ashamed of. Not ever."

"I'm not." She swallowed. "Why don't...I'll make us some lunch. Would you like something for lunch?"

It was a desperate plea for space and she was relieved when he smiled and stepped back, though he kept his hands on her, as if to keep her aware of his impending claim on her flesh. She should be offended by his presumption, his easy command of a situation where she was out of her depth, but she couldn't seem to find such an aggressive reaction, not with her physical self so off-balance. Perhaps she had been hit harder than she thought by the rock, and all this was an unusual dream, a dream of things and responses she had not thought possible.

"You may choose to live away from the noise of people's thoughts," Laraset had told her. *"But do not close yourself off from your own growth. Don't shut yourself off from the love people will give, no matter how much or how little. Just a moment of love, freely offered, is a powerful magic."*

"Let's eat," Conlon said.

* * * * *

"I don't understand."

He broke off a piece of bread, offered it to her. Marisa took it from his fingers, which brushed and held hers for a moment before they relinquished the food to her. "What don't you understand, kitten?"

"You just…" She shook her head. "I'm sexually inexperienced, yes, and you're overwhelming." She scowled at his grin. "But I'm not stupid."

His smile disappeared. "I don't believe you're stupid at all, Marisa."

"So why are you *really* doing this? This isn't the type of thing a person like you does. I can tell you've given your heart to this woman. How can you—"

Offer me so much that I can't think straight, and yet utterly convince me that you're pledged, heart, mind and soul, to the woman for whom you seek your potion?

His now bare foot moved, curled over her smaller one under the table. "I can't really answer that, Marisa. I trust you, and I trust the potion. Seems to me, if the potion demands a night with you as the price for the woman of my dreams, I should devote my whole heart to it, and to you." He lifted a shoulder, tried out some of the bread, gave a grunt of male appreciation that amused her. He swallowed.

"When you have the True Sight, it takes the guesswork out of decisions. You still have free will, but you don't have the option of rationalizing. You can see what's right and wrong pretty clearly. It may seem to you that our being intimate is a betrayal, but the Sight tells me it isn't. Maybe it's not even about me." He pointed his spoon at her. "Have you considered that the force that guides the potion may have been thinking of *you* this time? Maybe it decided it was time for you to know a man."

Her brow furrowed at the startling observation. He reached across the table, smoothing the wrinkle away, and he winked at her, a curl to his sensual mouth that made the bite of bread she had just taken do a slow somersault in her stomach.

"How did you know you had the True Sight, what it was?"

"Irish gift. My great-grandmother recognized it early on, told me what it was. The family used me more often than the dog to determine if business associates could be trusted. If my sister's boyfriends had honorable intentions." He gave her a wolfish grin that made her own mouth lift in a smile.

"I feel sorry for your poor sister."

"Don't. She married a good man, and she's mean as a pit bull." He took a swallow of water. "Let me ask you something now. How long have you lived here like this, disguised as an old woman?"

"Five years."

"Five years?" He put down his cup. "Marisa, you're only, what? Twenty-one?"

"Twenty-three. I'm twenty-three."

"You've lived here, by yourself, since you were eighteen years old?"

"I'm not defenseless, Conlon, despite what you saw." Her spine stiffened. "I usually hear visitors coming and can ward the house for intruders. I was just distracted today."

"I don't think you're defenseless, Marisa. But you're alone. Why? Why stay here? Don't you want to travel, to see different places?"

"This is a beautiful place."

"Yes, it is. But home is where you live, not where you hide."

"I'm not hiding," she snapped. "Sometimes people choose to be alone, Conlon. Sometimes that's their destiny."

He reached out, his large hand cupping her resentful expression. "I don't think it was meant to be yours, Marisa." His eyes were as fixed and steady as the center of the earth. "In fact, I can guarantee it."

She drew back from his touch, refilled both their water glasses from the jug on the floor, quelling the urge to conjure an invisibility spell and vanish. He would see through it anyway.

"Who hurt you?" he asked quietly.

"No one. Everyone." She gritted her teeth at his expression. "I just always have this hope when I travel that I'm going to find a place beyond the cruelty, and there is no such place, not where people exist."

"Maybe it does. You just haven't found it yet."

She inclined her head. "Maybe. I haven't traveled much." *But I can't endure the repeated disappointment of not finding it.* "I think it's much better to watch the Discovery Channel."

"I didn't see your satellite dish."

"I don't have a television here, but I have watched TV," she informed him, suppressing the itch in her palm to slap him. "When you watch a documentary, you know the dark underside exists, but you can filter it, absorb the beauty without being drowned in the darkness. You can at least imagine it might be a wonderful place, instead of a place like any other."

"Sometimes good wins, kitten."

"Yes, and often evil triumphs, because the human spirit isn't strong enough to fight it. Or even worse, it can't pay attention long enough to stick with the fight and win it." She propped her elbows on the table with a thump, like a sentry setting the butt of her weapon before a closed doorway. "I don't want to talk about it anymore. My turn again. Have you had to take a life?"

At his startled look, she pointed her spoon at him, mimicking his gesture. "Seems to me," she said, "if you're going to ask me difficult questions, it's only fair that I be able to do the same."

He sat back, eyeing her. "Yes," he said at last. "During a riot in Peru. The mob tried to pull my client out of the car." His expression flickered. "I had to fire into them to break it up, push them back so the driver could get through. I remember the faces of the three men I killed. There might have been more. When you're shooting at close range, it can happen. I fired seven shots."

Marisa reached out, covered his hand. "Oh, Conlon. That must have been awful. I'm sorry."

He lifted a shoulder. "It wasn't one of my favorite days. Truth, kitten, it was probably the scariest moment of my life." He turned his hand and closed it around hers, though his other hand traced the condensation on his glass, his eyes following the track of water there. "There's a claustrophobic heat when you're surrounded by a crowd that's become a mob. Their desire for blood is so strong it presses down on you. It's surreal, because the same people a few minutes ago were shopping in the market or talking to neighbors. Suddenly they've transformed into something else. For a moment I thought it wasn't going to be enough to drive them back and we'd be torn to pieces. It didn't work out that way, fortunately. I got Grace Fielding, that was my client, back into the car, and we got out of there."

Her grip tightened on his hand. "You took care of her, brought her home again."

"And thanked every deity of the Western and Eastern world for it, because there was no way in hell I did it alone."

"But you still do it," Marisa marveled. "It didn't turn you from it. Did you ever protect someone you felt didn't deserve it?"

"Yes. That's when I left the Secret Service, though I stayed until he left office."

He offered her a bite of bread. He held it away when she reached for it, and nodded at her mouth. Marisa hesitated, then opened her lips and he placed the bread on her tongue, as if she were a baby bird. He withdrew, touching her bottom lip, and then watched the movement of her mouth, the quick flick of her tongue to catch the crumbs. She found it hard to swallow, but she managed it.

"So you don't take on clients not worth protecting."

He nodded. "I spent the first part of my career sometimes having to do that, but once I made enough, I stopped. I only take jobs now that my conscience tells me I should take."

"Where they need the best."

His gaze lifted to hers. "Where someone of my experience is needed. Someone who can be trusted to do the job or die trying. Once I commit to protect someone, I'm there, as long as they need me. If that means forever, then forever it is."

Marisa rose from the table, turned away from him to the basin of water and dipped the bread knife, rubbing her fingers over it to loosen the bread cuttings. "She'll be very lucky, this woman you love," she said, trying to keep the longing for something she would never have out of her voice.

"No, I'll be the lucky one, if she'll have me." He pulled on his hiking shoes, laced them, then leaned forward, lifting a wooden spoon out of the arrangement of cooking utensils she kept in a clay pottery piece in the center of the table. "So." He caught her attention by waving it at her. "I think we've both had enough of questions for now. When was the last time you played, Marisa? Other than playing footsy with your cats? When was the last time you played with a human?"

She studied the glint in his eye warily. "You're a little grown up to be playing games, don't you think?"

"Mmmm. Maybe. But you're barely out of girlhood, and I don't think you got enough time to play with dolls, or play tag." At her blank look, he lifted a brow. "Tag? One person has to catch the other, then says 'You're it', and gets chased in return? 'Course, it's best played with more people, but if it's just the two of us, I think we can still make it fun." He twirled the spoon's handle in dexterous fingertips. "For instance, if I catch you, I get to bend you over my knee, lift your skirt and spank that pretty bottom of yours with this spoon."

"What? Conlon, you're teasing me. I…"

He rose from the stool, deliberate intent in his sparkling eyes. Marisa was distinctly reminded of Beezle, right before he pounced. A startled laugh bubbled up into her throat. She dropped the knife in the basin, circled left as he dodged right, a grin crossing his features.

"Really," she said. "This is very childish, and—"

"Run, Marisa," he suggested, and lunged after her.

She shrieked and ran through the open door to the yard outside. He was right behind her, but she ducked behind the hedge of roses where a small woman had plenty of room to do her pruning and a large man would be pricked mercilessly. She giggled as she heard him swear. The sound of her mirth shocked her. It spread warmth through her chest and stomach like a special spell. She scuttled to the corner before he could cut her off and headed for the copse of pine and cedar trees that shaded the side and front of the house.

The damn corset restricted her breathing, which suggested a man had invented the thing. She paused, uncertain which way to go. He stalked her, weaving through the same trees, that same menacing grin on his face, the spoon in his hand.

"Now, Conlon." She scampered around a cedar as he made another grab for her, and then danced left as he went the other way. Laughter made her hiccup out words and it felt wonderful. "This is silly."

"Mmm-hmm," he acknowledged, and kept coming. "It's worth it to see you laugh. But, Marisa?" His expression sobered and he came to a stop.

She stopped as well. "What?"

"I've been holding back."

She had time for a short squawk, an aborted dash. He came around the tree, too fast to follow his movements, and had her about the waist, tumbling them to the ground. He rolled so she landed on him, keeping her from harm. It made her body come to a state of high alert, that combination of physical mastery and gentle protection at once. When he sat up with her in his lap, turning her face down, not face up, her cheek pressed to the soft earth of the forest floor, the alarm increased. The fresh smell of fallen pine needles was there as her fingers curled into them. Panic lighted on her like the tickling brush of falling leaves, and something else, something that sent an instant flood of reaction between her legs.

His hand pressed firmly into her back, holding her there. The long fingers of that same hand gathered up her skirt, inching the fabric up the back of her legs. Marisa drew in her breath as his hand beneath her body turned and cupped a breast. The play of his fingers on her bare nipple was shocking, making her aware that her position had brought her breasts spilling fully out over the top of the corset.

"Conlon—"

"God, you've got a beautiful ass."

She quivered as the air and the stillness of his hand told her she was fully exposed. Her thighs were draped awkwardly and split open by his knee, so when his hand dipped into the crevice, finding the wetness of her pussy, she could only writhe and whimper helplessly.

"I want to spank you, Marisa. I want to see that pretty little backside you've got thrust in the air turn red and know you'll think of me when you sit down. So hold on." His tone roughened, sending shivers up her spine. "I want it to hurt a little."

Her stomach pressed against his jeans and his cock felt enormous, making her cunt weep for him even further. She was shaking like an autumn leaf, unsure when it would lose its connection to its branch. When it let go, the leaf would journey to places never seen before, places that it never imagined existed, except from the fanciful whispers of the wind.

The slap of the spoon on her bottom reverberated to her toes. It hurt, but in a way that made her crave more, craved him to use more of his strength, make her bottom red as he said he would, as if in controlling the response of her skin he was branding her, making her his in truth. Her image of a bookish, quiet man to fulfil her needs was obliterated by the rage of need in her mind, connected to the hand wielding that spoon.

Again. Again. The thwack was loud in the silence. After twenty strokes, the pain got genuine, but he was rubbing her bottom with his broad, gentle palm between each blow, soothing the skin, preparing it for the next. She was weeping, she realized in shock, though her body shivered uncontrollably from pleasure. His blows seemed to be drawing forth tears to wash out emotional refuse gathered in the bottom of her heart, things she couldn't understand or name.

By thirty strokes, she flinched at each strike, and he stopped. His fingers stroked her abused skin, and then the spoon's flat, round head was pressing her clit, caressing it. Her blood pressure rebounded, pounding deep in her womb like her clit and pussy had a heartbeat that matched the one thundering in her chest.

The spoon slid to the forest floor and he turned her over, cradling her. She lunged and brought her mouth to his, clutching at his body with both hands. Appeasing her hunger was the only demand in her mind as she attacked his mouth, pulling his tongue into hers, biting his lips, sucking on the moisture and heat of him.

She twisted without breaking the oral contact, and wrapped her legs around his waist, depositing her bottom into his wonderful waiting hands. The position brought his cock against her swollen clit. Layers of fabric, the folds of her skirt and his jeans, separated the two, but that did not matter to her straining body. She had no experience, only a complete surrender to the primal urges of her long denied body. She rubbed against him, panting, needing. Just needing. His hands slid up to her hips, pulling her closer, helping her move up and down along his length, though her undulating hips did not seem to need any assistance.

"Don't leave me. Please don't leave me alone."

She heard the words, but it was a full minute before she realized it was she who had said them, pressed them against his mouth.

The realization was as effective as if a hand had picked her up and dropped her in the creek in mid-winter. She shoved back and away, startling him with her abrupt departure such that she was out of his embrace before he could stop her. She scrambled backwards several feet and then stopped, the world tilting so she gripped at ground that was no longer steady beneath her.

He'd done it. He was working his way under her shields. She could feel him, feel his desire, his tenderness. Yet he wasn't hers. He wasn't ever going to be hers.

"Marisa—"

"No. *No.* Don't—"

Of course he paid no attention to her. He was beside her, and she shuddered when he touched her.

"It's all right…"

"No, this can't possibly be all right. Don't touch me…"

"That's the problem," he said. "No one's touched you enough." He somehow had pulled her back on his lap and was holding her cradled there. Even stranger was the fact that, despite her protestations, she was holding onto his waist, her cheek pressed against his chest.

"It's okay," he murmured, stroking her hair, letting her sniffle against his shirt.

His comforting hold and his tenderness were as unbearable to her as they were hard to resist.

"This is appalling behavior." Her voice hitched. "I'm sorry."

"Nothing to be sorry for, kitten. Nothing at all. A good spanking works that way sometimes. Hasn't anyone been there for…don't you have parents?"

She shook her head, kept her hand curled in his shirt, all too aware she was clutching at him the way a child would a parent, for comfort and the reassurance of his presence, the undeniable connection between their life forces.

She knew that humans were social creatures who longed for physical and emotional contact. She had trained herself to do without it, because her life depended on being able to stand on her own two feet.

That's what you'll have to do tomorrow, no matter what, her inner demons pointed out slyly. So why not lean on his strength while it's being offered?

What if I lose the strength to face the world alone tomorrow?

"Marisa, your parents?"

She sat up, pushed against him. "I need…let me have some space, Conlon. Please."

He reluctantly let her ease into a cross-legged position on the ground in front of him, but he held onto one of her hands. She wiped at her nose and eyes gracelessly with the back of her other one. He found a damp handkerchief in his pocket and offered it to her, and she used it, hiding behind the action until he put both hands on hers, bringing them and the kerchief back to her lap. "Tell me."

"I wasn't well when I was young, Conlon," she said, focusing on the kerchief to help her say the words. "I had an illness no one could diagnose. I couldn't bear to be touched. The only place I could achieve any type of calm was…" She hesitated, wondering at how difficult it was to say the words. "In an isolated environment, an institution."

His eyes narrowed, his grip tightening. "A padded cell?"

She nodded. "By the time I learned to cope with my problem, I was nearly eighteen, and they hadn't come to see me for years. What was the point? All I remembered was their pain, how helpless they felt.

"When I was five, my mother, she tried to kill herself. That was when my father…" She drew a deep breath to get it out in a rush. "He had to decide. They always made sure I was in the best facilities, that I received the best care. The nurses told me they adopted two children. They were terrified that it was genetic. I sent them a letter when I got out, thanking them for making sure I was safe all those years, but I never could bring myself to go see them. I sent them the letter because I wanted to bring closure to them, to let them know I wasn't angry with them, either of them, that they shouldn't feel they had failed me, because they did everything they could."

He tipped her face up, studied it. "You really believe that. You're not just saying it."

She nodded against his hand. "It's difficult for me to live with my…illness at times. How can I blame them? What would I do with a child that always seemed to be in pain when I touched her, who seemed as if she couldn't bear to be in the same room with me? Year after year, with no change."

His eyes were dark with thoughts, his jaw tight. She swallowed, pushed herself onto her own two feet, even though the desire to crawl back into his lap was overwhelming.

"You made my bottom hurt," she accused, rubbing the offended area, and eyeing him. "Didn't you say once a person is tagged, she gets to chase after the other person and catch *them*?"

At her words, his expression eased a fraction. She reached out a hand, a courteous gesture to help him to his feet. He studied her hand as if the curve of her fingers, the pale skin of her palm, were a mystery to him, then he surprised her by placing the spoon in her hand, like a scepter being given to a queen. He rose to his feet. "I did say that."

"Well, I had an unfair handicap, with this corset." She tugged it up and wiggled until her breasts were covered as much as they had been before she had landed face first on his lap. When she looked up, she found him watching the play of her breasts with a wry twist to his mouth.

"If you think you had an unfair handicap with the corset, kitten, I think you just balanced it." He caught her hand and before she could guess what he was about, he placed it on the erection starting to swell back hard and firm against his jeans. "Trust me, running with this between your legs isn't easy." His grin flashed wide and bright. "Catch me if you can, kitten. You going to give me a head start?"

She sniffled, swiping away the last evidence of her tears and tucked the kerchief fastidiously into her skirt's waistband. "If you think you need one."

He bolted and she was after him, her bare feet sure on the forest floor. She had played such games with Beezle, and she knew how to anticipate the feint and double back of a lithe cat's body, but Conlon Maguire had a panther's dangerous grace and the long legs of a giraffe. He widened his lead on her despite her ability to anticipate his movements around the trees, down to the brook, splashing through the shallows, scrambling back up the banks.

She saw no reason to physically compete with those long legs. She concentrated, and a moment later a dead branch on the forest floor spun into his path. He leaped over it, and she gained a stride. A mass of vines fell from the canopy of a water oak and tangled around his shoulders. He got out of that, cursing, but missed the root she pulled several inches out of the ground. He stumbled, and she latched onto the waistband of his jeans and hung on like a small burr. He swung around, and caught her deftly about the waist to help her keep her feet.

"You cheat," he laughed. "You witch."

"I'm not a cheat," she said with dignity. "I leveled the field between us. You never said I couldn't use magic, and debilitating factors or no…" She waved at his crotch, making him grin wider as she flushed. "Your legs are much longer than mine, so it was fair for me to do as I did."

"Well then," he drawled. "Since we're being fair, do you want me to drop my pants? After all, I gave you your spanking on bare skin."

Her color climbed to her hairline, but she lifted her chin at his teasing, challenging look. "Yes. That's what I want."

His brow raised, but he inclined his head and unbuckled his belt, pulled open the button of his jeans. When she swallowed, and her embarrassed color started to drain from her face, he turned with a cough that might have been a chuckle. He pushed the pants and underwear beneath down to his thighs, and she saw a pair of muscular buttocks, revealed as he gathered up the tail of his shirt. Buttocks that flexed as he shifted his weight to his hip and glanced back at her. "Well, kitten?"

His small witch stood there with the spoon clasped in her hand and a look of something between fascination and terror on her features.

"I just…just…" She stammered. "I just wanted to catch you, to show you I could. I don't need to do…the rest."

"Maybe you'd like to do something else," he suggested, his eyes warm and gentle, but apparently aroused at her innocence as well. "Would you like to touch me, Marisa, any way you wish? Have you ever been able to touch a man's roused body, Marisa?"

"Of course not."

His eyes flamed hotter, surprising her with his reaction. He drew his pants back up, covering himself. He zipped them but left them unfastened and the belt loose, and took her hand. "*Good*. Come on."

He led her back into the quiet seclusion of her home, took her through the doorway into her bedroom. He released the tieback on her curtains at the door and windows, so the fabric swung closed, enclosing them in a cozy, dimly lit nest, where there was little room for more than the bed and them, standing there facing each other.

"What do you want, Marisa?" he asked. "Anything. I'll do anything you want. There's nothing we need to rush. Ask me anything."

"Why does it…you seem to like it, very much, that I've never had a man, never touched one. Why?"

"Because it means I'm the first to know you, that you're mine, that my cock will be the first to fill your sweet cunt, slicked down with your warm juices when I slide into you." His voice was rich, like the honey he was coaxing from between her legs.

"Oh," she said faintly. The room had gotten much warmer, she supposed because the curtains did not allow as much air to circulate.

"Would you like me to take off my shirt?"

She nodded, and his fingers rose, slipped the second button, the third, and the rest. He tugged the shirt out of his waistband and shrugged out of it, baring the broad shoulders and wide chest, the defined muscles that marked his stomach, the low ride of his jeans on his hips.

Living so close to nature, Marisa had a highly developed appreciation of beauty. Whether it was the tiny artistic perfection of a ladybug's wings or the complex symphony of a tree's canopy as the wind brushed strokes through its leaves, she understood each was a miracle. She had never had occasion to study the male form, but that heightened awareness rewarded her now. For a moment all she did was look. He did not move, letting the dim light settle onto his muscles, limning their perfection for her pleasure.

He was so different. So much bigger, not just in height, but in the span of his shoulders, the more developed upper body, the size of his hands, the length of his fingers. Small nipples, surrounded by those fine hairs of gilded bronze. The diagonal slashes of muscle from the hip bones, pointing the way to the groin area, still covered by his jeans. Her gaze could not help but settle on that heavy bulge of his genitals contained in the juncture between his long thighs.

"You're beautiful," she said softly. "The most beautiful man I've ever seen."

She moved toward him, and he did nothing, remaining still as he promised, those green-gold eyes watching her. The lack of lighting shadowed his expression, except for the quiet ease of his mouth, inviting her to do as she would to him.

Marisa reached out, and his flesh quivered under her light fingertips. She stroked his fur, felt the texture of his nipple. She took a shallow breath, and watched his eyes automatically go to the swell of her breasts, barely tucked back into the tight corset. "I'd like…" She pressed her lips together. Instead of speaking her desire, she reached for it.

She touched the open button on his jeans, traced her finger into the zipper, and took it down. She did not look up, absorbed in what she was doing, though she could feel his head bent over hers, his breath on her neck.

"Marisa." It was a husky caress of heat against her skin.

She managed to work the zipper over the head of his engorged cock, moving carefully, instinctively aware of how sensitive that powerful looking organ could be, and noticed the spot of thick fluid on the tip. Fluid like her fluids, wetting his dark underwear as evidence of his desire for her. She could smell it, that musky scent, and it was new to her, so she bent close, inhaled it, breathing softly on him.

"I want…" She wasn't brave enough to go further.

"What, kitten?" His voice was a rough whisper. "Anything you want. Tell me."

"Can you take all of it off?" She straightened, looked up at him. "I want to see all of you."

"I wouldn't know how to tell you no, Marisa."

He bent and unlaced the hiking shoes. As he worked the strings she reached out, traced the movement of his back muscles, felt the soft short hair on his nape. She envied the person who got to cut his hair and run her fingers through it, feel the texture as she was feeling it now. It would be a woman, she was sure, because he was a man who enjoyed the touch of a woman.

He straightened, catching her fingers and kissing them so she did not feel he was drawing away from her touch when he turned to toe off the shoes. He slid the jeans and underwear down his haunches, and rid himself of them and his socks, so he stood before her in only the glorious creation of skin and muscle with which the Lord and Lady had blessed him.

He had heavy testicles, covered with the same soft down of dark hair that covered his chest in a light mat, and his cock was fully erect above the scrotal sac. He was large in all ways, and it gave her some trepidation.

She placed her fingers against his rib cage, followed the channel between two of them around to his back, and spread her hand out, a fan against his firm flesh there. She felt the life and strength pulsing within him. "I can barely breathe," she whispered. "You're so wonderful."

A ripple went through his skin and it took her a moment to realize he had swallowed, and his hands had closed into tight fists. She hesitated. "Did I say something wrong?"

"Never." He kept his head averted, but she saw his profile. "You just don't know, Marisa. A virgin in…the outside world, for lack of a better word to call it, is different. She may not have had a man inside her body, but you wouldn't be able to call her sexually inexperienced. She would know so much already. To you, all of it is new, wondrous. It humbles me." He turned then, his body held rigid against some enormous feeling he appeared to be holding back. "A man would look all his life to find someone as special as you. Let me pleasure you while you touch me. I can't keep my hands off you."

"How?" she asked, not certain of his intent, but certain she would not deny anything he asked of her in that ragged voice.

"Come here." He drew her to the bed and stretched his long body out on it, laying his head on her pillow. If he stayed there long enough, she'd be able to smell him long after he was a memory. She was glad she had made the bed oversized for her and all of the cats, because his feet were almost at the bottom railing.

"Come here," he repeated, tugging at her, at her skirt. He pulled the drawstring, untied it and loosened its fit, so the skirt went tumbling to her ankles, leaving her only in the corset and shirt beneath. From his point on his back, he took her elbow, guided her up onto the mattress and then brought one of her legs over his chest to straddle him, with her head facing his feet.

"What—"

He slid her back, his hands on her thighs, and she was on her knees, her hips over his face, her hands braced on the bed on either side of his ribcage.

"Touch me however you wish, Marisa," he told her, his hands closing on her waist as she tried to twist about and look at him. "While I bring you pleasure this way."

She understood then, and before she could become embarrassed or ask desperate questions, he brought her down full on his face, her pussy onto his waiting mouth.

It was like the exhilarating shock of cold water on a very hot day. Pleasure shot out in all directions through her bloodstream from that point of contact between his mouth and her body. She couldn't think of a proper analogy for it, the feel of a man's hot, hungry mouth on her wet, aroused cunt. He flicked his tongue back and forth like the lash of Beezle's tail, then around in a circle. She struggled, not to get away, just unable to be still. He seemed to understand, for he held her more tightly. His tongue made a slow, broad lick, from back to front, up and down, again and again, all while he made soft, wet sucking noises against her skin that inflamed her body and her senses.

Marisa fell forward, unable to sit upright, and found a feast waiting for the ravenous hunger he roused in her. She opened her own mouth and used it upon him. She started with his flat stomach, using her teeth to taste the roll of muscles there, biting and licking wildly like Beezle did when she scratched his back and hit the spot he liked so much. If it felt anything like this, she now knew why he got more and more aggressive as the pleasure continued building, until the best expression of appreciation was savagery.

Conlon used his greater strength to show her how to enhance her pleasure, manipulating her hips in low grinding circles, allowing him to stab his tongue deeper into her heat.

Her arms stretched, her fingers biting into the tops of his thighs. She sucked on his hipbone. His tongue probed and she mewled, curling her claws into him, her knees straining to clamp onto either side of his head. His hands held her wide, so her body shuddered in the grip of an unbearable level of arousal, unable to go forward, screaming to be pushed over that pinnacle he had shown her in the forest. Her clit was aching for his mouth, but now when she wanted it most, he offered only the smallest rations to that aroused center. A brief nuzzle, a quick lick. She cried out at the teasing contact, throwing back her head.

His cock brushed her cheek and her hand slid back, to the crease between thigh and testicles. Marisa turned her head and rubbed her nose and the edge of her lips against the broad head, tasting wetness and salt. She marveled at the peculiar velvet softness of skin stretched over steel.

Conlon settled into a rhythmic nursing at her pussy, so slow it felt as if her cunt were the eye of the storm raging through her body. Every slight movement of his mouth and every hot breath were as excruciating as an electric jolt.

Quivering, her breath sobbing in her throat, she tasted him again, more boldly, running her tongue along the ridged base of the head of his cock. She used a hint of teeth, as he had on her.

He groaned against her slickness, and the convulsive clutch of his fingers on her thighs told her he liked it.

She cupped her hand under his testicles, feeling their weight, and licked his cock again, from the base up to the tip. She wanted to hold it, this staff that would take her maidenhead, and so she wrapped her fingers around it. She slid her grip up, feeling the unusual give of the soft flesh over firm rigidity. It had incredible heat, warming the skin of her palm. She rose up and put the head fully into her mouth, just barely able to close her lips over it, touching it lightly inside the cavern of her mouth with little flicks of her tongue, learning his contours.

He stilled, his lips motionless on her pussy, but still *there*. His fingers lightly stroked the inside of her thighs, making her tremble even more.

He was very thick. Her index finger and thumb were barely able to meet as she grasped him to slide her mouth further down on him. She went as far as she could go before the head touched the back of her throat. His thighs quivered, just a shiver of movement, but it flooded her with a sense of power. She could do to his body what he did to hers, make him helpless with pleasure. She slid back up his length, feeling the way he stretched her small mouth, and she used her teeth, scraping, and sucked on his skin.

"No, Marisa…" His breath rasped hard over the words, and she felt his heart pounding beneath her thighs. "You'll have to stop, or I'll be no good to you at all."

She shook her head, made a murmured protest, her mouth still firmly fastened on him. She had no intention of relinquishing her new toy. He answered her willfulness with his mouth. He clamped his lips back over her soaking cunt, only this time there were no gentle licks or nibbles to draw out her pleasure. His hands shoved her thighs impossibly wider, and he suckled her clit hard. He lifted her hips off him and then drew them back down in a pumping motion, to give his tongue room to stroke in and out of her labia, emulating the act they would eventually do with the organ in her mouth. He alternated the sucking of her clit and the invasion of her pussy with his tongue with long, thorough licks from the top of her clit to the tiny opening of her bottom. He delved deep into her pussy on each downward stroke, an amazing feat of coordination that shot her up a ramp toward orgasm like a slalom skier. His afternoon beard rasped against her delicate skin, tightening the coils in her lower belly impossibly further.

The banked heat while she explored him now leaped high. She whimpered, her mouth still upon him, but unable to coordinate a sliding motion to tease him as he was tormenting her. In fact, she could do little other than hang on, her hands clutching his legs, her mouth panting on his cock, vibrating it with her soft cries. The head bumped the back of her throat as he mercilessly undulated her body toward a shattering peak.

"No...no..." She did not know why she was saying no, denying him, except it felt like too much, too frightening and overwhelming. The power that grew in her pussy coiled in her lower belly with the power of a diamondback about to strike, and then it did, in a blinding flash as brilliant as venomed fangs. She saw hues of silver, and light sparking in the back of her eyes as his teeth scraped her convulsing clit, consuming her heat and juices as if he dined on a meal of flesh prepared just for him. Indeed, at the moment she could not imagine belonging to anyone else but him.

She could accept that, would have to accept that. As unlikely as it had been more than a couple hours ago that he would be her first love, Conlon Maguire would likely be her last, with her life being what it was. She let go and was ripped away from the edge of reason, spiraling into the world of silver, her cheek pressed against his thigh, for she could hold her mouth on him no longer. He continued to drive her higher, even as she begged him for mercy. His arms were banded on her waist and hips, and his mouth worked her hard, bringing forth a primal passion and need she had not suspected were there, stored like a thousand unshed tears in her subconscious, just like the emotions released by his spanking. She sank her teeth into his flesh and the blood of his thigh gave her the anchor she needed, her cheek pressed against the heat of his erect cock and nest of testicles.

The pounding rhythm of his blood matched hers, but hers slowed first as she came down. She focused on herself with wonder, feeling the way her climaxing body contracted on his tongue, then pulsed down to an easier cadence, like a settling heartbeat. His hunger became a nibbling, just a feather touch of his mouth that made her wriggle a bit against his hold as the sensitive tissues were tickled.

His hands at last let her go, but only to lift and turn her.

"Come up here, Marisa," he murmured. "Taste your pussy on my mouth."

She let his hands guide her so she lay full on him, his cock trapped between her belly and his, her response trickling down her thigh onto his leg.

He lifted her under the armpits, slid her up to where he could kiss her, which meant his cock sprang up between her thighs and nudged the crease between her buttocks.

His mouth was warm, and gentle, and she could taste his leashed need beneath the flavor of her cunt, a slippery exotic taste. His hand came up and cradled the back of her head, his thumb stroking her ear. She loved how he liked to touch her face when he kissed her. She was reduced to a still peace by his gentleness, and a desire that was more than physical, though she could feel a stirring in her lower belly. She felt like a languid cat who had enjoyed her supper so much, she might want more sooner than expected.

"Conlon," she whispered, shyly meeting his gaze. "I'd like to take off the corset, so I can feel all of you against me."

His fingers worked the laces free and the pressure eased. She sat up so he could pull the garments away, leaving her soft and bare sitting upon him. As she sat up, she lifted, so his cock came forward through the opening of her thighs and lay on his belly again. When she lowered herself, she found it nestled against her pussy, the long hard length of him channeled between her wet lips.

Conlon reached up, fondled her breasts, rubbing his thumbs over her still aroused nipples. "Holy Mother, I want you. Can you feel how much, kitten?"

She thought he meant his cock beneath her, but he took her hand, laid it over his heart and held it there, as he stared up at her through the dim light.

Blessed Lady, what was the man trying to do to her? When she started this day, she could not have imagined she would be sitting on a naked man by late afternoon, but here she was, and now he seemed determined to crack open her insides the way he had pushed past her physical defenses.

He had roused powerful emotions in her, and perhaps that was what happened during sex. For just a few moments, you got to be everything to one another, even if you were nearly strangers. She had never been anything special to any person, not for a second, much less for an afternoon, so how could she resist it? This moment was a gift, a memory she could polish every day so it would not dim, like a lamp in her soul. She had always accepted darkness there, but she was afraid he had made it impossible for her to accept it anymore.

"I want you to…" She paused, her fingers resting beneath his, her other hand holding her up on his body. She loved the way his eyes coursed over her, again and again, as if he was trying to memorize everything about her, and then his gaze returned to her face, studying it with equal intensity. "Do you say, 'have sex with me'?" she asked.

She had certainly read books, but she had stayed away from modern literature. It was a world she could not join, and so reading those books caused her only longings for things she could not have. Her naivete and innocence were real things, her questions to Conlon genuine, his every answer a new wonder for her to ponder.

He reached up, cupped her face in both of his hands, bringing her down for a kiss on her forehead, her nose. The tips of her breasts brushed his bare chest, making them tingle.

"Sometimes." He kissed her lips. "But when you especially want it, and there's just an overpowering physical need inside you, you say, 'I want you to fuck me. Now.'" His lips brushed over her brow again. "Hard." Her ear, to nibble. "Long." Back to her lips, this time for a much longer kiss, during which her world spun off its axis and drifted away on a cloud.

He raised her face and she caught hold of his wrists to keep her balance, staring into his eyes. "Then, sometimes it's more, so much more, and you say, 'Make love to me.' Say that to me, Marisa. Please."

She closed her eyes, turned her face into his hand, pressed her temple there. "I can't," she whispered. "You're going to leave. You can't take everything from me, Conlon. You can't." She brought her gaze back around to him, her lips trembling. "Fuck me, Conlon." She stumbled over it, but she drew a breath and strengthened her resolve. "Fuck me. Now. Hard. Long. Make me yours for today, and I will live with that, if you can, and your potion will be served."

The last was a challenge, and her anger surprised her. It wasn't supposed to have gotten personal, but it had, because there was no way to get this close physically without it becoming that way, a painful lesson she would not forget. She didn't have the experience to be casual about it. He did, but his husky words, begging her for verbal intimacy, had not sounded casual. Neither was his reaction now.

There was a flash of frustration, a deep disappointment that made her want to withdraw, break the physical link of flesh with him, but he stopped her, his fingers biting into her arms. He pulled her down, put his forehead against hers, and she kept her palms open and light against his chest as he fought a battle for control she could feel quivering through his body.

"Before we do that," he said at last. "We need to take a little break. Your body will need some time to get roused again, to make certain you can receive me as comfortably as possible. After climax, the tissues are very sensitive, too sensitive."

"I can bear it," she assured him.

He shifted his grip and collared her throat, giving her a hard look that swallowed anything else she had intended to say to goad him to finish, to be done with it.

"I won't let you rush this, Marisa. You'll open every part of yourself to me, not compartmentalize to protect yourself. You never need to do that with me."

Didn't she? Why did he act as if he was not going to leave her when the day was done? Why did he want her to act the same way?

He gave her ass a friendly squeeze as if he had not just insisted she put her heart in his hands.

Lifting her off of him, he put her on her feet on the floor next to the bed. "Right now, I need to answer the call of nature."

She knew they were serving a Will greater than her own desires, but he irritated her beyond the capacity for speech. She wanted to tear out her hair, or better, his. As he rose and turned to leave her small bedroom, she snatched up the spoon and gave him a solid whack on his muscular ass.

Conlon jumped and spun, shock flashing over his expression for one delightful, vindicating moment. Then a wicked grin crossed his face. "You're going to wish you hadn't done that."

Marisa dropped the spoon and bolted, but he snatched her by the waist and hefted her over his shoulder, kicking and shrieking. She used her hands and smacked him again, taking out her frustration with a cheerful enthusiasm on his handsome backside all the way from inside her house to the creek. By the time they got to the water, she was laughing at his mock sounds of pain and missing every other blow. He tried to lift her, she was sure to toss her into the water, but she wrapped her arms around his neck and her legs around his waist as he brought her forward. "I'm not going in unless you are," she informed him.

"All right then," he said, and plunged in with her locked in his arms. He took four strides and dove below the surface of the deeper water.

It was marvelous, having him hold her, water rushing over them both. Even when he rose, she continued to cling, water pouring off their naked bodies, the melting afternoon sun warming their skin as they emerged. Beezle sat on the bank, watching them with yellow eyes rounded in amazement.

"Kitten, you've got quite an arm." He grinned, pushing her hair back from her face as she did the same to him, smoothing it back on his temples. "You'd be a hellcat of a mother."

The light in her heart died, and he saw it, for his face sobered. "What, Marisa?"

"I'll never have children, Conlon. My…problem, it makes it impossible."

"I thought you said it was cured. Is it life threatening?" He gripped her arms. "Are you sick? Tell me."

"No, I said I learned to manage it. It's not something you cure."

"Why won't you tell me what it is?" He gave her a firm shake. "I want to help."

"No." She shook her head. "Please don't ask me to talk about it. It's nothing that threatens my life, not that way. I just want to swim. Go…do what you need to do, and let's swim. Okay?"

She was grateful when he let her pull away, when he didn't push. She knew how difficult that was for a man who wanted to protect all those around him. Remembering that, she couldn't seem to hold onto her anger against him.

She knew Conlon didn't mean to upset her with his insistence that she open herself to him. He didn't know how susceptible her emotional well-being was. He was simply encouraging her to offer herself fully to the passion between them.

When he splashed back into the water, his face was more composed.

"Come on." He retrieved her hand, pulling her into the deeper water, beyond where her feet could touch. "Keep me company out here."

He let her go and sank below the water, then came back up, tossing his hair out of his face. He could touch bottom here, the water lapping at his collarbone, so she stroked over to him. His fingers linked with hers and he pulled her in, guiding her thighs so they wrapped around his waist and she could use him to keep herself afloat without treading. His waist was firm beneath her soft thighs, the hair on his belly brushing and tickling the hair of her pubic mound. Her calves pressed down on his muscular buttocks, her crossed heels resting on the backs of his thighs. She realized if they were lying down, this would be the position of coitus, and it turned the emotions fluttering in her stomach to liquid heat.

"I can see why you live here," he acknowledged, looking around them. "It is peaceful. But don't you get lonely, Marisa?"

"Sometimes." She used her arms to keep herself upright, her upper body leaning away from him. "But I have Beezle, and six other abandoned cats that come here to eat."

"Who built the house?" He studied the simple log cabin construction.

"I did," she said, with some pride at his look of surprise. "I studied survivalist manuals, everything from Robinson Crusoe to Walden Pond, and modern journals. Especially those written by women. Then I just followed the blueprint of what they did. Laraset and Kohana are the healers that helped me learn how to cope with my illness, and got me to the point where I could leave the care of a medical facility. They're married, and they came with some of Kohana's cousins and helped with the heavy lifting when I was constructing the cabin."

"Why didn't you stay near them? If Laraset and her husband helped you reclaim your life, they must be good friends."

"They were my healers." She nodded, tightening her thighs on his bare hips as he shifted. "They cared about me as physicians care for those they heal. But I spent my whole life under medical care, Conlon. I wanted to see what it was like to have my own home and my own life, as much as I could. My parents set up a trust fund for me so I could choose where to live and what to do with my life, and have whatever level of care I needed."

"But you're so isolated here."

"Not so much." She shrugged. "People like you are company, those who come here looking for potions. I go into town," she added, laying her head back in the water to float her upper body, though she continued to hold onto him with her legs. "I see people then."

"Well, it's obvious how often you go there." The flatness of his voice had her raising her head. "All the window shopping for trinkets, the pretty dresses you buy."

"I don't stay that long." She dropped her legs from their hold around his hips and swam away, rolling in the water, rewetting her shoulders. He swam alongside her.

"You strike me as someone who would enjoy looking at lovely things, Marisa. Trying on a pair of earrings, a hair comb. Do you go in as yourself? Or do you go in as an old woman to keep anyone from noticing you?"

"Stop baiting me," she snapped.

She had retreated enough that she was back on solid ground and she faced him, anger in her eyes. "You want to hear what you're fishing for, Conlon? I go to town once a month, for about two hours. That's what I can handle, okay?"

"Until what?" He stood up, his shoulders broad enough to block the sun setting behind him, making the wind raise a chill on her upper arms a moment before his hands closed on them. "Tell me what happens, Marisa."

"Why do you insist on making this about me?" she said, jerking away from him. "This is about *you*. Your potion, your life, your woman. I will never see you again after today. I am an instrument of other people's fates, not part of fate itself."

She saw it in his face. Pity. Pity for her. Marisa snarled and she spun away from him. "We'll do this *now*, and then you and your potion can be gone."

He caught her about the waist and she whirled on him like a cat, clawing at him. He caught her wrists and she resorted to teeth, snarling at him, fighting the needs he had roused. Needs that exposed her terrible isolation and the inadequacies of the world she had been forced to create to survive.

"Marisa—"

"Bastard!" She wrenched away from him. "You pry and pry, because you think I'm interesting and different, because I'm beautiful, but you don't live in my head every day. You don't know what it's like to live in fear of the pain coming back, the constant hammering of a million dark voices raised in threats, anger and pain until you can't hear the voice of a good person standing next to you shouting. Do you have any idea how shielded I must be to survive? How much effort it takes every day to hold those shields in place? And you come here with your patronizing attitude and your sexist assumption that I'm some weak, stupid female."

"Marisa, no—"

"You want to know what happens if I stay in town longer?" Her lip curled derisively. "My shields break down and all the ugliness pours in. Everyone's meanest, most petty thoughts and deeds, the things deep in their heads that no one knows about."

"Jesus. You're an empath." The light dawned in his eyes.

She nodded, a short, sharp jerk. "Yes. A very *special* type of empath, Conlon. I only sense emotions motivated by evil. And guess what? Almost all of us have them, even if they're dormant within us. I can sense them. Greed, petty selfishness, unjustified violence, the dark yearnings that everyone harbors deep inside. You know those primal instincts that turn a group of pleasant shoppers into a murderous mob? Well, I feel it in them in the marketplace, while they're still shopping, even if all they ever do is shop." She set her jaw to keep her voice from trembling. "Only the shields I've learned to build protect me, and the moment I come into town, it's like my mind is a fortress under siege by an army. Those with true Darkness in the active part of their minds make it far worse."

He reached out but she shook her head, stroked back from him. "That's why I spent all those years in an institution. Can you imagine being a child, and all these terrible images are pounding into your head from everyone you know? It's like one of those horror movies, where people look normal, but you're seeing them as demons, their innermost gremlins exposed on their faces, in their voices."

"Oh, Marisa."

"Laraset was a volunteer in the children's ward. She's a witch, and she brought her husband, Kohana, to see me. He's a Sioux medicine man, and he figured out what I was, looked beyond the physical and chemical to the spiritual. They helped me, helped me learn how to shield myself for short forays among others, and taught me the things I needed to do to cope. One of them is living apart from civilization, where I can keep it down to just a murmur of static in my head."

"There's no permanent cure for it."

Somehow, she knew he was going to ask. "There's only one permanent solution for it, a reference in a book that might or might not be true. When Laraset found it, and told me about it, I wished for it so much I almost put myself back in the same state again. Just like the shields, I learned to protect myself by not wishing for it any more."

Liar. His presence here had brought it to the surface like a predator floating in the shallows, just waiting for her fragile psyche to put one vulnerable leg into those dangerous waters.

"You won't tell me what it is?"

She shook her head. "I don't speak of it. I won't. I can't." She could not keep the desperate note from her voice.

"And the potions?" he asked quietly.

"An act, a joining of love, eases the drain on my shields. The success of my potions, no matter how far away, fuels the wards around this place, around me."

"So your potions are for you as well as for them."

"They make the world a better place, so everyone wins." She set her jaw. "I live alone, and maintain my wards and my illusion, and I survive. It's the life I have been given, and it has many blessings in it."

"Marisa." He reached beneath the water, caught her hand, and stepped closer. His other fingers touched her chin, lifting it so she would meet his intense hazel gaze. "You don't have to tell me what you and Laraset found, but I know faith grows weak. I know it." His hand tightened on her, and she saw the truth in the shadows of his eyes. "My faith nearly broke, after Peru. I never thought that kind of darkness was in people. But I learned that as long as your faith is still inside you, even just a thread of it in your heart, it can call your heart's desire to you, if your intent is pure. You have to believe."

"I have to survive," she said flatly. "And enjoy what I've been given rather than always wishing for what I can't have." *A man in her life exactly like Conlon Maguire.* "Anyway, by nightfall, I'll no longer be such a pure vessel, will I?" The porous ground beneath her feet sucked her down, sliding her closer to him, despite her struggle to pull back.

"Innocence is not purity, Marisa," he said seriously. "Physical intimacy doesn't taint the soul. In some cases, it can enhance the shine." He drew her closer, so her breasts and her stomach were pressed against his wet skin. She had to tilt her head to look at him, which put their mouths distractingly close. "You have every right to be proud. I wasn't trying to pick that apart. You just have an incredible amount to give, Marisa." His hands slid up her sides, palms resting on her rib cage. "I wish there was someone in your life with whom you could share it all. Not someone to nurse you. Someone to be with you, be your helpmeet. Share your life."

"You think I don't wish for that?" she demanded, stiffening against his hold. "Laraset said…"

"What? What did she say?"

"She said that maybe one day I'd find someone." There, she'd said it. "Someone who might get close enough to me that they could lend their strength to my shields. But it can't be just anyone. So it's impossible."

He opened his mouth to respond, but she'd had enough. Marisa wrenched away. "You see, you've got me messed up about this again. You're just like Laraset, always pushing, always wanting me to offer more. Well, none of you are in my head. It isn't about what all of you want me to be able to do, it's what I can do to serve the Lord and Lady, and still survive from day to day. So as far as I'm concerned, the whole bunch of you can just go to hell. This is my life."

She stormed out of the water, leaving him there, and snatched up her towel from the basket. She wrapped it around herself and plopped down on the bank, deciding he could finish his bath alone, and if he got his legs tangled in some water weeds and started to drown she might just wait awhile before deciding to fish him out.

After a few minutes he joined her. She chose not to look at him, though she couldn't help her peripheral vision, which noted the way the sunlight played off the water sluicing down the muscles of his body, the dark pelt of pubic hair, the movement of his genitals as he strode from the water. He picked up the other towel she had provided and knotted it loosely on his hips. He sat down next to her, joining his hands around his bent knees.

"If you were one of your cats, your tail would be lashing and your ears would be laid back."

Her gaze shot to his face. She could feel the fire inside her shooting sparks from her eyes, but his expression was open and apologetic. "So," he ventured. "Want to have sex now?"

The anger slid away with her glare and she looked away, her lips twitching. "Idiot."

"Yeah, it kind of goes with the whole male-female dynamic." He carefully laid an arm around her shoulders and she felt his warmth, the comforting touch of something she'd rarely had, a friend.

"I didn't really mean I wanted you to all go to hell," she said after a moment.

"Even me."

"Even you. I did kind of want you to drown, for a second or two."

He chuckled and she laid her head on his shoulder, let herself lean for just that moment, because, after all, once the moon rose, it wouldn't matter.

"Does that mean I can talk you into having dinner with me?"

"Didn't we just eat?"

"That was a snack. This is dinner."

"What are you fixing?" she asked, a smile touching her lips, curving against the skin of his shoulder.

He nudged her so she lifted her head.

"You tell me what you have, and I'll make it into something worth eating. I'm a great scratch cook."

She considered. "Well, I've got fresh vegetables, bread, and…" She slanted him a glance. "Hershey chocolate bars. A case of them, one a day to last me until my next trip into town."

"My God, you've fallen in love with me."

"What?" She jerked back.

"A woman doesn't offer her chocolate stash to someone she's not madly in love with."

"Perhaps I just have a generous nature," she said, recovering her dignity.

"I've no doubt you do about most things, but a woman and her chocolate? Kitten, you'd be the first."

He grinned and rose, offering her a hand. When he tugged her to her feet, he brought her close, so her towel-clad body was pressed against his bare upper torso. She was suddenly aware of how loosely that towel draped about his lean hips. But he stepped away after a moment and just held her hand as they walked back to her house.

* * * * *

"Play 'what if' with me."

"You don't play 'what if' if there's no possibility you can ever have what you're wishing for."

"With all you do to ensure the success of your potions, you don't think anything's possible?"

"Are you trying to be cruel?"

"I want you to share your dreams with me, kitten. That's all."

Marisa studied him across the table. He had indeed prepared an excellent meal, concocting a spicy light soup of vegetables from her garden. She had sliced up more of her wonderful bread. Now they faced each other, and the candles she had lit upon the table were becoming necessary to illuminate the room, every flicker of the flames like the ticking of a clock, tightening a coil of anticipation in her belly. She saw the awareness in his eyes as well, though they kept up their conversation as if they were both oblivious to the significance of the impending twilight.

"It's more than the empathy that makes me choose isolation. I'm not a prisoner of this place, Conlon. The noise of towns, the way no one pays attention to the natural world except as an accent to their possessions, it's not for me. Here, I'm connected to the Lord and Lady, as part of the cycles around me, and I can hear Their Voices, and my own."

"So that's why no electricity."

"I don't need it." She shrugged. "People get far too dependent on such things anyway."

"Hmmm." He rose, collected the dishes and deposited them in the basin of water in a considerate gesture that had as much of an impact on her senses as the physical implications of the moon rising. It made her think of his words.

Someone to be with you, be your helpmeet… Someone to share your life.

Someone to share mundane tasks like washing the dishes. Another person to stand on the other side of the wide bed in the morning and help her make it. Someone to help her take a jar off a shelf just out of reach of her fingertips.

He lifted his backpack to his shoulder and extended his hand. "I think it's time, kitten. Will you come to the bedroom with me?"

Her throat suddenly went dry, but she nodded, rose and took his hand, let him lead her into the bedroom.

Conlon set the backpack down. "Will you lie back on the bed for me, Marisa?"

They had worn their towels at the table. His clothes were wet and he did not want her to put on one of the shift dresses. She lay back on the pillow and pressed her cheek to it as he rummaged through the bag. She smelled him on the pillow, just as she'd hoped.

She opened her eyes to find he had removed a small item of pale blue rubber, shaped like a butterfly. He was using his fingertip to spread a fluid from a tiny bottle onto the butterfly's wings.

"What's that?"

He sat down on the bed next to her hips and slid his hand holding the butterfly up her thigh, nudging the terry cloth out of his path so her leg from knee to pussy was exposed to his gaze. "Spread your legs for me, kitten," he murmured. "I have a surprise for you. Courtesy of the Eastern invention of the alkaline battery."

She trembled but obeyed, trusting him in a way she knew she had never trusted anyone.

His fingers touched her, pressed her gently, and the wings of the butterfly closed over her clit, the substance he had spread onto them adhering to her skin so it stayed in place, like a hood for the tiny bundle of excited nerve endings.

"What is it?" she repeated again, breathless.

"Something to change your mind about electricity."

The whir of the tiny motor was almost noiseless, but its impact was immediate. Marisa stiffened as the vibrations kissed her clit, little frissons of current drawing the blood so it began to swell in arousal again.

"Ah." She caught her lip in her teeth as he watched her, his eyes steady on her face, his hand on her thigh, his fingers achingly close. His hand held the control at his hip and he turned the knob. She bucked up as the sensation intensified.

"Your nipples are hardening," he said quietly. "They have jewelry for them, did you know? Rings to go around them, make them stay stiff and large. There are even vibrating shields for them so they can become as aroused as your clit is now. I can turn this up to its highest setting and you'll come instantly, Marisa. You're getting wetter even now. I can smell it. You're ready for it again."

"Conlon." She clutched the covers, sensations shuddering over her skin. She opened her legs wider, lifted her hips toward him. She felt like a wanton, wanting to offer all of herself to him, but she couldn't help it. From the flare of heat in his eyes, she could see he didn't mind.

However, he turned the control down, easing the vibrations so she could think somewhat again, and stroked his hand down her trembling leg. "You could come that way, but I want you to come this time with my cock inside of you. It's just about dusk," he murmured, glancing toward the open window.

The crickets were starting their evening serenade, and the air had the soft quality of early summer evenings. It was a lovely time of day to embrace a change to her life, for she knew that was what this was. The price of the potion was never set without deep purpose, and the amethyst color, the color of the crown chakra, had underscored its significance.

"Conlon, could you…would you mind stopping it just a moment? I have to…it's important I tell you something."

He acquiesced to her wishes and even went a step further, leaning forward to take the butterfly off her. The touch of his fingers peeling it off her clit was enough to make her gasp, her thighs tighten. He bent, pressed a kiss to her pubic bone, nuzzling her soft hair, then he straightened, met her gaze.

"Are you afraid?" His voice was soft, though she could feel the tension in his man's body, the ache of wanting her so close to the surface it emanated from his skin. It helped, knowing that.

"Not of the act. Just of what it might mean. Conlon." She pressed her lips together. "It's possible, when we come together, that I won't be able to maintain my shields. Great emotion widens the scope of my empathy, and…" She stopped to steady her voice, felt his hand close on hers. "I know this will overwhelm me. If the negative emotions rush in, promise me you'll finish the consummation, no matter how much pain I appear to be suffering."

His expression hardened. "I'm not going to cause you suffering, Marisa. If there's any danger to you, we're not going to do this. I don't care what—"

"No, it's important to the magic that sets the price that we come together in this way. I wish to serve its purpose. Please, you must promise me, despite your strongest instincts, to do this."

It was she who turned over her hands and gripped his, hard, her expression beseeching. "I serve the Lord and Lady.

Don't deny me the right to control my own destiny. That's far more important to me than anything else, do you understand?"

He studied her. "All right," he said at last. Knowing it cost him to go against his own inclinations to support hers, she lifted his hands to her mouth, kissing them.

"I'll do as you say," he said. "But I will do everything I can to keep you safe. You'll have to be satisfied with that."

Would he talk to his chosen woman so possessively, so arrogantly? Marisa closed her eyes and imagined that woman's lips lifting in an indulgent smile as his hands and mouth and words asserted his dominance over her, all the while knowing she held his heart and soul in her gentle hands. It was the way of the Lord and Lady, the unique way male and female expressed their sense of belonging to one another, their mutual reverence and devotion. She understood it now, after only one afternoon with a man. Not just any man, but the right man, to teach her such truths.

She nodded, not trusting herself to speak further. He drew her forward, into his arms, all the way in, pressing her into the curve of his body so she was sheltered there. He wrapped his arms around her back so she was in a cavern of male heat and strength. Tipping her chin back with a nudge of his jaw, he kissed her.

They'd had a whole afternoon of love play, so she had anticipated that he would quickly move to the intimacy of baring both their bodies again, stripping away the towels, claiming her breasts and thighs with his mouth and hands.

Instead, he seemed to want to take his time now, seducing her only with his mouth. He started with a persuasive rubbing of his lips against hers, pushing her bottom lip down with the pressure of his so his lips were moistened by the inside of hers. He rubbed that moisture against both of her lips. The tip of his tongue came out, making a delicate touch here and there, as if he was marking each tiny crease of her lips that enabled their movement. Marisa's fingers uncurled and fluttered onto his abdomen, pressing against his hot skin. She caught the light covering of hair there, a reflexive clutching for balance, as he took hers away.

Her lips parted, welcoming him deeper, but he would not take the plunge. His tongue touched the edge of her bottom front teeth, delicate licks to her gum line, his large hand coming up to hold her jaw still for him.

She made a noise at the back of her throat, and her body pushed against his, insistent.

"Tell me you want me to make love to you, Marisa," he said, his harsh whisper no less a demand because it was a heated breath along her cheek. "This is not sex, not fucking. No matter what happens after this night, you know that's the truth. You serve the truth, and love. Let me in. Trust me for this one moment, the most important moment in the world."

The hard-won mental wall she had built crumbled like a sandcastle against the onslaught of the ocean, just from those few coaxing words. His strength and goodness surrounded her, made her feel desired and protected, revered and enjoyed at once.

Marisa now understood why desperation for this feeling bloomed in the many hearts that visited her door. This was the greatest of magics. Even if a person had never had this blissful feeling herself, the sacred Joining of the Lord and Lady to renew the cycles of life emanated outward and encompassed all Their creations. All who were a part of Their Body would feel those emanations, and long to have it for themselves, be a part of it. As above, so below, as within, so without. It could be measured in an hour or a second, but it would never be enough until it became a state of existence, an infinite instead of a finite experience.

"Yes." She looked up at him, his beautiful, handsome spirit, the desire waiting to be unleashed in his eyes, his hands, his cock moving against her. "Make love to me, Conlon."

She gave a glad cry as he plunged, mating their mouths in a full penetration, his hands moving down to hold her hips firmly against him.

He slid onto the bed, covering her body with his own. She lay down in the comfort of this bed every night. Lying down in it now, with his body settling on top of hers, felt more welcome than the best dream she had ever known in it. Her thighs opened to cradle his body, and her towel slid to the floor as he unknotted his own, so there was nothing but the waiting precipice between the meeting of their flesh.

Their sexual interludes to this point had been flashes of fire. This was a slow, hot burn, his kisses upon her throat and lips taking an eternity until she was only sensation in his arms. She couldn't think past each place his mouth pressed and held, tasting her flesh with bare movements of his lips that rocketed through her nerve endings from the point of contact to her toes. She gripped her fingers in his hair, holding him to her, and realized her body was moving with a life of its own, her hips rising, circling, stroking against him in insistent demand.

He lifted his head, his body lying upon hers, his arms sliding up so his elbows were on either side of her shoulders, holding some of his weight off of her.

"How does this feel?" he asked, his fingertips doing a light stroke of her cheek, his eyes darkening as her head turned and she caught his finger in her mouth, biting him with sharp teeth. She curled her tongue around the imprisoned digit and let him withdraw it slowly, glistening with the moistness of her mouth. He groaned and caught her face in his hands, pressing his body down on hers to keep her still. "I need to know if you're okay. You're trembling."

"I'm not afraid. I want this. I want you." She reached up and touched his face, tracing his forehead, the slope of his nose, the curve of the bone under his eye. He brought his lips to the pulse point on her wrist, and she rested her hand on his face. Her blood pounded against his mouth. His cock moved against her, a bump of movement, and she felt wetness against her thigh, her wetness mixing with his. Something in that place between her legs was pulsing as hard as the blood through her wrist, and thousands of years of instinct told her what it wanted. It was an ache connected to the tightness in her chest, the trembling in her body. If this was merely lust, she could understand why it was so often confused with love, but she knew Conlon was right. Whatever this was, it was more than lust, even if it was too sudden to be called love.

Her hips rocked up, brushing her pussy against him, and he groaned against her wrist.

"Slow down, kitten," he muttered. "I don't want to rush this."

He moved down to her neck, and she arched her whole body, telegraphing the ancient female message of surrender and trust, that she was open to him, his to claim.

His arms curled under her waist, holding her in her arched position as he bit her neck, then tortured it with his tongue, the rough afternoon shadow of his beard rasping against the pale skin of her breastbone. She could do little with her arms but let them lie on either side of her. All her energy seemed to be drawing toward one place. Her hips pressed up, circling, rubbing in a manner she couldn't stop, a continuing call to his body to come into hers, to bring her to that place that the magic, and now her own desires, demanded.

Instead of succumbing to her body's plea, he heightened it, by sliding down her body and bringing his lips to her breast, nibbling the skin to her nipple, and then covering it with the warm, sucking pressure of his mouth.

Now she did catch hold of him, her fingers gripping those massive shoulders. "Conlon," she said. He murmured, an incoherent noise of desire against her flesh.

She closed her eyes, and suddenly the world turned over. She surfaced in the hot spring of Conlon's body and mind. The red heat of his desire rolled over her, through her. She felt the tightening of his body, preparing to take the woman beneath him, as clearly as if it were her own body. Her mind seesawed between shock and the muddled confusion of arousal. Her empathy had never received anything but negative emotions, emotions of darkness. This was a melding of two desires in a heated rush of sensation, and she felt both of them.

Her muddled mind tried to make sense of it. Perhaps as this physical act opened her mind, her empathy gave her the gift of being able to merge in this way with her lover. She had never done this before. Anything was possible.

It was a very plausible explanation, and her moment of fear turned into wonder, and then a wild craving, for now she felt his desire as well as her own, and the demand was overwhelming. For the first time in her life, she experienced joy in her ability to experience what lay in the mind of another.

I feel it, too. Marisa, I feel you. In my mind, in my body. In my heart.

She had a brief flash of his intense hazel eyes focused on her own before his mouth was on hers again, driving away any rational thought. His hand moved in between them, guiding himself to her.

He had brushed his cock against her as he suckled her breast, but now his intentional navigation brought his broad head firmly against her moist lips. She had no fear of this. He had taken that away. Now, she just wanted. She opened her legs wider and he murmured hot approval, biting at her lips as she answered with a soft cry of encouragement.

Her pussy stretched to take his head in, her thighs spreading and lifting. The warm wetness of her body eagerly welcomed him. The shaft of his cock followed, that impressive column of flesh and steel she couldn't get her fingers around. He was widening her, but taking his time, moving in slowly, his fingers sliding up off his shaft once he had it inexorably in its track to gently pinch her clit, making her hips wiggle and move faster, her breath coming in pants at the sensation that spiraled through her in rhythm with the pump of her hips.

She felt the tremendous control he was exercising to hold back, and she didn't want that. She wanted him, all the way inside, now. Her hands slipped down, finding the slick muscles of his buttocks. She clutched him, lifting her hips as if she could impale herself.

"Jesus," he rasped. "Hold on, kitten. I don't want to hurt you. You're such a little thing."

She didn't listen, her clutch insistent. Her legs rose to fold over her hands on his buttocks, her muscles inadvertently squeezing, tightening on him in her channel. Being in his mind at the same time she was in her own, she knew how much he wanted to be inside her, and exploited every image she could see through his mind's eye to try and make him surrender to her will.

He met the shield of her maidenhead and stopped, resisting her with his greater physical strength and a mental control she would have admired if she didn't want him so desperately.

"No turning back," he whispered, his face above her, framed by the soft light of a dying day. "Hold on, kitten, and trust me. Let yourself go."

He surged forward, breaking through her innocence in one sharp, clean movement, seating himself to the hilt in the same motion. Marisa cried out, but it was a short pain, one that could not detract from the overwhelming experience of having a man's body so deeply within her, so irrevocably connected to hers. It was an intimacy she had never had, never hoped for. In that one act of burying his cock in her, he had filled the empty place in her heart.

He whispered to her, the words not important. He held still, his powerful body trembling as he let her get accustomed to the feel of him, and then he pulled back. One inch, another inch, the thick shaft teasing her clit, the head stroking her inside. Then he came forward again, as if he was drawing a bow over the strings of an instrument, and her body tightened, rippling with the music he was creating.

"Oh," she breathed. "Oh."

He smiled then, a faint gesture, as dream-like as the twilight air, and he did it again. And again. Just as slow each time, even though the fire burned exponentially hotter with each stroke, and her body screamed with the desire to push to full conflagration. He kept her smoldering, hotter, hotter, his teeth gritted, the tense muscles of his jaw giving his handsome face the appearance of smooth creek rock, slick with his sweat.

"You need the slowness, kitten. I know you want to go over, but you need an easy pace."

And she did. He was so large that her newly stretched muscles needed time to learn how to ease and tighten on him in a way that brought them both pleasure. So she wavered on that pinnacle, and focused inside herself, marking the give of her muscles as he pushed inward, then their jealous squeezing as he pulled back, communicating her desire to hold onto him and which made her gasp with the mutual pleasure she gave them both. She found the rhythm, matched him, stroke for stroke, and felt the beat of their hearts, the pump of their lungs and the motion of their bodies become aligned.

"Trust me, Marisa," he repeated, his words lost in a groan of restraint. "Let go, kitten. Let go."

Why did he keep saying that, when he would not let her get to that wonderful precipice of sensation? His hips changed their angle so that his thrusts rubbed a seesaw motion against the opening to her cunt, her clit, and a circle of pleasure inside that seemed no bigger than her pinkie print. Each rub of his head against it, and the stroke of his shaft out against the clit, drove her higher, but not over.

As her arousal grew, her consciousness expanded as she had predicted, but also much further than she had anticipated. Beyond the room, beyond the clearing, it flung itself out like a roll of clouds, farther than it had ever been able to reach, into the nearby town and beyond. Marisa felt the height as if she was on top of a mountain, looking down on thousands of souls. As suddenly as she became aware of them, they became aware of her.

Her fingers clutched on his skin. "Conlon."

She tried to speak further, but she couldn't get the words out. He pressed his lips against her ear, and it felt as if his voice spoke from deep within her. "I'm here, kitten. Don't be afraid."

They were coming toward her from all directions, like a tidal wave from which there was no escape. She could not move, frozen in their sights as they descended upon her, shoving aside her shields, trampling them beyond repair, leaving her completely vulnerable.

Their darkest emotions poured over and into her like a flood of bright flashing lights, hurting and blinding her inner eye. Her body stiffened. That pinnacle of pleasure so close a moment before was now lost in the confusion, blasted away beyond her reach.

Use me, Marisa. Look. Use me. LOOK.

Conlon's voice was a roar in her head, a command that she thrashed around within herself to find. As she turned, amidst all the light, she saw a point of blessed darkness. She fought toward it, her survival instinct shoving down her panic enough to make her focus on getting to it.

As she kept it within her sights, it grew larger, a dark vortex before her inner eye. The harsh lights surrounded it, but none penetrated that welcoming blackness. Her subconscious ran for that shelter, scrabbled for it, urged on by his voice in her head, calling her, over and over.

Come to me, kitten. Come now.

She stumbled and fell into the darkness, wrapped its protection around herself like a cloak. As abruptly as she had been sucked under by fear and despair, she exploded back into her consciousness and gasped, gripped by spiraling strokes of pleasure in a dizzying wave of sensation, for Conlon was still moving within her.

Only now, his movements were fierce and strong, as he pulled her to him with the demands of his body and her own, breaking the power of the invading force over her will and desires.

Her body arched and all those complex nerve endings in her pussy began to vibrate, a warning, a promise of the strength of the magic sweeping over her. The climax struck with the power of a summer storm, rumbling out of the depths of the sky and earth, taking her over, opening her mouth in a scream she could not stop. It erupted from her, the force of her orgasm electrifying the lights gathered like hungry demons just beyond Conlon's protection and driving them back even further.

Conlon's hands tightened, a bruising but welcome grip on her body and he let go, pouring hot seed into her. It shattered her emotional shields, her personal defenses against his impact on her emotions, galvanized the yearnings he had raised in her. Their bodies moved together as one, synchronized by mysteries that were centuries old.

In the amazing link their joining had forged, she could feel the limitless space within him for her spirit to turn and draw his essence around her. With that around her unprotected psyche, she could face the world she so often had to shut out. She sensed them, those many consciousnesses, but they could not attack her. They could not come within the circle of his protection without her permission. She could filter them. She felt the ones genuinely in need of healing, the good soul gone astray, and the ones who had willingly succumbed to the petty desires of the selfish heart. However, without the attack on her senses, the cacophony from the negative vibrations could be dimmed, and she could see how best to help, how to set any of them on a better path. Not just with her potions, but with her empathic understanding of their needs.

She could not see him physically on this plane of awareness, but it was a place where emotion was more powerful than physical sense. He was there with her, his soul and mind, seeing what she was seeing, standing with her, lending his protection to her power. That was Conlon Maguire's gift, a limitless well of protective power to offer, fueled by his pure spirit and the accumulation of a life spent protecting others, a White Knight in truth.

When the powerful grip of the orgasm started to ease, like the ebbing tide of a sparkling ocean at sunset, something even more amazing happened. She saw all those flashing lights fade away, back to their respective souls, and yet she was still warmly ensconced in Conlon, their spirits intertwined like their bodies.

Yet it was no spirit, but a human male under her fingertips, with sweaty, muscled skin pressed against the inside of her thighs. Who even now scratched her neck with his stubble as he nuzzled her, his heart thundering against hers. A real man who could answer the quiet desires of her woman's heart and stand by her for the life the Lord and Lady had given her.

The miracle Laraset had promised was in her arms. Her soulmate. Capable of giving her the strength and shielding to live the life she chose, not the life forced upon her to survive.

Marisa was so overcome she could not speak, and the shudders of her body were now fueled as much by her tears as the post-coital aftershocks of desire. Conlon didn't speak for a long while. He simply held her, kissed away each tear. He let her see the knowledge in his eyes, the promise that had been there all along, that she had not recognized until the magic was released by their joining.

When the emotional and physical tumult had ebbed enough that she lay quiet in his arms, she spoke at last in a voice hoarse with emotion.

"Why didn't you tell me?" She held onto him as if he might vanish if she let him out of her body, and he tightened his hold around her, understanding her need. "Why the potion?"

"I couldn't have told you, kitten. Something like this, I had to show you, and I could only show you if you let it be more than sex. Your heart had to be open to the possibility of love between us, of forever. If you had closed down, only given me your body, it wouldn't have worked."

She ran the palms of her hands down the muscles of his broad back, arched with a sigh as his thighs tightened at her touch, driving him more deeply within her. "How did you find me?"

"It's been a thirty-two year search." He smiled, rubbed his nose against the side of her face. "It ended when I went to a Sioux medicine man by the name of Kohana." He pulled back so he could face her surprised look. "I went there to do a sweat lodge, after Peru. To heal."

Now it was her turn to press upward, put her cheek against his rough jaw, caress his ear and neck with her fingertips. His jaw moved against her skin.

"In my vision in the sweat lodge, I saw you clearly for the first time, but at that moment, I knew you had always been there, in me. Like that moment when you find your destiny and you think, 'ah, there you are.' You were it for me, kitten.

"No, no more tears." He raised a lock of her hair, pressed it to the corner of her eye. "Imagine my joy at having a vision of you when I'd been locked in a sweat lodge for three days with a bunch of other unwashed guys." She managed a smile and he used his lips to catch the next tear that fell. "There you were among us," he said. "But I was the only one who could see you. You were like Snow White. Ruby red lips, pale, perfect skin, raven hair falling forward over ripe breasts cradled in lace and velvet. I wanted you so much that from that moment forward you were a constant ache in my heart, and my cock." He wound his fingers around her hair, tightening his hold. "From the first moment I saw you in my dreams," he murmured. "I wanted to spread your legs and make you mine."

He kissed her neck, bit. Marisa trembled in his arms, aroused and overcome by his words, but he showed no mercy, taking her from laughter to tears to passion to joy. "I wanted to curl my arms around you, shield every part of your body and soul with the strength of mine, reassure you, be your lover and your friend, be everything you needed, forever. Your shadow was already printed on my soul. I wanted the real thing in my arms."

He lifted his head, their eyes less than a finger width apart. "I told Kohana all I saw and he said, 'This woman is your calling, your true destiny, and your lifemate. I will tell you how to find her, but winning her will not be easy. You will have to approach as the true hunter who respects and reveres his prey must. With strategy, and stealth.'" Humor flitted through his eyes at that, reflected in her own, as Marisa could well imagine the eccentric Kohana laughing at them both.

"He told me to go halfway across the country, to this tiny hole-in-the-wall town, and find an old woman living in the woods on its outskirts. This woman, he told me, would be the key to finding my soulmate. It was the only warning he gave me. He didn't tell me I'd find you here. It took everything I could do not to fall down at your feet and beg when I first saw your face."

Marisa smiled. "Strategy and stealth." She cocked her brow, bit her lip when he shifted within her. "Well, Mr. Maguire, you did a very good job with both." She placed her hands on his face, held him there so she could stare at him, this miracle that she didn't quite believe wasn't a dream. "With you, I felt what people were feeling," she said. "But I could control it. I could pick and choose, and I could feel the bad *and* the good, not just the bad. It's like I always could, but the volume knob on the bad was just turned up so high it drowned the good out." She blinked more tears from her eyes and he smiled, kissing them away again.

"I know. I felt it when you turned it down, took control. It was marvelous, kitten."

With a groan she found endearing and amusing, he rolled off her, taking her with him, so she lay on his chest. "We don't have to be joined physically to do that. Laraset and Kohana told me, if we made it work, we'd eventually be able to link spiritually and I'll be able to protect you, even if we're not together. Like if one of us is traveling, or at the grocery store," he added, seeing her sudden look of apprehension. He reached up, touched her cheek. "You can go anywhere, kitten, anywhere you want to go. Though I'll admit, I kind of like doing it the physical way."

She found a tiny smile, her worries easing. His large hand cupped her face. "Forever, Marisa," he said quietly. Firmly. "I'll talk you into falling in love with me. I might even confuse you enough to get you to marry me in a weak moment. Maybe have my child."

He looked at her steadily, waited for her reaction. Marisa swallowed down a lifetime of fear and chose to believe in miracles again, accept his reality.

"Yes," she said.

His eyes darkened and he raised up on his elbow, taking her down to her back to kiss her, long and hard, curling his arms under her to pull her up against his body. When he lifted his head, he kept her tight within his embrace. Her arms were folded against his chest, between the two of them like a pair of delicate bird wings, and her fingers fanned out on his collarbone, touching him.

"I'm scared, though," she admitted. "The idea of children."

The corner of his mouth lifted. "That's the thing you can fear least, kitten. When I had my vision in the sweat lodge, I saw you in three images. First, I saw the face of the old lady, your illusion. The Crone face, Kohana called her. Then I saw the raven-haired beauty, as I said. The Maiden. But my soul knew neither of these was the true face of the woman I loved. It was when you appeared to me as a Mother, I knew I was seeing your true self. The mother of my child." He shifted, laid her hand on her stomach. "A child we may have just planted in your body."

Marisa felt a thrill flutter through her as he laid his hand on hers. He stroked her knuckles, traced the delicate skin of her bare stomach in the open spaces between her fingers. "But more than that, you're a Mother in the sense of capital M. A Mother and healer to the souls of many, as many as your generous heart and what you call the Lord and Lady will bring to you."

She turned her hand, linked it with his and wiggled around so she was lying on her side, facing him. Her mind could not digest the enormity of it all, so she chose to focus on a random thought niggling at the edge of her mind. "So, that butterfly thing. That was part of your strategy?"

He grinned at her, stretched his free arm over his head. "Never know what methods you'll need to convince a woman to see your point of view. It worked, didn't it?"

"Ooh, you…" She scrambled, snatched the spoon off the floor and went after him with it. They wrestled in the bed a moment or two, him laughing until he got it away from her and set her on his loins, seating his cock firmly against her. She quieted like a child given a pacifier, her hands braced on his solid chest, feeling the beat of his heart as he lay beneath her.

"Eventually," he said, "we'll go see your parents."

"Oh, Conlon, I don't know."

"Kitten, if your mother and father got the chance to hold you in their arms once without causing you pain, it would do more to bring healing and closure to their lives than a thousand of your letters, no matter how well written they are. You've got adopted siblings out there. They deserve to know you."

She shook her head. "But, I don't know—"

"There's no rush on anything, Marisa. None. We have time. We definitely have tonight." He smiled, a slow, sexy gesture that made her stomach somersault. "And I'm in no hurry to leave a bed with you in it. You remember me talking about those threads? They'll guide us, and they're strong. They'll bear us up no matter where we go, even if we decide to spin all our dreams from here. Fate finds us anywhere. All you have to do now is think about tonight." His fingers eased down her spine and his gaze descended as well, considering her naked body. He cupped her breasts, brushed the tips of her nipples with his thumbs. "I'm thinking—"

"Conlon, you couldn't." She felt him hardening beneath her pussy and her gaze flitted to his intent one. "Or, I could be wrong."

"Any objections?"

A smile crept onto her face, its light coming from her heart and the growing warmth of her own body. "I hope those are REALLY strong threads," she said, as he banded his arms around her, bringing her body down fully on top of his. "Because if we spin them from this bed, I don't know of a potion strong enough to hold up the frame."

"I do," he murmured, bringing her breast down to his eager mouth. "Let me show you how to make it."

Make Her Dreams Come True

&

Make Her Dreams Come True

ဢ

"Honey, that's not a dress, that's a personality change."

Meg glanced over her shoulder at the woman who'd spoken, a woman who wore motherhood and menopause as comfortably as her padded Reebok walking shoes. Her companion cackled.

"Earlene, you're too much. Let's go get an ice cream cone."

They drifted away, bumping Meg's elbow. She stood beside them, looking at the same magical creation, but neither woman had noticed her.

The gossamer silk fabric draped over the high tip of the mannequin's breast in storm cloud blue and merged into lavender at the waist. The two colors joined hands to dance and whirl in the folds of the skirt, so light it shimmered in stillness. Reminding her of the touch of a sunrise on ocean waves, the dress transformed the mannequin into a silver-skinned goddess, frozen in the peace of perfection.

"A long time ago, when we believed in fairy tales…" Warm breath and an oddly familiar voice filled her ear, "…a legion of fairy seamstresses wove this dress for their beloved princess."

Meg turned her head, but the voice moved to her left shoulder, evading. "The dress was stolen by a jealous mortal woman. She couldn't wear it, of course, because fairy clothing can only be worn by a fairy. She tried to destroy it, but it was magic and couldn't be destroyed."

She tried turning her body. Hands, so strong her muscles couldn't tense against their grip, came down on her shoulders, made her face the dress. "The jealous woman finally put the dress here." Lips brushed her ear. "In the least magical place she could imagine. The princess can only retrieve it by becoming mortal. But, if she does that, the experience of mortal suffering will destroy her fragile, fairy heart."

"There's not a lot of hope in your story," Meg murmured.

"That depends on whether or not you believe magic can happen in a mall." The hands released her and she turned to look into a stranger's eyes, so intense in their pull that they almost drew her forward. Meg swayed against it, startled, and took a step back.

A flash of humor moved briefly through his dark gaze, then burned away in pinpoints of flame. She felt like a creature of snow standing too close to a fire elemental, thinly disguised as a mortal man.

He reached past her, his arm brushing her shoulder as he unhooked a matching dress from the rack beside the mannequin. His shoulders were wide enough to keep her trapped between him and the decorative, shrimp-colored pillar next to the rack. "Go put this on. It looks like the right size."

"What?" She blinked at him, then the dress. "I beg your pardon—"

"You'll beg for something from me today," he said. "But it won't be my pardon. You'll never need that from me."

Her gaze shot to his face. There was nothing oily or pretentious in his tone, no implied come on. His soft voice held the confidence of someone with the ability to control and direct others. There was also an intimate undercurrent, somewhere between the warm possessiveness of a father and the unpredictable aggression of a lover. His voice alone cracked the yearning within her, and the dress and the story magnified it, leaving her vulnerable to the searing touch of the madness.

"I can't—" She shook her head. "It's… it's not my size."

"Yes, you can, and yes, it is." He laid the dress over her shoulder and fanned it out over the front of her red sweatshirt. A scent of lavender rose from the movement of the cloth and

Meg's hand, nervously rising to defend herself from his advance, settled uneasily on the garment. She held still, afraid her rough skin would tear the web of delicate threads. It felt like she rested on the surface of a cool lake, the currents tickling the nerve endings around the circumference of each finger.

"I saw you earlier today." She spoke with her eyes on the dress, her breath quivering along the fabric.

"I saw you. You looked frightened." His fingers brushed her chin lightly. His eyes opened hers like a tomb and shone on all the treasures that should have been there.

Meg looked back down at the ripples of silk immersing her. Her cheek brushed the folds of the dress and the smell of lavender rose again. She wanted to do more than try on the dress. She wanted to absorb its energy, feel the silk against her bare body, discard the conventions of slip, hose and bra, and stand in it on the edge of a cliff of hopes like a Maxfield Parrish painting. The older woman had been right. This dress was an alternate reality.

The man brought his heat a step closer and lavender wound itself around the lingering scent of rain that clung to his coat. There was also a faint trace of male cologne, rich like a palace tapestry. The aroma drew her gaze to his jaw, and the pulse in his neck below it. He bore a late afternoon shadow and the contrast intrigued her, silk clutched in her one hand, the possibility of touching that roughness with the other.

Panic flooded her veins. Meg turned, stumbled into the rack of dresses, and groped for the empty hanger. "I can't try—"

His hand curled over hers, and she felt his chest and ribs press into her shoulder blades.

"What's your name?" he murmured.

"Meg. But—" She pulled her hand from his grasp and turned back to him, executing an awkward hop so her breast wouldn't come in contact with his chest.

"Meg." He recaptured her hand and placed it back on the dress, over her right breast. He molded her fingers over her curve, then he drew his hand away, sliding from the channels between her fingers so he caressed her breast through the cage of her hand. She couldn't tell whether the gesture had been intentional or not, but his touch prickled all the way from her collarbone to her waist.

"I want you to put the dress on, Meg, and you want to. What harm would that do?"

There were a dozen answers, not the least of which stood too close to her, but no answer seemed as compelling as the scent of lavender. "Okay," she said quietly.

She bumped the rounders of clothes between her and the dressing room like a scratched pinball, while the dress didn't catch on the jutting tip of a single rack. She went behind the curtain of the changing area and tripped through a cream pair of plantation shutter doors, stumbling into a dressing room framed by three walls of mirrors.

Laying the dress over the heart-shaped back of a blue velvet chair, she smoothed the fabric. She'd try on the dress because she wanted to. If the man didn't leave her alone, she'd ask the store manager to call security. She was in control. Meg nodded to herself in the mirror. She pulled her sweatshirt over her head, watching all the images of herself do it.

Prominent ribs and pale, loose skin assailed her. Up until a year ago, she'd fought fifteen pounds of excess fat most of her life. Now she didn't remember to eat unless Deb put it in front of her. *You can achieve all your personal goals, you just won't get them until they don't mean anything anymore.*

It sounded like the Eastern philosophy she'd loved so much in college—let it all go and you'll be truly free. An idealistic, fresh college student saw a person sculpting away the excess to define the shining soul within; in reality, vital organs dropped off like pieces of a rotting corpse until only dust remained.

She shoved the jeans off her hips and kicked them free, stubbing her toe against the curved mahogany leg of the chair. "Shit." She hopped around, gritting her teeth as the pain intensified, reached its peak, then faded into that post-anguish, tingling numbness that was strangely pleasurable.

Why was she doing this? Was it because of how she'd felt when she'd first seen the stranger earlier that day?

She'd gone into the card shop to get an anniversary card for Deb and Jeremy. It was a simple, manageable goal, something she was sure she could do, one less thing she'd have to apologize for not doing. But she'd forgotten that card shops were the torture chambers of the dysfunctional, with racks and racks of mocking sentiments. The anniversary cards flowed into an ocean of sympathy cards, a macabre sense of arrangement. She'd floated from "congratulations on another year together" to a graveyard of "sorry for your loss". She'd fled the store after ten minutes.

It was when she'd pressed against the iron rails of the mezzanine, gasping for air, that she'd seen him. A waterfall of silver ribbon icicles had sparkled before her, hung from the steel rafters of the glass dome ceiling above. People had clattered and chattered around her, some hurrying to finish their shopping, some using their surroundings as an avenue to stroll and socialize with friends, some ambling alone and gazing into store windows with the faintly guilty expression of self indulgence. The currents of air created by the different paces and groupings had moved the icicles against one another in a rustling, discordant music. Following their descent to the ground level with her eyes, she'd seen him.

He sat on the glossy tile wall circling the mall's wish pond. His body, in a black duster, tweed slacks and white dress shirt, had the deceptively relaxed look of a panther. One of his large hands rested casually on the ankle he propped on his opposite knee. His other arm stretched along the rail behind him. The pose enhanced his size, and Meg was certain he stood well over six feet with shoulders practically half as broad. His thick, black hair fell away from his forehead to sharply define the precise, strong angles of his face. A few loose strands of his hair scattered over his lined forehead. He was solid attraction at a primitive level, the predator so magnetic that a rabbit would willingly walk into the range of his jaws. And he looked directly at her.

She had drowned in the impact of his dark eyes. Normal people didn't look up at the mall, too self-conscious. A person who looked up wasn't afraid of drawing attention to himself.

He was man in the original sense, sure of who he was, what he was, and emanating the fierce certainty that could light a woman's soul, protect her and give her the peace to find herself again. It could also stir dangerous anticipation.

An image had flashed through her mind. A male mounting a female beneath a canopy of interlaced foliage deep in the forest, pressing her palms and clutching fingers into the earth with his hard thrusts, the scents of heat and earth filling her nose as he filled her body, mind and soul.

Meg had backed up from the rail, stumbling into a man pushing a baby in a stroller. She'd spun away from them and staggered into the crowd.

Maybe that was why she stood in the dressing room now. For a moment, the stranger had made her feel something other than fear and guilt.

She snatched up the dress and yanked it over her head, thrusting her arms through the sleeves. The fabric snagged on her bra, caught on her elbow, and she writhed in the dress, a fragrant straight jacket. Wiggling an arm free, she released the waistband of the skirt from her bra. The dress settled over her body, rubbing against her cotton underwear like fingers against styrofoam. Meg stared at all three images of herself in the mirror, and three scarecrows with vacant brown eyes and limp chestnut hair held back with battalions of bobby pins stared back. She felt as transformed as the dress hanger.

She sank into the chair and dug her hands into her hair, dislodging pins. The pose could hold in the madness or summon it. She waited to see what would happen, since the choice was entirely out of her hands. If she was lucky, a banshee shriek might erupt and shatter the glass on all sides, destroying her image forever.

"Ma'am? The gentleman sent me to check on you."

She lifted her head enough to see the polished burgundy toe of an elegant Italian heel outside the dressing room doors.

"Tell him I've changed my mind. Tell him to go away."

The foot in the shoe rose as the woman peered above the top level of the doors, but Meg didn't lift her head. The foot sank back into the heel, then turned and whispered away softly on the carpet.

She was a sucker for the promise of magic, fairy godmothers, and handsome princes. She was the type of idiot who'd go to Disneyland ten times in a row, even knowing it wouldn't be as good as what she wanted it to be. Meg bared her teeth at her images. "Bibbidi-Bobbidi-BOO."

"Is she dressed?"

"Yes, sir, but—"

"Meg?"

She jolted upright in the chair. He stood before the doors, easily able to see her and her crumpled pile of clothing. She found her mouth open, closed it. She'd lost her grasp on outrage, and had no strength to do anything but sit and despise her body in the hated perfection of the dress.

"Stand up and let me see you."

"No." She shook her head. "I'm not playing anymore."

"This isn't a game, Meg." He pushed open the doors and she started up from the chair in reaction. He stopped and his hard eyes slid from her apprehensive face, down her throat, over her breasts, and rested on the flare of her hips. His eyes retraced their path just as thoroughly, and her muscles tightened wherever his gaze lingered.

He advanced another step. She stepped back from his energy, too large to be contained in this small room. It held her against the center mirror, surrounded by dozens of their images.

When he laid his wrist above her head, she had to tilt her face to look at his. His white shirt smelled of fresh starch and rain. Faint impressions of drops still marked the shoulders of his coat, which lay against his body with the same fluidity as the dress had lain on the mannequin. Dark curls showed at the open throat of his shirt, promising a pelt of dark hair covering the skin beneath. The pulse along his neck was slow, steady. Hers wasn't.

"Speak to me, Meg." His voice resonated against her ear. His breath passing off her cheek like heat off brimstone.

"What? Yes?" She cleared her throat.

"Good. I was afraid you'd lost your ability to talk." His eyes glinted. "Patrice, the scarf, please." He turned his wide shoulders and revealed the woman with the burgundy shoes.

Her gold-plated pin declared her the store manager. Meg wondered if the stylish thirty-something was really a store mannequin switched on each morning. It sounded—and looked—like an appealing fate. To be only one thing, expected to be nothing else…

Patrice laid a silver scarf shot with black threads and edged in black and silver tassels over his extended palm. She inclined her head to Meg with warm professionalism, then breezed away on her heels.

"Meg, I'm going to tie this scarf around your eyes."

She put her hand up, halting the advance of the cloth he held between them. Meg could see the lower half of his face through the silver mesh, like a reflection beneath the surface of water. "I don't even know your name."

"You're not in any danger here," he said. "I don't want you to look in the mirror again. I'll be your mirror. I want you to take off everything you're wearing under the dress. You know that's how it was meant to be worn. You knew it when you first saw it. When you're ready, call to Patrice, and she'll come get you."

He moved forward and Meg raised her hands again, but not high enough to stop him. They twitched, frozen in mid-air, as he brought the gauzy fabric against her eyes. Then he stepped closer to tie it behind her head, and her fingers rested against his shirtfront, her rib cage brushing his stomach. The folds of his duster fell against her hip. His living, pulsing warmth washed over her as darkness descended and her other senses multiplied.

He tied the knot beneath her hair, then his fingers slid to her shoulders, bringing the tasseled ends of the sash sliding against either side of her neck. One of the tassels tickled Meg's nose and lips and she wrinkled them in reaction, dodging it with a turn of her head. A chuckle reverberated out of his chest and into her. He rested his hands on either side of her face, enveloping her cheeks. The base of his thumbs pressed her lips because his hands were so big, his index fingers pressing the silken fabric of the scarf against her temples.

"Don't be afraid, Meg. Everything will be all right if you do as I tell you. Call Patrice when you're done."

The doors squeaked as he passed and the air became hollow, as it does when a room becomes empty. Meg swallowed. Jeremy had said she shouldn't be eating Jell-O by herself, much less wandering around loose in a mall. He'd whispered it to Deb in the supposed privacy of their kitchen, but Meg had heard. She heard everything now. It was surprising how loud everyone became when your own inner voices died.

She gathered the skirt and slid her fingers under the waistband of her panties to push them down her thighs. Her skin shivered beneath the trail of her fingers. She didn't use sight to dress and undress herself, but now the lack of it made her feel awkward. The silk skirt slid down the cheeks of her bottom, dimpling in her crevice, her awareness of that intimate opening enhanced and coiling in her stomach. The silk felt like feathers over the curls between her legs, and she worried that they might show, a dark smudge of tight coils poking through the thin cloth.

She unhooked her front-clasping bra and worked the straps down inside the loose sleeves. Meg could hear the hum of the lighting in the dressing room, and the vague murmur of voices drifting in from the mall outside the store. Patrice murmured efficiently, helping another customer, but expectant silence filled the space immediately around Meg. It pushed her own noises against her, the rustling as she struggled out of her clothes, the soft inhalation of her breath, now quick, now normal, as she freed the left strap. It made her skin prickle at the touch of her own hands against her body. She felt as aware of herself as… as if she were being watched.

She froze in the act of pulling the bra out through the tunnel of her right sleeve. Was he standing near, watching her over the doors? Maybe it only sounded as if he'd left, and he really sat in the chair, watching her push her panties down her calves and maneuver out of her bra within the span of his knees. The lack of space in the dressing room would necessitate the splaying of his long legs. It scared her, trickling nervous sensation down the line of her sternum. The accelerated pounding of her heart drowned the sound of her breathing, and she flung out her hand.

Her knuckles rapped the smooth mahogany scalloping on the back of the chair. She whirled to the doors and pushed. They swung out and creaked back, unimpeded until they bumped gently against her.

This was idiotic. All she had to do was take the scarf off to be sure. Meg put her hand up to the cloth, curled her fingers on it, then stopped and lowered her hand.

She liked how the dress felt in darkness. Her skin replaced her eyes, savored the silk, and told her she was beautiful.

She pulled the bra free and dropped it. The moment the waterfall of silk settled over her nipples, they hardened. When she took off her short socks, her bare toes sank and curled into the Berber carpet.

There was still something wrong, though. She set her mouth and pulled the plain gold band and the diamond off her left hand. What did it matter? She flung them on the carpet, and one of the bands pinged off the fiber and landed back on her bare foot. She shook it off, kicked at it, heard it bounce off the wall. It wasn't good enough. She wanted to hurl it, make sure she didn't step on it, or feel it, ever again.

"Ma'am? Are you ready?"

Meg unclenched her fists. Her breath rasped in her ears like a rabid dog's. *Stop. Stop. Don't lose it here.* Oh, God, what had she done?

She dropped to her knees, scrabbling blindly on the floor.

"My rings—"

"I have them, ma'am. It's all right." Patrice's hand touched her arm, her fingers briefly pressing the rings against Meg's cheek before they disappeared. Meg's hand closed on air.

"I need those."

"It's all right. I'm putting all your things in a carry bag. The gentleman said I should hold them for you."

"But I don't know if I'm going to get the dress." Actually, she did know. She knew what the price was.

"He's already purchased it, madam." There was a tissue-like rattling as she assumed Patrice put her things in one of the store's stylish silver foil bags, the kind Meg had seen carried around the mall. The rattling stilled and Patrice's cool hand took Meg's arm in a light hold, leading her out the swinging doors.

Meg balked. "I don't want to walk through the store like this." She reached for the blindfold.

"He didn't intend for you to. Here, let me help." Patrice's hands were at the knot under her hair, her nails lightly scraping Meg's skin. "He just wanted you out of the dressing room before I removed it, so you wouldn't be tempted to look in the mirror."

Meg wanted to ask Patrice how she thought she looked, but she knew she'd look like a scruffy orphan even if she walked out of a full body makeover at Neiman-Marcus. It wasn't just that holding the question back, though. The stranger had said he'd be her mirror, and she wanted to know his reaction. She wasn't sure what would be reflected in those dark eyes. Most gazes were a pathetic mirror of what was in her own.

The light made her squint a moment as she adjusted. She faced the entrance to the dressing rooms. Beyond the threshold, he stood at the sales counter, completing the purchase. His coat was folded over his arm and the white shirt pulled across his wide shoulders as he signed the receipt with a gold pen. His short dark hair, layered on the sides, enhanced the planes of his jaw, the shaved nape of his neck. He pocketed his wallet and saw her.

Come here, he mouthed. No words, just the movement of his lips, compelling her. She took a breath and moved toward him.

The dress caressed and stimulated her with every movement she made, and it gave her its fluidity. Meg turned her body at just the right moments, and the racks of clothes brushed her hips like waist-high meadow grass, gently parting to let her pass. She held his eyes the entire way, and they brought her to him as if she'd never had another destination in her whole life.

Lord, she was losing her mind. If they found her headless body in a ditch tomorrow, it would probably be no less encumbered than it was now, with nothing bouncing around her skull except trapped air currents that had wandered in through her ears. Meg stopped before him.

"Let's take care of this." He reached into her hair and removed the pins and combs, stuck there to keep the different lengths from her face. Once, her hair had fallen to her waist in thick glossy curls she'd thought other women might envy. She'd burnt it off with vicious efficiency with a curling iron, one hank at a time. It was growing back fast, refusing to respect her violence, just as weeds refused to respect the gardener.

He laid the pins on the counter as he went, and Patrice put them in a smaller bag. Meg's eyes followed the lacquered nails, but it was an automatic, unfocused gesture to hide her nervousness. All her senses responded to his fingers, so powerful that their gentle questing through her scalp felt like stroking.

Against her better judgment, she closed her eyes to feel his touch from the inside out, the lesson he'd already taught her with the scarf and the dress. She hungered for touch, craved it so badly that she daily suppressed the urge to ask Deb to stroke her hair the way he did now. She wanted Jeremy to hold her against his side, his fingers playing absently along her hip as he did with Deb when they all watched a movie together. Touch affirmed existence, affirmed connection, and it simply felt good. She might have acted as she did now, turning her head into his hand like a cat, almost purring with the pleasure of it. Deb would have thrown her out for making moves on her husband and they'd end up on a talk show. Based on how her day was going, she might end up there yet. Or on a milk carton.

She opened heavy-lidded eyes when his hand drew away.

"So, Meg," he said softly. "How does the dress feel now?"

She cleared her throat and found a voice thick enough to petrify skeletons into fossils. "You said you'd be my mirror. How does it look to you?"

He tipped up her chin with fingers brushing her jaw. "How it looks isn't nearly as important as how it feels. You went into the dressing room slumped over, dragging your feet, bumping into anything that got in your way."

She tensed her neck, but his hand held on, strong enough to hold her still with just three fingers, two along her jaw and one under her chin.

"You came out of the dressing room and walked to me like a Jaguar with rack and pinion steering." He lowered his hand, grasped her fingers, and laid them on his chest. "Just talking about it makes my heart beat faster. You feel that? " She watched his unsmiling mouth, the movement of his shaved jaw. "If I wasn't certain you'd run like a deer, I'd put your hand on my cock and you'd feel how much it likes the way you wear that dress."

Meg jerked her hand back. "You're trying to shock me."

"No." He shook his head. "I told you honestly how the dress... How you, in the dress, make me react, how any man in this mall who sees you will react. Now, I ask you again. How does the dress feel?"

She took two steps back from him. "It's...fine," she said faintly. She turned away, but, of course, it wasn't that easy. His hands were on her shoulders before she could take another step toward escape.

"Why are you afraid of your feelings?" He spoke against her ear, his voice frustratingly familiar, wine-sensuous.

"Because I drown in them." She twitched, but he didn't let go. "Because God didn't give me enough of what other people have to survive their emotions. I'm like one of those babies born without an immune system to protect themselves from disease, only my immune system can't build walls to protect me from floods of emotional pain."

"Well, then..." He folded his arms around her waist, holding her against his body. "I'd say you need to concentrate less on building walls and more on developing gills."

She saw the two of them on the rack of mirrors outside the dressing room. She avoided her image, transforming it into a blur of blue silk in her peripheral vision. She liked the image he'd created in her mind, but the mirror would return her to reality. She patted his hands inanely and started to pull away.

"Meg, I have a proposal for you." He held her with one arm and removed something that glittered from his left pocket with his other hand. She turned to see, but he bumped her slightly with his thigh. "Be still."

His hands came down over her head and, before her, she saw a choker of silver and gold-tone braid, no wider than a ribbon for a child's hair. It was so elegantly understated, it had to be real and expensive. Her pulse pounded against its slim restraint as he nudged her hair aside with the point of his wrist and fastened the clasp against the nape of her neck.

The stranger settled his hands on her waist again and bent his head back to her ear. He gazed at her in the mirror, so she had to face herself to look him in the eye. "Give me today to help you develop gills. You don't have to worry that I'm a psychotic killer. We won't leave the mall." He drew a loose curl back behind her ear and she shivered, her head full of his voice, her body heated by his closeness.

"What's the necklace for?"

"The necklace says you're mine. Leave it on and obey me in all things until I free you tonight when the mall closes."

"Why — "

He shook his head, placing a finger on her lips. "No more questions, Meg. The only act of free will you have is the right to take off that necklace and reclaim your independence. In everything else, I'm your Master. If you refuse, take off the necklace and walk away."

She turned to face him, and he let her this time. His eyes were remote, almost stern, but she still felt his heat and remembered the smile that had brushed through his eyes, the scarf tassels teasing her face.

In twenty minutes, he'd drawn a dozen different feelings from her without breaking her Pandora's box. Well, not totally.

What did she have to lose?

Deb wasn't picking her up until closing and the card store had proven she didn't have the emotional strength to handle shopping. So, why not go for the less stressful tack of turning over her will to a complete stranger, a dark angel who offered her something different, a change of perspective, for just a little while? If she did end up headless in that ditch, she'd be no worse off than the present sarcophagus her life had become. If the worst happened, her friends and family could bury her and get on with their own lives at last.

Meg looked into his eyes and the fire he'd banked surged into her chest and stomach, making her feel excited, and a little sick.

"Okay," she said. "I... I belong to you for today...until the mall closes. Or... until I take the necklace off." She shifted under his level gaze. No surprise showed on his face, not even a relaxing of muscles to say he might have doubted her response. She wasn't sure if that disturbed or comforted her. "Please say something."

He laid a hand on her neck, collaring her throat just below the choker. "Relax, Meg," he spoke. "You haven't signed a pact with the devil."

"That's exactly what Satan would say at this moment."

A full, wide smile flashed. It sealed the evidence, in Meg's opinion. Only a fallen angel could have a smile equally balanced between sin and the remembrance of heaven.

"Consider me one of his lesser demons." He molded her fingers into the crook of his elbow and clasped a hand over them. When he led her toward the arched opening of the store, Meg balked.

"I don't have any shoes."

He glanced down, and she curled her toes reflexively into the carpet. She should have known it would be over as quickly as this, reality intruding on an intriguing fantasy, like Dorothy waking up without ruby slippers, realizing it had all been a dream.

"It's okay," she managed, backing away. "It's probably just as well. I shouldn't be—"

He snagged her arm, and her breath whooshed out as he scooped her into his arms. She'd been picked up before, that one giddy moment before stepping over a threshold as man and wife. It had been awkward, with Tommy struggling for balance, and her feeling like an oversized cow. She'd felt relieved when he let her feet touch the floor on the other side. They'd laughed at it then. Meg had deprecated her weight and he'd held her hands and assured her it was his lack of "buff". Now, the moment stuck in her mind with a different symbolism, him too weak to carry her burdens, her too heavy to be carried, or cared for, by anyone.

In this stranger's arms, though, she felt no sense of weight. He held her easily, his long arms cradling her back and knees, cuddling the angle of her body in toward him. Her skin tingled, just a thin slip of silk away from the touch of his fingers. The curve of her left breast swelled above her neckline, pushed up by the solid muscle of his chest.

"Meg, I want you to understand something."

"What—yes?" She struggled to adjust and his arms contracted, keeping her still.

"You belong to me today. That means you'll tell me when you have a problem, and I'll handle it. You don't worry, I do. We'll get you some shoes."

"Sir." Patrice stood at the store entrance. "There's a very good shoe salon around the corner. If you wish, I'll call Marcus and tell him you're coming."

"I do wish, but it'll be an hour or more. We have another stop to make first."

Meg tightened her fingers on his shoulder. "Where are we going?"

He stopped at the opening to the mall's main avenue of people and noise. He tightened his arm, bringing her up his chest, and dropped a kiss on the bare curve of her half-exposed breast. "You'll just have to wait and see."

Her nipple peaked instantly at his brief, almost casual gesture and pressed stiffly into his chest. She suppressed a startling urge to cup her hand over her breast and keep the sliding pressure and dampness of his lips focused there, rather than lose it to the cool, indifferent mall air.

His move had been deliberate, executed with the confidence of a man who owned the right to touch her intimately. She hadn't shrunk away or been outraged. He'd drawn her into his fantasy with as little effort as he carried her. The whole situation should have frightened her, but the thing most people feared—the unknown—no longer had any power over her. It was what she knew—the familiar—that scared her to death. Meg knew what tomorrow would bring, and the next day, and the next, and a more terrifying hell she couldn't imagine.

He stepped into mall flow. His height made her feel as if she were on a pedestal, displayed in his arms. Teenage girls giggled and pointed from the mezzanine railings. Men's eyes grazed the curved turn of her hip, then rose to her escort's face. Their gazes skittered elsewhere, conceding ownership and declaring non-territorial neutrality. One woman, loaded with bags and two snarling children, saw them, and the tired lines of her face froze in a stone mask. Meg almost could hear her heart shut, as the woman jerked her eyes away. She didn't want to see a tall, handsome man carrying a caterpillar in a butterfly's garb. Where was the tall, handsome man to carry her, to give her the attention she secretly desired but didn't feel she deserved?

The mask that locked in the woman's pain closed around Meg's heart. She wanted to scramble down, run to her and bring her over, offer her the man's wonderful arms, a carousel ride which would bring back the magic of childlike wonder and romantic dreams. She had no right to be in this dark angel's arms; she'd done nothing so worthy. Embarrassment flamed conspicuously in her cheeks and she wished he'd put her down.

She turned her face into his throat, and through the tunnel of his jaw and throat, her eyes landed on another woman, sitting on a bench next to a bored teenage son. Tugging his hair, the woman gestured toward Meg. He shrugged, but then she flicked his nape with playful fingers, and a smile twisted at his lips. He made a face at his mother, making her laugh. When the woman's eyes turned back to Meg, there was a secret joy in them, as if the sight had brought the memory of an imperfect but well-loved husband and the peace that only a heart equally open to pain and pleasure could bring.

Then she was gone and they passed a cookware store. A brace of old men leaned against the glass storefront, three sets of eyes trained on their progress. Stepping forward abruptly, the main in the center put his hat over his heart and swept her a bow, a wistful smile on his lips.

Her mouth curved and she fluttered her fingers at him, brushing her carrier's nape. He glanced at her and the old man, and shook his head. "Buy her a dress and she's already flirting."

Meg laughed, and it sounded harsh, unused. She cut it off, startled. "What's your name?" she asked to cover the moment.

He stopped and lowered her bare feet to the cool tile floor. He left one arm at her waist, keeping her close to his body, though there was a slight cushion of air between them to avert the certain risk of flammability. He slid the finger of his other hand beneath her choker, tugging gently. "Meg, if you want something from me, you'll have to ask permission for it."

"I...I don't understand." The fingers of the hand resting at her waist stroked the outline of her hip. Without underwear, sensation trickled wherever the silk touched her.

He toyed with the necklace. "I mean, you don't tell me your desire. You ask if I'll give it to you."

"Oh." Her pulse treadled against the pad of his index finger. "May I know what your name is?"

"Yes, you may. My name is Daniel." He withdrew his hand from her throat, but left the other at her waist. "What do you like best about having your hair styled, Meg?"

"What?"

She'd lost track of how many times his unexpected questions had wrested a snappy retort from her.

He'd set her down in front of Victor's. Most mall hairdressers were open to public view like arcades, patrons parked in a double row of swivel chairs along a black and white tile floor, made more stark by harsh strobe lights and loud music intended to create a hip atmosphere. Victor's gave its patrons sanctuary behind panels of textured stained glass divided by black Gothic-styled columns. The entrance was a hallway, guarded by an antique Victorian lady's desk bearing a crystal compote of wrapped gold chocolates.

Soft track lighting spotlighted a gilt-framed print centered between two mirrors over the table. A Renaissance nude reclined on a deep burgundy loveseat, her neck arched and mouth opened for a chocolate held just out of her reach by her fully-dressed lover.

"It involves the senses, doesn't it?" Daniel guided her to the picture. "At first glance, it looks gaudy and melodramatic, something you might see at a drag queen's yard sale."

She chuckled, startled at the image.

"Keep your eyes on the painting, Meg."

Daniel picked up a chocolate, closed it in his hand, then passed behind her. "Look at it again. Something about it, maybe the way her hair falls down her back, or maybe how he has his arm around her waist, crushing her breasts into the fullness of his linen sleeve, holds you, arouses you."

Meg felt the lace and folds touch her own bosom as he drew his spell of words.

"Or maybe," his breath whispered against the bare skin beneath her ear, "what involves you is how she reaches for the chocolate, stretching her neck for a taste of sweetness from his hand. What do you think she's feeling?"

"She looks so absorbed," Meg said, staring at the woman's eyes. "As if that moment is all that matters. She's lost in everything sensual—his touch, the taste and smell of the chocolate, the way the velvet of the loveseat feels against her bare legs, and the way her hair feels on her bare shoulders..." She stopped, heat rising in her cheeks.

"No." Daniel placed his knuckles against her flushed skin. "That's good. Very good." He unwrapped the chocolate, peeling one corner at a time until the cube sat in a nest of gold. He extended it, and Meg reached her hand to take it.

"Uh-uh." He drew it out of reach. "Part your lips for me."

She looked around, and he brought her attention back with a firm hand to her jaw. "You're mine, Meg. The others don't matter."

Her stomach tightened uneasily. She didn't have to do it. She could remove the necklace and walk away. But why should she care if people thought she looked silly, mimicking a woman in a painting? She'd done more embarrassing things than that, though it was different when the madness made the decision for her.

She parted her lips and his dark eyes grew darker. He rubbed the chocolate along her bottom lip, then traced his way to the top. She smelled the rich, decadent flavor, tinged with the sharp, metallic odor of the gold foil. Her tongue came out and followed the path of his fingers.

Daniel stopped, watching her. His stare made her tongue trace the path of the chocolate even more slowly, weighted by the intensity of his stare and the power that uncoiled in her stomach as she saw the effect she had on him. She reached to touch him, but he stepped back and shook his head. He held the remaining chocolate just above her lips.

Meg tilted her head back. When she rose on the balls of her bare feet, she swayed forward, unsteady. His arm caught her at the waist and she smiled, closing her mouth on the chocolate and the tip of one of his fingers as her hands closed on his shirt front.

"Little trickster," he admonished, but he didn't make her release him. She licked the remaining chocolate off the wrapper and the sweetness filled her. She'd never had a better candy. She held the taste in the back of her mouth and let it melt down her throat.

Daniel rolled the wrapper into a ball and tucked it in his trouser pocket. "Now…" His thumb rubbed across her bottom lip, taking the last of the stickiness. "What do you like best about getting your hair styled?"

She couldn't remember the last time she'd gone to the hairdresser. Hell, she couldn't remember if she'd washed her hair this week. Yes, yes, she had. Deb had made sure she'd done it. It was hard to remember things like that, brushing hair, teeth, putting on deodorant. She'd run through the jungle of her mind for so many months, she had a hard time remembering why personal grooming was important.

"I've never thought about it."

"Close your eyes, then."

"But—"

"Obey me, Meg."

He turned her so she was looking at the Renaissance nude when she closed her eyes. She saw the outline and swirl of burgundy and gold colors against the dark canvas of her eyelids.

"You go to your stylist. You've worked it into your lunch hour or at the end of a long day, so you really don't want to be there. It's a chore, a task, one more thing to cross off the to-do list. You sit in the waiting room because he's not ready for you yet. You think about picking up *People* magazine, but, instead, you grab *Time* and read something about the Federal Reserve. When you're about halfway through, he's ready for you. You go to his stall, tell him not to bother with the shampoo, just do a wet cut. He's obviously pleased, being in a hurry to get to the next customer. You make uncomfortable small talk while he wets and cuts, the talk strangers make when forced to interact and act like pleasant acquaintances. You have no impression of your surroundings, just light, murmurs of voices, the smell of harsh sprays, and the passage of time before you can go home to your microwave dinner. He pulls the towel off your neck twenty minutes later, brushes your nape with horse bristles, and asks for eighteen dollars made out to the salon. Now, what do you like best about that experience?"

His words blurred and dissolved the colors of the Renaissance painting, creating a new canvas slashed with jaded realism. The picture made her feel the way television did.

Meg had learned that most bodies produced a natural, mind-numbing anesthetic that padded the jagged edges of television, edges created by the exaggerated emotional angst of teens, canned sitcom laughter and situations of "powerful" melodrama. With the anesthetic, the brain could spin them into a usable cotton candy substance, unoffensive and vaguely applicable to one's life.

Her anesthetic had run dry eight months ago. When Deb and Jeremy watched TV, she stayed in her room, her pillow squeezed tightly over her head. Her desperation for courage, loyalty, true love and friendship made it possible for a program like "Little House on the Prairie" to rip out her heart in one single hour episode. There was nothing designed to give rather than to take, no unconditional offerings. TV painted a picture that covered the way things really were, hid from view what had been lost, the great empty hole where the soul of the planet used to be.

"There's not much to like, is there?" he asked.

"You know there isn't. But it's the way life is."

"Close your eyes, and I'll make it better."

She shook her head. "I can't take any more."

"Meg—" He curled his fingers into the fabric over her bare hip. She tensed, but didn't pull away, though her spine stiffened and her shoulders rose defensively.

"You'll not argue with me or refuse me. Those are the rules. You don't think unless I give you permission to do so."

"A man who wants a woman that doesn't think. There's a shock," she muttered.

"When I tell you not to think, Meg, I'm not denying your intelligence. I'm telling you that I want you to react, to feel. When you think, your thoughts eat you alive. It's like watching ants tear apart a butterfly while it flaps helplessly on the pavement. Don't burden yourself with thoughts today."

The fingers of his left hand straightened, gliding down the slope of her thigh. They traced the joint between thigh and groin, languorously rose to circle her hip bone, then descended again. The knuckles of his right hand stroked the line of her ribs, his fingernails trailing the soft skin below her armpit. He repeated the path of his lower hand, this time with more pressure, this time with less, sometimes a straight line, sometimes a meandering path, while his right hand stilled just below her armpit, the pressure of his fingers only a whisper from the curve of her breast. The nerves in both places shimmered, yearning for his touch to expand its range.

"How does it feel, Meg?"

"Good," she whispered in a thick voice, full of the heat he created.

"Good, because you're going to stand here while I keep doing it for as long as I like."

She startled herself with a slight exhalation of breath, the embryo of a moan. His eyes studied her in the mirror to the left of the painting, and her body trembled beneath his regard. She reacted even more strongly to his eyes than his touch, though she wanted to turn her body against his hands and invite him into territory that, moments ago, would have been invasion.

"Are you thinking, Meg?"

"I'm trying not to," she breathed, and meant it. Thinking was overrated if a woman could feel like this instead.

"Good. I want you to imagine yourself at the stylist again. Close your eyes."

She obeyed.

"This time, you pick up the magazine that first catches your eye. What is it?"

"Gardening." Flowers and sunshine, lying against the earth as a man stroked and plowed, planted...

His fingers stopped, rested for a moment on the flesh between hip and thigh. She shuddered. "You dream of flowers and sunshine, warm earth, the low drone of bees, the smell of soil as you wait. You're at the whim of your stylist. You can't make him do your will, you must wait for his, so you have time to explore the limits of the world he, as master, gives you.

"When he comes for you, you follow him to his workspace and he lays you back, guiding your head into the yoke of the sink. His fingers work into your scalp, massaging until you almost drift to sleep, like a child beneath his touch. When he lets you up, he towels you dry, again like a child, then he takes you to another chair for styling."

Daniel pressed his body closer and his resilient strength pressed against her back. Meg expected the heat from his body to burn the flimsy barrier of the dress away. Or was it the heat from her own skin she felt?

"May I ask you something?"

His chin nudged her hair aside, and he dropped a kiss at the juncture between neck and shoulder. Another line of fire erupted. Soon her whole body would be engulfed, and still he stroked just a few inches of her thigh and the line of her rib cage. His fingers paused, longer this time, at the apex of her leg and hip. Her body quivered, and she quelled a primitive need to rock her hips forward, the way she would if he'd cupped her directly between her legs.

God, what had she been about to ask?

"If I had control, I'd want him to do it longer, the shampooing," she burst out. "It…just starts to feel good and then they stop."

Her words hung in the air, like a breach of etiquette at a dinner party, and the lovers in the picture seemed to be laughing at her. She averted her face from the mirror, but Daniel's hand cupped her chin, his forearm pressing against her left breast, and brought her face back where she had to meet his eyes directly in the glass.

"Meg," he whispered against her ear. "If you don't stop condemning yourself for every word that comes out of your mouth, I'm going to take you into the men's room at Victor's. I'll lock the door, bend you over the counter and put my mouth between your legs until you couldn't form a thought if your life depended on it."

Fire warred with fear in a searing burn from her stomach into her suddenly dry throat. His finger traced her breast bone to her jugular, following the path of her emotions, and rested on the choker. The reflection of his finger rested on the nude's breast, and Meg's jumping pulse created a strange overlapped image that made it seem as if the other woman's heart was pounding as hard as hers.

"I don't—"

"Don't think, Meg." His eyes promised it was the last warning before he did exactly as he'd threatened. "Close your eyes and don't open them until I give you permission. Tell me why you like the shampoo part."

She swallowed a confusing mixture of resentment and passion in the darkness. "I like the way it feels to have my head... massaged." *It's quiet and dark, an undemanding, human touch, intimate without the pressure of intimacy.*

"All right," he said, more gently. "What else would you like if you could have it done any way you wanted?"

"I'd like it if the stylist didn't talk, if he'd just touch me," she admitted quietly. "I wouldn't have to say empty, pointless things he's not going to remember the minute I leave the chair. I don't want to feel like I'm just another faceless task. I want to feel real to him." Her palms were sweating. Why did he have to keep asking her things? "That kind of contradicts itself, I guess."

"Not at all." His arm settled around her waist and his other hand collared her throat, holding her locked against him. She didn't resist. The muscular line of his thigh rested against her lower buttocks, his hip pressed into her right buttock. "You want to be touched for as long as it gives you pleasure, by someone whose pleasure comes from obeying your desires completely. Open your eyes, Meg."

He stepped to her side and threaded her fingers into the crook of his elbow. "You just described what it is to be a master. I believe there's a dominatrix lurking in that frightened heart of yours."

It startled a chuckle from her. "Not likely. I don't have any leather bustiers or chains."

Daniel slanted a smile at her and led her into the hallway. "It has nothing to do with what you're wearing, Meg." He stopped in the dimly lit corridor and turned to her. The narrow space pushed them closer together, physically and mentally, and she had to tilt her head to look at him.

"Look at yourself in your mind's eye," he said, so close to her lips she thought an indrawn breath would win her a kiss. "I told you to do nothing, but you turned to me the moment I stopped, lifted your face to me with your lips parted, and left your arms at your sides, giving me free access to any part of you I desire. Your nature has submitted to mine, and my will controls yours, and it gives us both pleasure. Domination and submission come from instincts far deeper than our conscious attitudes or what we wear."

"What — may I ask — what kind of instincts?"

His dark eyes glinted, acknowledging and complimenting her recall of another lesson. "I'll tell you that later if you don't figure it out first. Maybe after you learn that you could bring a man to heel wearing jeans and a t-shirt, silk and lavender, leather, or nothing, the most vulnerable garments of all." He glanced down. "Not that I wouldn't appreciate seeing you in leather and chains."

Her face pulled into the unfamiliar reflex of a smile. He took her hand in a firm grasp and led her down the hallway, turning the corner into Victor's main salon.

Daniel's first, dismal vision had been a perfect recreation of Meg's usual styling salon. Hair clippings falling on a glaring white-and-gray-flecked tile floor scuffed with shoe marks and stained with perm chemicals. Neon lights and incessant voices interrupted by bursts of strident laughter over piped-in radio music. She went there for maintenance, never to be nurtured in the manner he described in the second vision, in the manner she expected she was about to experience now.

Victor's main salon floor was carpeted in a marbleized purple and gray Berber, the walls painted a soft gray and hung with more paintings of lovers enjoying the luxuries of intimacy. In each, one of the lovers was unclothed, the other fully and fashionably dressed. Her eyes lingered on one where the woman was clad in the straight lines and laces of a riding habit. She leaned against a tree with her horse and stared at her lover, sprawled naked, relaxed and inviting on a plaid tartan laid across wildflowers and green grass beneath the spreading limbs of the same oak.

She tore her gaze away to face Daniel's amused regard, her automatic flush deepening to rose when she saw he wasn't alone.

A beautiful young man sat in the chair behind the front appointment desk. He had long blond hair, so curly it lay on his narrow shoulders in soft natural corkscrews. His legs were crooked into triangles, his heels holding the edge of the chair by virtue of the circle of his arms banded loosely around his knees. When her attention turned to him, he unfolded from his casual perch and rose from the chair.

"Madam, Sir," he nodded. "My name is Victor. May I help you?"

Daniel gestured to her. "I'd like to see some styles for my companion."

Victor's dove-feather eyes behind horn-rimmed glasses turned to Meg again, this time in assessment. With one thoroughly knowledgeable look, he dispelled her surprise that he was "Victor". Nothing seemed to be required of her other than to stand still, so she perused him as well. He had the sensual movements that appealed to men as much as to women. His long-fingered hands were perfectly manicured, his slim body clad fashionably in a loose cotton shirt and casual slacks.

He smiled at her regard, turned and opened a late nineteenth century armoire covered with the ivy and flower carvings particular to the Naturalism Period. There were hundreds of magazines on the shelves, but he withdrew one without lingering and handed Daniel the glossy, heavy stock styling magazine. "She'll find something in there to meet her tastes, I believe."

Daniel handed the magazine to Meg. "Victor, there are some rules you'll follow while styling Meg's hair. You'll wash her hair as long as she likes. She likes the way it feels to have her head rubbed."

He nodded. "Most women do."

Daniel inclined his head. "You won't speak to her. She's allowed to speak and receive instruction only from me. She'll let me know when she needs you to do something different."

He spoke to Victor, but looked at her to see that she understood. Meg nodded slowly. Victor accepted all of Daniel's commands without a trace of surprise marring his fine-boned face. Her apprehension melted, leaving her with a surprising surge of eagerness for what lay ahead. Daniel touched her arm. Butterflies startled her stomach and alighted with tickling brushes along the inner walls of her thighs.

"Have you chosen?"

"Oh." She opened the magazine with a sheepish grimace. Daniel steered her to a chair, sank her into it with a hand at her waist.

"Choose the one you want, Meg." He tapped her nose with his index finger. "Not what's easiest or safest. I'll know if you do." He bent, caging her in the chair with a hand braced on either arm. "I've already told you what I'll do if you disobey."

Her knees tightened. The image shot through her mind, Daniel's strong hand in the small of her back, pushing her so her body bent over the counter, her breasts hanging into the bowl of a sink and quivering with convulsive jerks when he spread her legs and explored her soft lips between with his hot mouth. She nodded and shuddered when the movement shocked her involved nerve endings. Daniel brushed his lips against her temple, sliding his nose across her loose hair, then turned from her to Victor.

Meg dropped her gaze to the book. His murmuring voice formed a background to her considerations. She couldn't hear his words, but her ears filled with his tone. She'd like to lie with her head on his chest, listening to those tones vibrate through his skin against her cheek, his breath stirring her hair.

What was he doing to her? She had major problems, huge emotional weaknesses, staggering obstacles to overcome, and a completely uncertain future. So now she was allowing a total stranger to fondle, kiss and stroke her anytime the mood struck him, which was a lot.

She'd given him control, but she was in control of her control. Wasn't she? *It's one afternoon. Pick a hair style.* Her lips twisted wryly and she focused on the pages spread across her knees. One crisis at a time.

When Daniel finished with Victor, she'd marked two places in the book with her fingers. She started to rise when he turned to her, but Daniel motioned her back down. "Did you choose?"

She lifted the first picture. He looked at it a long moment, then turned to Victor. "Where is the men's room?"

"No." She clutched his sleeve, panicked. She wasn't ready for what he was capable of doing. A perverse part of her had wanted to test him, to see if he really knew her as well as he thought he did. Meg let out a relieved breath when he lifted a brow, waiting. She let the book drop open to the other page in her lap.

The first picture had been what she thought was best for her hair type. Now she showed him the one she wanted, and waited, her toes gripping the carpet, waiting for him to laugh and Victor to say it was impossible.

Daniel took the book from her hands. The picture was a close-up of Jodi Foster, her beautiful sand-colored hair swept into loose waves from temple to crown, then pouring through the teeth of a carved mahogany comb and cascading down her back in a swirling mass of curls. Tiny, loose ringlets softened her angular face around her absorbing pale blue eyes.

It was ridiculously romantic and her hair would never do it. Daniel glanced at it, then at Meg. He handed the book to Victor without taking his eyes off her face.

"Better," he said. "No second chances next time. Go with Victor and, remember, if you need to speak, you speak to me." He slipped one finger under the braided choker and tugged it gently, pulling her to her feet. "Understand?"

She nodded and overbalanced, leaning into him and inhaling his wonderful scent. His hand slid down her back and then he directed her with the pressure of his fingers to follow Victor.

Victor led them behind the desk and down an avenue of styling rooms. Each space had a ceiling-to-floor gray or purple velvet curtain whose satiny silver tie back could be released to give the customer and stylist complete privacy. The first one was closed, and Meg heard the methodical snip of metal scissors and a pleasantly off-tune voice humming a song that reminded her of a lullaby.

A stone archway at the end of the hallway framed a tapestry of a woman cutting blooms in an English garden. They stepped through the opening and Victor pulled back one wing of the heavy fabric. He gestured courteously for Meg to precede him into the styling area.

She stepped under the fall of the curtain and caught her breath, afraid any voluble expression of delight would shatter the fantasy before her.

An octagon of etched glass formed the ceiling over the chamber like a sparkling, translucent umbrella, permitting the sun to soak the room with natural light. Six tall Gothic pillar supports circled the glass dome. Stone sculptures of a dolphin, a mermaid and a seahorse were mounted on the sides of three of the pillars. Water arced from the creatures' lips and the urn held within the slender arms of the mermaid. Falling to a rock ledge, the streams of water poured into a small pond framed with junipers and azalea blooms in fuscia and white. Red tropical water lilies rose from the water on slender stalks among aimlessly floating lavender hyacinths. Several incandescent goldfish swam lazily in the water garden.

The other three pillars bore planters overflowing with white, pink and purple petunias, pansies and begonias tangled with strands of mint and dark green English ivy. The styling chair, upholstered in gray velvet and trimmed with antique brass arms and footrest, was positioned in their crescent embrace, facing the pond.

As Victor drew her to it, Meg saw a pedestal sink braced against the lower part of the center pillar, its satin enamel stalk painted with mauve and cream lilies matching those painted on the glossy interior surface of the sink. Mounted in the space on the pillar, between the planter and the sink, was an antique brass mirror with an hourglass shape. A natural pine garden cart held an assortment of colored glass bottles with magnolia-shaped pewter stoppers.

"Wait." Daniel took her arm before she took the seat. She looked up at him.

"It's so beautiful."

His eyes softened on her enchanted face, and something else moved in them, something that made her swallow over a hard lump in her throat. "You deserve beautiful things, Meg." He glanced at Victor, a command for a moment of privacy.

"I'll get you a chair, sir." Victor excused himself and slipped by them.

Daniel put his hands at her waist and drew her toward him. His hands shifted behind her and his fingers curled over the swell of her buttocks. He began to gather the back drape of her skirt.

"Daniel—" She moved against him and he made a noise in his throat, both command and warning. She steeled to immobility, but her hands gave her uneasiness away, trembling at her sides.

"You're scaring me," she whispered.

His hands stilled for a moment, but she found no compromise in the line of his jaw or his dark eyes. "I don't want to scare you, Meg. But I need your trust. I want you to be absolutely certain that, if you flung yourself off the edge of a cliff, I'd be the one to catch you."

"That scares me more."

Victor would return and see her on display. Meg raised her hands, unable to help herself, but she stopped short of pushing at him, instead resting them on his chest, a quivering reminder of her worries.

"Trust, Meg." He breathed it against her temple. His fingers gathered, stroked, gathered. Cool air struck the backs of her knees and ran up her thighs until that soft layer of air was the only thing covering the heart-shaped curve of her bottom. His fingers kept tugging, though, until he held the dress just above the small of her back. She felt the press of his hand, holding the material in place. His other hand moved, and his finger traced the bare channel of her spine.

"There's nothing so beautiful as a woman's back," he murmured.

She tilted her head up to look at him. He gazed intently beyond her at the mirror. She couldn't see what he saw, pinioned against him by one strong hand, but she could look at his face, and it made her wonder at the nature of a God who had thought of so many details to break down a woman's resistance. Her thighs trembled with the desire to open and welcome his plunging heat into her slick, musky marsh. That desire she could still control, barely, but the lips of her mouth opened as she looked at him, craving the wet penetration of his tongue for a mouth as dry as the lips between her legs were wet.

"It's time to sit, Meg." Daniel shook out a soft, thick towel with his one free hand and placed it on the crushed velvet of the chair. As if he knew her knees wouldn't hold her much longer, he passed the drape of her skirt to his arm and pressed her into the chair.

The soft towel stroked her bare bottom and sensitive folds of flesh like animal fur. He arranged the surplus of her skirt in a swirl like a flower's petals around her. He finished just as Victor entered, followed by two men bearing a heavy wooden chair that would have been at home in a lord's hall. They placed it several feet away from the styling chair, facing Meg.

Daniel sat and laid his ankle on his opposite knee. He laced his fingers over his calf, his eyes remaining on her with the contained energy of a patient panther.

Victor placed a smock around her throat, just below the necklace, and freed her hair from the neckline. "You have beautiful hair."

"Thank—" She stopped, looked at Daniel.

Victor followed her gaze, then cleared his throat. "I'm sorry, sir. I meant to tell you that your lady has beautiful hair."

"Yes, she does." Daniel inclined his head. "She thanks you for the compliment."

They both found it so easy to do as he wished. Meg had met controlling men, but Daniel was different. Both she and Victor wanted to obey him, to submit to his magnetism, his dark flame eyes and the sure strength and purpose they held.

Victor lowered the back of the chair and guided her neck into the curve of the bowl. Her head lay over the sink and she looked up into a cloud of flowers hanging from the planter mounted on the pillar. She turned her shoulders to accommodate her position.

The pain jabbed her where it usually did, below the right shoulder blade. It shot through her back muscles, as if the chair had metamorphosed into a bed of nails that speared and held her in immobile anguish.

She tried to shift, make herself more comfortable, and lancing pain sucked her breath into her throat. If she stayed still, she could wait it out. She couldn't ruin this moment…

"Meg." Daniel stood over her. "What's the matter?"

Victor's brow wrinkled in concern. "Sir, if she's uncomfortable, we have cushions in the cabinet. We want her to be completely at ease."

Daniel's eyes stayed on her. "Tell me."

"My back—" She felt foolish as anguish and pain spiked her syllables with high, squeaking notes. "I hurt it a little while ago, and this position—" Couldn't she have anything that didn't lead to this? She tried to rise and her breath hissed through her teeth.

"Meg, lay back." Daniel's hand pushed into her shoulder. She obeyed and his arm was under her. "Victor, bring the cushions. We need to raise her knees and take the pressure off her back. One for the neck, too, to soften the sink for her."

He lifted her, again, so easily Meg felt she must weigh nothing to him. Victor adjusted the cushions, then Daniel lowered her back into the chair. A small pillow supported her lower back now and an herbal neck pillow cushioned the grasp of the sink. She inhaled fragrant rosemary.

Daniel leaned close, his lips an inch from hers. "You'll tell me immediately next time something hurts you, Meg. All right?"

She nodded. Her lips parted despite her attempt at control and his gaze lingered, as intimate a touch as if he'd kissed her. But he didn't kiss her lips. He just looked, studying, and if her muscles hadn't still been throbbing, she might have arched up to him, compelling him to touch her, to kiss her.

Meg followed the temptation and reached up to trace the light sandpaper of his three o'clock shadow over the hard, smooth planes of his jaw. Her touch and gravity brought his smell even more strongly. When this fantasy ended, she'd hunt down his aftershave and keep it under her pillow, even if she had to snort every man's fragrance in a department store like a coke addict to find it.

His eyes softening, he pressed a kiss against her fingers, took her hand and laid it back on the other folded over her abdomen. He disappeared from her vision as he went back to his chair. Victor turned on the water.

The warm spray soaked into her hair. Meg closed her eyes and listened to its soft whishing noise as Victor's hands moved through her brown tresses, weaving the water among the strands with skillful, deliberate turns of his fingers.

If people were paid equitably for their gifts, a hair stylist with Victor's fingers would be a millionaire. She'd mortgage her soul for him. His hands hadn't looked that strong, but now they massaged her scalp with gentle power, rubbing in small, slow circles. He took his time, lingering over the task. Meg made a soft noise of appreciation.

Eight months ago, before life as she knew it had changed forever, she'd had a dog, a Scottish terrier whose body stood no higher off the ground than a skateboard. Sometimes, she'd wondered if dogs ever grew tired of a life revolving around a master's attention and wishes. Now she marveled at Skate's life. He'd responded to tone and a few basic commands, but most of all, he'd responded to touch. He'd gone to college with her, and she remembered him napping in her lap while she'd studied, her fingers playing absently in his fur. He'd lain quiet beneath her hand, content with simple tactile acknowledgment of his presence and importance.

A cool grip took one of her limp hands from her stomach. Meg turned her head. A blonde in a loose blue silk blouse over a gypsy skirt had come in and set a manicure tray on the pine counter. Another stylist appeared on the horizon of Meg's vision, a black woman with long, dark red braids and a form-fitting red knit dress. She rolled a small table to Meg's left side with similar tools and took her other hand.

"I thought you'd like a manicure." Daniel's voice came from beyond her feet.

Meg nodded. Neither woman spoke nor lifted her eyes from her task, and the slight elevation of tension from their intrusion receded. The light, feminine fingertips gliding along Meg's skin awakened nerve endings in her palms and in the grooves of her knuckles. The black woman's thumb whispered over her pulse on the delicate underside of her wrist and Meg's body rippled with a jolt of sexual pleasure. She froze, mortified at her uncontrolled response, and darted a glance at the woman.

The black woman didn't raise her eyes, but the corners of her full, sensual mouth lifted slightly. Her thumb, brown and tipped with a long, ruby nail, changed its direction and stroked the vertical line of Meg's pulse, moving back and forth over less than a half inch of throbbing vein.

Should she do something? Turn her hand, make the woman stop? Maybe Daniel had arranged this. Did he watch the woman touch her, those dark angel eyes noting every response, the quickened breath that caused her breasts to rise and fall more? What should she do?

How about nothing?

The thought jolted her like a broom handle thrust into the overdriven machinery of her mind. Everything stopped. In her mind, Meg stared at the strange thought, examined it and considered what she never had before. Daniel had said it himself. He was in charge. If something displeased her, she need only let him know. If it pleasured her, it gave him pleasure. If it displeased him, he'd take care of it himself.

Daniel's fingers touched her calves and Meg jumped, jerking her wrists from the women's grasp. She smiled in nervous apology and gave them back. His hand glided up and down her quivering right leg, gentle strokes that eased her muscles. Victor leaned across her and depressed one of the pewter spouts to pour an emerald green liquid into his palm. Jasmine fragrance saturated the air.

Daniel's strokes grew longer, sliding under the fall of her skirt, up the sides of her knees. He came back down, went back up, this time with the hem of the skirt in his grasp. Meg felt the silk run up her leg and over the knees.

The humid air of the styling chamber advanced curiously into her newly-revealed territory. Daniel smoothed his palms over her folded skirt, marking its resting point so she knew it lay at mid-thigh. Then his fingers insinuated themselves between the closed line of her thighs and pushed them apart, holding her for a moment with a slight tightening of his fingers, a mute command that her legs should remain where he placed them.

Meg obeyed, though when he withdrew his touch, she feared the nervous quivering in her thighs would slide the silk back and completely reveal her to the others. She lay in a position of utmost decadence, her hands manacled by the ministrations of the manicurists, her head bound to the pleasuring of Victor's fingers. The man who'd ordered it all sat beyond her line of sight with total access to her bare sex. She could almost feel the heat of his gaze resting on her. The trembling in her legs increased, wanting to draw her thighs back together, not out of modesty, but to protect herself, to hide the fact that she was so aroused.

But why? That broom handle penetrated the normal machinations of her mind even further. Obviously, everything he did was designed to arouse her, so why did she want to hide it? He'd asked her to choose and she'd chosen to belong to him for today, a person she'd never met. Possession was by its very nature a sexual motivation, a relinquishment of defenses. Her continuing protestations had nothing to do with her decision to relinquish those defenses to him. She feared her own responses, feared it would allow the madness to take over and cause those she loved greater harm than it had already.

Fear had become the strongest motivation in her life of late, keeping the beast in the cage. But with Daniel, she felt safe. He wouldn't allow her to be embarrassed before others, and he could keep the madness from rearing its head and taking over. Was it wishful thinking, another strain of the madness, or truth?

The black woman went to answer the phone. Meg opened her eyes and looked up into Victor's face. He smiled slightly, feeling her regard, but he didn't meet her gaze. One of the long locks of his hair fell forward over his shoulder and swayed near her face. Meg dared to reach out with her free hand and catch the corkscrew curl. It was soft, like a child's hair, delightful. His gray eyes brushed hers, but her touch didn't seem to bother him. She twisted the curl around her fingers and tugged. Victor smiled at her foolishness and tried to free himself, but only succeeded in shaking several more of the corkscrews off his shoulder. Meg closed her eyes, threading them through her fingers, his soft hair sliding through her knuckles and springing back to spirals over and over again as his hands continued their magic. It was like being an infant in the crib again, touching a parent to reassure herself of his presence. The black woman came back, gently untangled her hand and returned to the manicure.

"Daniel," Meg murmured, after a long while.

"Yes?" She heard the rustle of his clothes as he rose. He bent over her and she raised her eyes. She took her time, starting with his dimpled chin and strong jaw, working up his aristocratic, lord-of-the-manor cheekbones and sliding into the embrace of his incomparable eyes. "I'd like for Victor to cut my hair when the manicure is done... if you're ready."

He kissed her nose, surprising her. When the women moved their tables away, she lifted her arms so he could raise her to a sitting position. Her heart dropped to the soles of her feet when a smile that didn't use his lips crossed his eyes.

"Why are you— May I ask why you're smiling?"

"Because you expected me to take care of you. Why are you smiling?"

Because your smile makes me want to smile. But she didn't say that. Even admitting she was capable of smiling seemed a dangerous exposure. She looked down at her bare feet. "I was thinking about Marco Polo," she said.

"Really."

"Mm-hm. He said he met princesses on his travels so spoiled that they didn't need shoes because their servants carried them everywhere. You've been making me feel like that."

He squatted next to her chair, bringing him to her eye level. Victor removed a dark green towel from a warm press and toweled her hair with the scent of gardenias.

"Were they carried in covered lounges or in their servants' arms?" Daniel asked softly.

133

"I—I don't know. I think in lounges."

"Pity." He blew on her lips and Meg parted for him.

"Why is it a pity?"

"Well, imagine it. You're forced to carry your princess behind a wall of veils when you'd rather carry her in your arms with her legs wrapped around your waist. You could hold her soft bottom in your hands and gaze at her breasts, resting on your chest, the skin like firm, ripe fruit, ready to be tasted by the press of your teeth, the flick of your tongue." His brow raised thoughtfully and he leaned closer, his breath on her cheek. "I suspect it would be torture either way."

The child-like moment of play with Victor evaporated in the steam coming off her skin. Her body simmered in its own juices, as if she were a feast Daniel was preparing to satisfy his appetite.

"I don't think a servant would carry her like that," Meg said hastily, not daring to look at Victor to see his reaction to the conversation. "Even if he carried her in his arms, he'd carry her more... more like you carried me."

"My mistake." His eyes flickered with dangerous currents. "Which way would you prefer, Meg?"

She caught the loose ends of the towel and pressed them to her face, inhaling the rich smell of magnificent white flowers. Victor cloaked her shoulders with the rest of the towel, protecting her from the dampness of her hair, and turned to arrange his tools.

"The lounge," she said abruptly, pushing a wet lock from her brow. "I'd watch the muscular bodies of my servants behind my veils and they wouldn't know I was looking at them."

Daniel nodded, unperturbed. "How would you dress them, Meg?"

She rolled the thought around her head. An impish smile tugged at her mouth. "A short battle skirt of studded leather, like the Romans wore. Nothing... under it."

His eyes flashed with delight. "What would you do behind your veils, watching these scantily-clad servants of yours?" His finger stroked her jaw, traced her lips. Meg licked them in reaction after his touch had passed. "Would you slide your fingers under your silk and brocade and touch yourself, imagining the hand of one of your servants?"

"We shouldn't be talking like this," she whispered, glancing at Victor.

"I set the rules, Meg," Daniel reminded her, guiding her attention back to him with a firm finger along her jaw. "Your face is flushed. I suspect it's not the only part of you that is." He straightened before she could respond and moved away, leaving her to Victor.

Meg *was* flushed, but the fire coursing through her body and her mind didn't feel like the madness. The madness was the insanity of an animal imprisoned in a cage. This felt like she'd burst free of the cage and now savored her first moment without chains. How was it possible that she could suddenly feel so free when she was in thrall to Daniel? Enthralled by him.

She couldn't dispel the image she'd conjured for him. As Victor styled her hair and then began to dry it, Meg imagined one of the servants who carried her.

He was her favorite. He supported the lounge on the front right corner where she could see him clearly through the gap in the embroidered curtains. Beads of sweat glistened on his muscular shoulders and gathered at the nape of his neck. The moisture rolled down the channel of his spine, trickling under the battle skirt where she knew it would slide between his bare buttocks and rest on soft, down-covered testicles. He was strong enough to bear her to the ground and take her as he pleased, yet he was her servant, sworn to obey and protect her in all things. When they reached the market and he lowered the chaise to the ground, he knelt before her. She stepped out, onto his curved back, her bare sole grasping his slick skin. The shortness of his skirt clearly revealed his balls and muscular ass. He'd remain in that kneeling position, his head down, until she'd shopped for her trinkets and was ready to mount him again.

But would he obey? Or would she buy him a gift and return to find him gone, abandoning her amongst a mob of hostile strangers?

Victor misted her face with a water bottle and Meg looked at him, startled. He imitated her pensive expression, then aimed the spray bottle at her again, threatening. She smiled, pushing the shadows away. He'd propped the picture of Jodi Foster on the pine cabinet. She discovered a complete set of Mutant Ninja Turtle™ figurines tucked discreetly behind the antique glass — his collection, she guessed — items that personalized the styling room for him.

He flicked one of her short curls onto her face and she shook it off, wrinkling her nose at the itch. She batted at her face through the smock and he twirled her in the chair, distracting her. Snatching up one of the turtles as she came around, she pretended she'd twist off his head if he didn't behave.

Victor held scissors and comb in open-palmed surrender. Then he held up a finger with the dramatic mystery of a circus clown and took the turtle from her. Setting a rubber band mechanism in the toy, he carefully stood it on the flat wood surface of the garden cart. The turtle's staff twirled in a circle and the character emitted a piercing "Haaaiii – ya!!"

Meg burst out laughing. She hiccuped over the unexpected noise, which made her laugh again. Looking around for Daniel, she found he stood several steps behind her chair.

At that moment, the black woman and the woman in the smock returned, bearing a large Victorian mirror framed in gold leaf cherubs and flora. Meg realized only then that she'd avoided looking directly at the hourglass mirror Daniel had used to look at her. Now, at Daniel's insistence, she looked at herself as Victor turned the chair to face the new mirror.

A girl with her eyes smiled invitingly from beneath a riotous waterfall of chestnut curls wisping softly around her laughing face. Meg reached out and touched the reflection, absorbing the vibrancy and beauty of what looked back at her. It might have been a memory of her girlhood, but it wasn't, not entirely. This was a new creation, a phoenix rising from the ashes, the same soul surely, but reborn in the promise of a new day, a new life.

She looked away, to Daniel. She liked it better his way, letting his eyes tell her everything she needed to know about herself. If she kept looking in the mirror she was sure she'd find the flaw, the key to undo the whole spell.

He reached out and touched her cheek with a gentle palm. "I'll be right back." He inclined his head at Victor and they left the chamber together, to settle the account, she supposed.

Meg rose from the chair and the woman in the mirror rose and came closer, wearing a silk dress that left nothing—or everything—to the imagination. She recalled a makeover she'd had over a year before. She'd been an inanimate doll being dressed by others. She hadn't recognized herself when it was done, though she'd exclaimed to spare feelings and hide her horror at what she'd seen in the mirror, a glaring apparition of her reality, a woman never who she really was, but who everyone wanted her to be. Or who she thought everyone wanted her to be.

This reflection was different, created from what was inside of her, coaxed from a storeroom of forgotten hopes, untouched by adjusted expectations.

The black woman with red hair smiled and beckoned her to come closer to the mirror. Meg reached up and touched her new hairstyle, slid a soft curl through her fingers and watched, fascinated, as it sprang back into its styled curve.

"You're beautiful," the black woman whispered. "So fascinating."

Her companion, the woman in the smock, nodded.

"Touch yourself some more," the black woman encouraged, her gaze sliding down Meg's body. "So soft, so irresistible."

Meg managed a nervous smile, shook her head, began to turn away.

"Wait." The woman stopped her. She and her companion propped the mirror in Daniel's vacated chair, at an angle so Meg could see herself from the hips up. The black woman stepped to her side. A good deal taller than Meg, her statuesque elegance complimented rather than diminished the petite, fairy-like wonder of Meg's appearance. She took each of Meg's hands in one of her own, curling skin dark as fertile earth around Meg's much whiter fingers. Raising Meg's hands, she threaded their fingers together under the curtain of Meg's hair until they found the nape of her neck.

"Feel how soft, how beautiful." She applied pressure, and Meg followed her lead, her fingers penetrating the skeins of chestnut, warm and soft, that lay on her neck beneath the outer pelt. "Your neck is so delicate, chére. A man couldn't help but wish…"

She gently guided and Meg obeyed, a willing marionette, her hands gathering in tandem with her companion's. They pulled her hair in a sinuous curve over her right shoulder, leaving the left side of her neck bare and inviting from the right tilt of her head. The black woman bent to her left ear, whispering, her breath tickling the fine hairs on the exposed jugular.

"A man would go crazy, ma chérie, watching you stand like this. He must kiss your throat or die. And should you do this…" She linked her fingers loosely in Meg's and brought them out from under the hair. Meg's breasts peaked and rose like her pulse as their joined hands slowly followed their downward slope. The black woman's hands turned, and she scooped Meg's palms up in her own, a spoon cupping a spoon, so Meg's palms cradled her own breasts. Her white, thin hands looked like the lighted crescent of the first quarter moon, holding the shadowed sphere of the full moon to come.

"You haven't loved yourself enough, sweet chére." The French accent and full red lips caressed her ear. "A woman should love herself often, keep her passions close to hand, not locked in a box like good china too expensive to ever use."

Meg swallowed. The woman's hands flattened beneath her own and drew away, stroking her skin as the woman stepped out of view. Daniel filled the mirror behind Meg.

She dropped her hands from her breasts, turning crimson.

"You've done nothing wrong, Meg," he assured her quietly. "She's right. I can think of nothing better than to sit back and watch you pleasure yourself, but…"

His chest filled her vision as he approached and turned her to him. The women carried the mirror away as Daniel's hand lifted her face. While he studied her long and intently, his thumb rubbing her cheek, her self-consciousness faded under the aroused fire in his eyes. She had a sudden, surprising desire to touch her breasts in front of him as she had for herself.

"Time to get you shoes, princess."

He bent and she looped her arms around his neck as he scooped her into his knight-errant arms again. She passed through the fading dream of velvet, flowers, and Victor's beautiful child-like smile of farewell. As they went by his desk, he pressed a kiss to her hand.

The mall was the same, a gentle roar of echoing noise and footsteps, people traveling from experience to experience in a manufactured world of possibilities, props to each person's individual reality, including hers and Daniel's.

The Sole Finder Shoe Boutique had a more familiar layout, open wide to the public, displaying a back wall of shoe boxes stacked to the ceiling and pyramid displays of the store's best placed at different points on the floor for customers to navigate. Spotlights and soft jazz earmarked it for a more expensive clientele, as did the framed picture of shapely calves in elegant heels standing next to a masculine pair of legs in slacks and Italian loafers, backdropped by a red car door gleaming with the Ferrari logo.

Daniel let her feet touch the carpet once they were in the store, but he kept her body close to him with one hand pressed to her lower back. "Meg." He tilted his head down to her. "Are you wet for me?"

She swallowed and glanced around her.

"Meg…" He jerked her chin so she was looking into his stern eyes. "I told you before. What others think doesn't matter. Answer my question or I'll find out myself."

"Please, don't embarrass me," she whispered desperately.

His eyes softened, his touch becoming a caress instead of a restraint. "I'd never do that, Meg. Now, answer me, sweetheart. Are you wet for me?"

She licked her lips, swallowed. "You should know I am."

"No caviling, Meg. Not with me. 'Yes, I am'."

"Yes. I am."

"All right, then. Come here." Daniel linked her fingers in his so her fingertips brushed the soft hair layering his knuckles. He surprised her by drawing her out of the store. To the right of the entrance was a long hallway leading to a mall exit. The hall was deserted, a service exit, and a moment of doubt trickled through her stomach. But then he turned into a narrow corridor off the main hallway. The smaller alley boasted a locked maintenance closet and was crowded with a small grove of potted fir trees and life-sized, cotton-haired, glitter-cheeked elves, soon to be used in the mall's Christmas display.

His arm curled around her waist and his deft fingers gathered her skirt in his hand as he'd done in Victor's. He pressed his body against her and Meg jumped as her bare bottom met the cold wall.

"Put your arms at your sides, Meg, your palms against the wall. Open your mouth and look at me."

She laid trembling palms against the rough cinder block and opened her lips. Lifting her head without the familiar, gentle force of his hand was difficult, and meeting his eyes was nearly impossible. His expression gave her no clue, though a thousand possibilities of his next move went through her mind.

She didn't know what to expect—violence or gentleness. His kiss was both. His teeth scraped her skin as his lips came down on hers, but tenderness laced raw passion. He cherished and devoured in the same movement. He didn't kiss her; Daniel pulled her soul into him, making every part of her his. Her mind clung and clawed with everything she had, trying to get into him as desperately as he pulled her in that direction. When her palms lifted, he shook his head against her lips, forbidding it. Her fingers dug into the cinder block and a moan escaped her lips. Keeping his body away from her, his hands cradled her face as he kissed her. God, she wanted to touch him, so much that no other thought could get past the wet possession of his mouth, his fingers pressing on her throat and jaw.

When he pulled back from the kiss, he stared at her breasts. Her nipples were hard and stiff, her aureoles clearly visible against the sheer cloth.

"Who do you belong to, Meg?" There was a rough intensity to his voice.

She raised her eyes to his. "You," she whispered. It took concentrated thought not to say it over and over again. *You. You. You.*

He stood back and gathered the front of her skirt. She started to look right, to check the main hallway, but a sound from him stopped her. He pointed at his eyes. "Right here, Meg. My desires are all that matter."

He touched her sex lightly, a faint touch that shot through her vibrating nerves and jolted her hips off the cement blocks in a convulsive shudder. Daniel took his touch away with a light smile at her reaction and pressed his damp fingers to his mouth. He inhaled her scent through flared nostrils. Meg colored, but he shook his head. "It pleases me that you're wet."

He reached into a pocket of his duster and drew forth a blue velvet bag. He loosened the drawstring and pulled out a handful of silver and black silk. "You're going to wear this."

"What is it?"

"You'll see." His hands reached for the front of her dress. Meg shrank in reaction, but his hands were already spreading the overlapped neckline and pushing it off her shoulders. She caught his wrists, but he didn't stop nor did she exert enough pressure to interfere. She simply clung to his wrists like a child holding an adult for balance while being undressed.

He pushed the silk to her elbows, and her breasts and shoulders were bare to his gaze. "Beautiful," he murmured.

"I'm too skinny," she said desperately. "Daniel—"

"Hush." He went to one knee. "Hold onto my shoulder and step into these."

The black silk was a lace thong, the crotch lined with soft cotton. When Daniel tugged it up under the skirt and fitted it over the swollen lips of her sex, a jolt of pleasure sighed through her. His fingers traced the crease between thigh and groin to her bare hip bone, pulling the side straps in place. Slender silver chains attached at the hip point on either side of the thong. He threaded these ends under the waistband of the dress and crossed them, looping them once around her waist. The two chains were tipped with a finger-sized circle of wire, strung with a tiny waterfall of small diamonds on silver threads.

His hands slid over her breasts like wings and Meg realized the function of the wire. "Daniel, I—"

"Hush, Meg. It won't hurt, I promise."

His fingers fit the wires over her nipples, and her breath caught in her throat as he tightened their hold, a starburst of sensation exploding from her taut peaks. Once he had the wires fitted, he fastened a serpentine length of chain between the two nipple rings. A teardrop diamond pendant swung on the chain against her breastbone.

Her nipples had thickened to the point of pleasurable pain, and they curved upwards in their silver restraints. The gems caressed the underside of her breasts like the playful fingers of fairies. When Daniel stepped back from her and crossed his arms, putting her on display before him, her arms automatically rose to cover herself.

"As long as you wear the necklace, Meg, I'll look at your breasts when I wish. Put your arms down."

Tears swelled behind her eyes. She wanted him to be soft and gentle, to reassure her that this wasn't more of the madness. She wanted him to tell her again how she could trust him. But trust given in words was a chocolate Easter bunny, something that would cave in and prove itself hollow at the first pressure. Meg met his gaze, tried to forget what she wasn't wearing, and moved her arms away from her breasts. She went a step further, straightening her arms to either side of herself along the wall as if she were stretched and manacled before him, giving him free access to all he saw.

Total submission had a power of its own. His eyes fired with desire, Daniel knocked the breath from her, slamming her back against the cinder block with the pressure of his body. When his hips pushed her legs apart, his hardness against her, his tongue invaded her mouth. Her hands tried to come to him, but his strong fingers stopped her, keeping her manacled. The brush of his shirt across her nipples made her feel the binding of the jewels. Her reaction drove her over the edge of restraint. Bucking her hips against him, she rubbed herself shamelessly against the steel beneath his tweed.

When he pulled his hot mouth from hers, she strained against his hold, panting, her lips open and moist. Her fevered eyes focused on his mouth, wanting more. He lowered her arms to her sides and pressed her palms firmly against her thighs, commanding her to be still with a stern look. She glanced down, wanting to see the press of his arousal against his trousers, but he caught her chin. "Keep your eyes on my face, Meg. Don't make me have to blindfold you."

She wanted to snarl her frustration like a savage mountain cat. She'd lift her hands and pleasure herself in front of him, dip her fingers in her wetness and offer it to him, and he wouldn't be able to resist her. She could make him satisfy her need, like an ensorcelled knight at the whim of a succubus.

"No, Meg," he said softly, soothingly. "Bring it down, darling." He cupped her cheek in his hand, let her press kisses over his large palm. "We've got time for all of it. When the time comes for me to take you, you're going to take all of me, not just my cock and my mouth."

His words were a haze in her desire-fogged mind, but the soothing, almost platonic stroke of his hand did help. Her breath steadied, though little spasms of pleasure continued to spark through her body from the pressure points of her nipples.

Daniel stepped back from her at last, his eyes sliding over her quivering breasts like warm water. "I think it's time we did something about those nervous hands of yours."

The velvet bag came out again, and he produced two bracelets made of braided chain, like her choker. Each bracelet was strung with a small locking ring. He released the catch on the small rings, took them off the bracelets and threaded them onto the waistchain. The two bracelets fit close on her wrists, again like the choker. He attached the rings to the bracelets through tiny slits Patrice apparently had made in the sides of the dress.

If Meg tried to lift her hands from her sides, the chain at her waist would hold them. As long as she kept her hands at her sides, the dress would hang naturally and no one would know she was bound except him.

Daniel drew the dress back onto her shoulders and arranged the folds over her tight nipples, smiling slightly as a shuddering breath escaped her lips from the caress of silk on her skin. He adjusted the neckline differently, leaving the deep cleft between her breasts exposed. The diamond pendant weighting the chain strung between her nipples could be seen. To any who knew the adornment, it would be obvious she wore a nipple chain. He ran his finger along the inside curve of the chain, pressing slightly, and she gasped.

"How do the bracelets feel?"

"They feel… good." Her hips twitched. The folds between her legs shivered like the silver gills of fish in warm, tropical waters.

"The rings connecting the bracelets to the chain can be broken without too much pressure, but they remind you to keep your hands away from yourself." He ceased his idle torture on the chain and put his hand under her hair, tugging so she looked up at his face. "I'll stay close and won't let you lose your balance. If I want you off balance, I'll put you there."

Too late. Meg had never felt so unbalanced in her life.

He didn't carry her back around the corner. He made her walk and feel the binding pull of the chain on her waist and the gentle tug on her nipples that came from every sway of her hips. She felt helpless and uncertain without the balancing movement of her hands. Daniel's hand rested on shallow curve of her back, his smallest finger resting in the valley between her buttocks, along her tailbone.

A man in a double breasted gray suit had appeared in Sole Finders. He arranged a trio of elegant heels on tiny platforms amid a spray of fresh white gardenias and polished dark greenery. He hadn't seen them yet, and now he stood back, considering the arrangement.

The GQ cut of his clothes, the youth of his build, and the carefully arranged hair was familiar to Meg, a typical sales clerk with a fancy suit and moussed hair, a sharp pitch and no real interest in customer or product. He came to the job to make money and advancement, all the while thinking of what he'd do when he got back into jeans and a T-shirt at the end of the work day.

Had Daniel's spell broken? Had they finally found their way back to the world of the anonymous and uncaring?

Slipping a casual hand into the pocket of his slacks, he tapped his thigh restlessly. When the hand came back out, the head dipped once in acknowledgment of some internal debate. Plucking up three of the gardenias, he crushed them and scattered them haphazardly over the gleaming footwear.

The artistry of his display, the way he studied it a moment longer before he turned and saw them, chased away the mold of indifference. Meg imagined a woman coming home from a hard day at the office. While she absently flipped through bills and sat in a kitchen chair, this man knelt in his business suit, slipped a shoe off her foot and kissed her arch, inhaling the mysterious perfume of woman and gardenia.

Had Daniel pulled Patrice, Victor and this man from some alternative universe where apathy and drudgery didn't exist, or had he merely awakened her senses so she saw things as she never had before?

"Sir." The young man came forward with a casual shove at his coffee brown hair and a welcoming, reserved smile. "Madam. Patrice told me to expect you." His gaze fell to Meg's bare feet, then rose to her face without a change in expression. "I suspect you need some shoes."

Meg bit back a smile, but her chest hitched once with the effort to hold the giggle in. Stars spun in his deep blue eyes for just a moment, long enough to convince her that it was a twinkle.

"I pulled the two styles Patrice told me you wanted," he continued, glancing back at Daniel. "Would you like to look at those now or browse the store?"

Meg looked at Daniel, curious, and his hand slid to her elbow. "I'd like to see them now," he informed the man.

"I thought as much. My name is Marcus. Follow me, sir."

Men as a general rule had no appreciation for the experience of shopping, and Daniel didn't appear to be an exception. However, given his taste thus far, Meg wasn't inclined to be put out by it. Having to choose also meant thinking about the different avenues of choice and free will, and she'd stumbled on that hazardous path with the greeting cards. She had no immediate wish to return.

The padded chairs in the store had been clustered in several intimate horseshoes, as if shoe shopping was similar to small group therapy. She suppressed a chuckle, startling herself.

For the past eight months, any expression of mirth had been a faked orgasm, constructed from memories of pleasure. Her mind had been a meadow of chirping commentary on the absurdities of life, but the sense of wonder had died, making her subconscious a barren field.

Until now. Interesting people, dresses, and jewels were fertilizing the earth again. The steady fire of Daniel's eyes warmed it, and the moisture he'd drawn from her body rained from a sky of new experiences. Smiles and quiet pink blossoms of laughter bloomed in her heart.

The chairs had been pressed close to each other, so the occupants could do the same. Daniel guided her into one, then sat beside her. He stretched his arm over the back of her chair, fitting her into the warm corner between his arm and chest. His fingers draped loosely over her shoulder, playing with the ends of her hair, and when he crooked his ankle over his opposite knee, his bent knee overlapped her thigh, rubbing a small expanse of skin as his foot tapped the air.

"The heels first," he ordered. Marcus nodded and withdrew.

"Oh, but, I can't—" His brow arched in her direction and she compressed her lips at his expectant, stern expression. "I'm sorry."

"As I said, Meg, you need never apologize to me. But you must obey and trust that I'll care for you."

The last time someone had handled her feet other than her parents, she'd been a little girl. The sales clerk had been a squishably round man and had measured her foot with a metal slide rule. The sliding portion had been shaped like a snapping turtle's head so he could pretend to bite her feet with it. His eyes had nearly disappeared in his face when he smiled, like coal sparkling in a seam of desert rock, and he'd let her rub her hands over his bald head.

Marcus drew a slanted wood stool to her feet and straddled it, circling her ankle with strong, long fingers to lift it onto the slope of his thigh. The wool of his slacks tickled the sole of her foot. He withdrew a supple black heel from the lavender tissue of one of the boxes.

The shoe had a scalloped line along its mouth, and the toe was reinforced with a polished triangle of etched silver. A black waterfall of silk fringe tipped with tiny bells was sewn in the edge of the back seam and the bells whispered through the senses like a breeze through chimes. The heel was nearly three inches high.

Marcus lifted her foot and Meg pointed her toe, sensation shivering from arch to groin as the soft silken lining slid up the sides of her foot and captured it. Her pinioned hands curled against her thighs.

The ability to wear heels was one of the many things the madness had stolen from her, and she missed it, that sauntering glide that swung the hips farther and made the legs feel long and equestrian. But there was nothing remarkable about the support of this shoe. She couldn't see what would make these heels more wearable for her than any others.

Marcus lifted and fitted the other shoe. "How do those feel, ma'am?" Even as he asked, his fingers were busy, pressing the insole, gripping her ankle and the back of the right shoe, determining slippage over the narrow bone of her ankle.

He straightened, sitting back with one knee crooked to support his elbow. With his vivid blue eyes and strong, earnest expression, he reminded her of a young knight, doing heroic feats of kindness to celebrate and earn the love of a fair maiden at home.

"Are you married?" she asked.

A sweet smile crossed his face. "Engaged, ma'am."

Meg smiled, drawing in a breath of delight. "That's what I thought."

He glanced at Daniel. "I'll give you a moment to get accustomed to this pair before we move to the next."

He rose and left them, going to the aid of a harried-looking business man.

"Meg, did you forget a rule?"

She turned her head, her hair brushing Daniel's shoulder. The movement turned her body so her breast touched his chest. The hand he had on the back of her chair slid to her back, his palm holding her still so his pectoral grazed just the tip of her nipple, tightening it inside its slender silver collar and focusing all her attention on the man causing her spiraling ache.

"What was the rule, Meg?" The hand he'd laid casually on his ankle now traced the sloped neckline of her dress. "Look at my face, Meg."

She raised her chin and shuddered as his fingertip brushed her bare breast bone. His thumb and wandering finger pinched the chain that ran between the two nipple loops, twitching it idly. Sensual waves rose between her thighs and she shifted uncomfortably, gasping as her movement increased the force on the chain.

"You're not paying attention, Meg."

"I'm not... I'm not supposed to talk to anyone without asking you first."

"Very good. Do you want my permission to talk to Marcus?"

"Yes." His fingers flicked and the jolt of pleasure broke the word into two syllables. "If it pleases you."

"Anything you desire pleases me, Meg. Do you like the shoes?" Daniel released the chain and placed his hand back on his ankle. "Put your foot against the stool so I can see how it looks."

Meg complied, though her leg trembled as she braced it against the cushion. With her arms bound to her sides, she felt as if her aching breasts were on prominent display. The need to arch her back to bring her foot onto the slope of the stool only increased that sensation.

He took his casual perusal from her erect nipples and leaned forward. He ran his finger over the top of her foot, around her ankle and stroked his knuckles up her calf. He cupped her knee under the skirt with his palm, his thumb brushing the soft skin on the back of her knee.

"Beautiful," he murmured. "How do you like them?"

She hesitated. "I like that you like them."

He straightened, wrapped his hand in her hair and pulled her head back with the tender force only powerfully physical men could demonstrate. "There's a line between an honest desire to please me and evasiveness. Don't push me."

She grimaced. Not since her mother had she known someone so perceptive. "I love them, Daniel. I just... I don't know how I'll walk in them."

"Is that all?" He relaxed his hold, turning it into a light kneading at the nape of her neck beneath her cloak of curls. His strong, gentle touch relaxed her tense muscles and made her want to turn her head into his hand. "They're not for walking, Meg. They're bedroom slippers."

At her puzzled look, he smiled, but continued his petting, making her lids droop heavily over her eyes.

"When I see your foot arched in that shoe," he murmured in a soft growl, "I see you lying in my bed against white satin. The only thing you're wearing are those three-inch black heels. Your body is shaved and naked, and you lie with your arms above your head with your wrists tied to my headboard. You're on your back, which tilts your breasts high, and your nipples are as hard as they are now." His gaze flicked down, dwelling, and Meg's breath caught in her throat. "You're turned on your right hip, and your legs are bent, close together like you'd sit in a chair. But then I turn you on your stomach and make you get to your knees, your sharp heels pointed at me, your beautiful ass rising into the air first. You hold your knees together, shy, but it frames your shaved pink lips and I stop you so I can sit and look at you.

He leaned in, his dark eyes never leaving hers. "As I watch, you become more excited, and your lips grow wet until I have to get close and taste your sweet oil." He rubbed the side of her nose with his, his lips brushing her cheek. "So tell me, Meg, are you going to forget my rules again or do I need to punish you some more?"

"N…no." Her breath shuddered out of her.

"I'm not so sure." His eyes branded her soul. "If I touched that chain holding your nipples and twisted it just once, right now, you'd come hard for me, wouldn't you, Meg?" His voice dropped to a whisper. "Harder than you've ever come for anyone."

"Oh, God…" She gasped as the wave rose, taking her against her will. Panic and passion warred in her rigid features and a strangled moan made it past her clenched teeth. Her thigh muscles contracted, compressing her throbbing center.

Catching her neck, Daniel swallowed her moan in a kiss. She fought the vibration of her body. She'd never had an orgasm come so hard or fast, so out of control. Bunching her dress beneath her hot fists, she squeezed as the waves kept rolling, her arms jerking, adding to the sensation by tightening the jewels and chains on her body. That pushed her climax up and over the flailing wall of her self-consciousness. His other arm circled her waist and pulled her tight so his body absorbed her convulsions.

Mortification and panic cut her climax to a short, blinding moment of intense pleasure that left her shuddering. As the orgasm receded slowly, leaving her weak, she pressed her forehead against the bridge of Daniel's nose.

His hand stroked her hair and he eased his kiss, making moth-like touches on her lips. When Meg opened glazed eyes to stare at him, his eyes were brilliant, raging with passion for her, and the fire rippled through her as an aftershock. He traced her quivering lips with his thumb.

"You're torturing me, Meg," he whispered. "Every time you get aroused, I want you. I want you so badly right now, I could pull you on my lap, shove my cock in you to the hilt and explode."

Her aftershocks expanded and she groaned, trembling against him.

"Daniel, please stop," she begged. "I can't... take it, it's too much, too much..."

Her voice quavered over the words and she dropped her foot to the ground because her leg shook so hard the stool rattled. Tears pricked her eyes.

"Meg." He cradled her face, soothing. "Sshh, calm down, sweetheart. You're all right. You're all right. I told you..." He stroked her cheeks with his thumbs. "You belong to me for as long as you wear that necklace. But that also means I want you to be happy. We'll ease up a bit, all right?"

"I can't do this anymore." She waved at the other box. "No more shoes."

He shook his head, secured her under his arm again and motioned Marcus to come attend them. "You'll like this other pair even better, I promise."

She buried her face in his throat, inhaled his rich cologne and male scent. "I can't do this anymore, Daniel. I'm scared."

"Why are you scared?" He pressed his head down on hers and she burrowed deeper. His fingers glided up and down her back.

"I just... you know what I just did. In the middle of a store. Daniel, I can't hurt the people I love anymore. I just can't. I have to stop."

"Do you want to stop, Meg?"

"What I want isn't the point. I owe people."

"What do you owe them?" He brushed a curl from her temple.

How could she explain what she'd put others through because she couldn't get her head straight? Sometimes having people love you could be a cage, because you couldn't, no matter how hard you tried, love them back the right way. You were so messed up in your head that you didn't seem to be able to do anything but hurt them, and all the while your true self was imprisoned inside your messed-up self, screaming out your love in a voice that couldn't be heard. The best she could hope was to train the madness to behave when company was present, try to channel the moments for the times when she was alone.

"I can't put them through anything else," she said quietly. "You don't understand. This is a game to you."

His hand hooked her chin and jerked up her head with a roughness that startled her, as much as the angry heat in his eyes. "This isn't a game, Meg. I told you that before. Now, you want to take off the necklace and call it over, fine. But if you do, you're the only one calling this a game. The necklace is a commitment, a promise, not a referee whistle." His hand closed on her throat, hard enough that she felt her pulse pound against his palm, felt strength in his grasp. "Can you see this day through, Meg? Can you give up control? Maybe you've spent your energy in the wrong place, trying to control something that shouldn't be controlled. Maybe you hurt those you love because you won't let go. Maybe it's time to see what happens when you let someone else take the reins."

His touch gentled as a tear from her eyes rolled over his knuckles. "The only way to learn about control is to relinquish it," he said softly, brushing the moisture away with his other hand. "You've given it to me. Trust me, Meg. I'm going to make sure you're not embarrassed in front of anyone. I'm going to make sure you don't hurt anyone, especially yourself. I'm going to be here in every way you need me. I can handle anything you do. All right?"

She swallowed and his finger compressed her rapidly beating pulse.

"All I want to hear you say is, 'Yes, Daniel'." His face was stern and uncompromising again, totally in control.

Her breath hitched in her throat as common sense warred with intuition. She'd never wanted to trust someone so much in her life. She wanted to believe in someone's strength other than her own, but she knew it was a lie.

"Is the lady ready to try the other pair, sir?"

"Are you, Meg?" Daniel's eyes did not move from her face, nor did his grip on her throat ease.

"Yes, Daniel," she whispered.

He nodded, released her and put his arm back over her shoulders. "The other pair."

Marcus resumed his spot on the stool, took her foot and slid it out of the heel. "How did those feel, ma'am?" he asked with a look of professional concern.

A flush came into her cheeks. She felt the hot prickle of it on her skin under the weight of Daniel's dark, sultry gaze, felt his thigh rub against hers. She knew she could never wear the shoes again without thinking of the picture he'd painted of her in them.

"They're incredible." She cleared her throat and ignored Daniel's abrupt, devilish smile.

"I agree," Marcus said. He opened the other box. "But I think you'll love these."

Nestled in a bed of crushed blue velvet was a pair of shoes the color of her dress. They were designed like ballet slippers, the upper sole lavender satin. A yard of iridescent ribbons nested around the shoe. "I've never seen anything so beautiful," Meg murmured.

"I have," Daniel said, his hand tracing the shell of her ear. She turned her gaze to his face. She looked at him, and kept looking, until he raised a brow.

"What is it, Meg?"

"You," she said, reviewing all his features, the stern authority pierced by the gentle light in his eyes, the strong jaw that could ease with a smile. "Thank you for this, Daniel. And for this day. It's the best I've had in a long time."

His eyes softened, the sternness almost disappearing. Marcus slipped the first shoe on her foot and began to criss-cross the ribbons, the light picking up a variety of lavender shades in the shimmering ties as he worked his way up her calf.

Daniel drew the hem of her dress past her knees to give him better access. Marcus' capable fingers slid around the crevice of her knee and finished tying the shoe by passing a double loop around her thigh just above the knee. He left the remainder of the ribbon twisting down, ticking her skin along the side of her calf.

"You have another customer," Daniel nodded. "I'll take care of the other one."

Marcus rose. "I'll be back, in case you have any trouble."

Daniel knelt in front of Meg, pushing the stool out of his way, and slid the other shoe onto her foot. His capable hands dwarfed her small foot as he cross-tied the ribbons. He wound them up her leg, and his fingers slid under the hem of the dress and crossed the ribbons as high as they could go, well past mid-thigh, then tied them off like garters. His fingers moved so close to her center that tiny electric pulses jolted as he lightly brushed her skin.

"Open your legs for me, Meg," he murmured, and she shifted slightly, giving his hands room to redo her other leg the same way, passing the ribbons under and over, under and over.

When he was done, he rested his fingers on the top edge of the bindings and looked up into her flushed face, his eyes running over her parted lips, the quick rise and fall of her breasts. "I should tie the ends together so you can only spread your legs for me." One corner of his mouth lifted. "A satin chastity belt."

She laughed shakily. "You're going to have every inch of me tied up in something–ribbon, gold, silver."

He leaned forward, dark eyes intense. "That's how I want you, Meg. Bound to me and by me in every way, with or without ribbons or jewels."

"Why?" She flexed her fingers in a motion that would have been a helpless gesture of her hands if she could have moved them from her sides. "Why would you want me? You're gorgeous, rich and confident. You could have anyone."

He drew back the stool and sat on it, splaying his knees so her legs were between them. "So that's how you see yourself." He lifted a brow, cocked his head, and crossed his arms. "You're the broken toy in a store, the one that gets shuffled farther and farther back on the shelf until you're forgotten, befriended by the occasional scurrying cockroach or impassive dust bunny."

Meg snorted.

He leaned forward, dispelling the air of playfulness. "You're the sick member of the pack, shunned and cut off. The only time you think you'll get noticed now is when you catch the attention of a predator. For one brief moment, you serve a purpose again. In the back of your mind, you're thinking maybe that's who I am, the predator come to end it all."

She stared at him, suddenly unsure of the ground they were treading.

His mouth lifted in a soft grimace. "You're no more invisible than a butterfly or a sunset, Meg," he said sharply. "People just forget to look for beauty or something different. They forget to savor, to sense, to look or feel. They go through life looking for the arousing in pornography instead of in the world around them. Fulfillment is a spiraling destination because, once you start noticing and experiencing, it grows until all of life is a sensual experience. It will almost bring you to climax, and then you'll notice something else and it takes you even higher, makes you want to savor it even longer before you succumb. You never get enough. It's so fragile, so easy to destroy by ignoring it. You can lose it forever and never even know you had it."

His hands shifted under the skirt until his fingers were at the top of her thighs again. "You're pure sense, Meg. Every part of you is open and, like a butterfly, you're heartbreakingly fragile. As you said, born with no protection against being ignored or taken for granted. If you put armor on the butterfly's wings, it couldn't fly, and it wouldn't be a butterfly anymore. You think the wall you're trying to build will protect you, but all you're doing is building a wall between yourself and your experience of yourself. You're really just suffocating yourself." He passed the ball of his thumb lightly across her clitoris, like feather-light kisses, flesh to flesh.

Her hips writhed sinuously. "Daniel, don't, there are people–"

"People would be mesmerized watching you come. Meg, you're a goddess when you give in to pleasure. I want to see it again, as many times as it takes before you learn not to beat yourself up in that head of yours." He stopped moving his thumb and pushed it firmly against her moistening lips.

She clenched her fists against the sensations that swept through her. How could he have gotten her so hot again so fast?

Slowly, keeping his eyes on her bright ones, he withdrew his hands, just as Marcus returned to them. "The lady will take both pairs," he said, and handed over his credit card.

Marcus nodded and headed for the cash counter.

"Now." Daniel lifted her satin-covered foot. "We should see about getting you something to eat. Do you like ice cream?" He laid her foot against his groin, on his hard, engorged organ, and checked the snugness of the ribbons on her calf.

She nodded, not even certain what question he'd just asked.

"This is what you do to me, Meg," he muttered. "That's all for you. And as important as that is…" He touched her chin automatically and her gaze slid to his. "It's nowhere near the most important reason I have for wanting you."

Marcus came back with the sales slip. Daniel guided her sole down the length of his cock to the floor and rose to sign the receipt. "We'll come back for the heels," he told Marcus. "Meg, are you ready to go?"

She rose carefully, and he immediately put his hand under her elbow to steady her. She nodded to Marcus and he smiled, watching them with curious eyes as they stepped back into the flow of shoppers.

She smiled up at Daniel. "Thank you–"

She cried out in pain as something hard thudded into her and she stumbled against Daniel. A middle-aged man shouldered past her. Emerging from the mall administrative offices, his moussed hair and pastel polo shirt identified him as an employee likely headed toward an overcast nine-hole Friday afternoon. He carried the briefcase that had hit her legs, but only spared her an irritated glance until Daniel's open palm met his chest.

"I believe you owe the lady an apology," Daniel grated, steadying Meg with one hand, and effectively restraining the man with the other.

She felt certain her protector could sword fight with one hand and offer a toast with the other if it came down to it, but the dangerous glitter in his dark eyes alarmed her. "Daniel, it's all right. It was an accident."

"Which is why he wants to say he's sorry."

"Yeah... Yes, sure." The man's expression changed from belligerence to deference when those eyes came back to him. "I'm sorry, ma'am, I didn't see you. No need to get upset here."

"I'm all right." Meg waved it off with a polite smile and glanced tensely at Daniel. After a searching look into her face, he released his quarry with a shove. The man stumbled back into the crowd and Meg hid a smile as he churned out a running profusion of apologies to the other shoppers he bounced against.

Daniel knelt and ran his hands up her dress to her thigh, lifting her skirt high enough to examine the mark right above her knee. "That's going to leave a bruise," he said, his voice heavy with anger. "He should have watched where he was going."

"It's that invisible butterfly thing, I guess." She stretched her fingers and managed to touch his hair. She could run her fingertips just below the surface, along his nape, and she liked the contrast between his silken overcoat of hair brushing her knuckles and the down-like texture of the hair shaved short along the tendons. Her fingertips itched for more range.

Daniel took her hand from his neck with a reproving look, but he pressed his lips over each of her knuckles, then touched the tip of his tongue in the indentation between them. Still watching her face, he turned her palm over and nibbled at the fleshy pad of her thumb, working down to the taut, pulsing vein in her wrist. It sent a surge of current that tingled up her arm, all the way to the breast that pressed against her arm. Her nipple elongated and shaped itself before his smoldering regard.

"Stop that," she whispered, though her command lacked force. Her breath pumped in her lungs as rapidly as her blood pounded through her wrist.

"Watch this." He leaned forward and blew gently on the other breast. The flood of cool air against skin warmed by passion sent a shiver of goosebumps prickling across her skin. Her nipple puckered.

"Did you ever think about the boys you knew in high school?" He rose from his knee, put his hands at her waist and drew her to the rail of the mezzanine. He leaned back against it and held her between his thighs, cuddling her against his chest. Daniel linked his hands at the small of her back while her fingers twitched nervously against the tweed fabric of his slacks. "Lean against me, Meg. Relax."

When she complied, it felt suddenly like a baby bird sinking into the safety of her nest. His strength and warm enveloped her, her body molding into his perfectly.

Stretching his legs to either side of her, he narrowed the difference between their heights. Her body shuddered with pleasure when he pulled her more firmly against him. His still-hard cock pressed against her damp center.

"Those boys," he persisted. "Did you ever think about them getting hard during class?"

She lifted a shoulder. "I guess so. I was a typical teenager."

He chuckled. "There's no such thing." One hand left her back and pushed her head onto his shoulder. He stroked his knuckles down the side of her face, tracing an ear. "So you know boys lived in mortal terror of getting an erection in algebra," he rumbled against her cheek. "Or while dancing with a girl at the prom. But what if the boy, instead of getting embarrassed, had pressed against you like this during the dance? What if he'd wanted you to know how you made him feel, what he wanted to do to you, with you?" Daniel shifted his hips, a slow friction, and a tiny mewl of pleasure escaped her lips.

"Maybe, instead of putting his algebra book in his lap during class, he used the book to block everyone's view but yours, and he rubbed himself, cupping himself in his jeans, and grew bigger and bigger just because you were watching. What would you have thought of that awkward, pimple-faced boy then?"

She raised her eyes to his throat and wondered if he'd ever been that boy. She brushed her nose against his Adam's apple. "I think I'd have given him the first dance at the school prom."

Daniel laughed, and Meg smiled at the pure masculine pleasure in the sound. Abruptly, he caught her throat in his hand, nudged her chin with his knuckle and covered her mouth in an open-mouthed, deep-throated kiss. His tongue stroked every silken crevice of her, and he drew out slowly, lingering, as if he'd drawn out of her body after lovemaking. She rested completely against him, her weakened knees as useless to her as her bound hands.

"Let's go get you some ice cream," he murmured against her quivering lips.

The spontaneous humor managed to gain a foothold in the dents he'd made in her subconscious and Meg let go of the nagging worries. Perhaps she did have the strength to put her feet in the still pool of happiness for awhile. She might even find the courage to go wading.

She enjoyed the hard clasp of his hand on her elbow, his knuckles brushing the side of her breast. The echoing voices in the mall rushed like ocean waves through her senses, and textures and temperatures crested through her mind, each filling her awareness, then ebbing to make room for the next tide.

A woman in a rich green and blue print skirt sat on one of the mall benches. She'd placed a cluster of bags at her hip, and the skirt trailed the ground on the other side of her like a peacock's plumage. Meg wondered what would happen if she hadn't put the bags there. A restless-looking man wearing a rugged, good-looking mid-forty as well as jeans and a black turtleneck was on the payphone behind her. Perhaps he would have finished his call and sat beside her. They might have struck up a conversation that could lead to dinner, a relationship, a first kiss and a first fight...then one night, a kiss might have turned into long, sweeping touches, gentle, murmured words, and an urgency satisfied by only one thing.

But what if what had started on a bench with a peacock-colored skirt became devoid of color, fading away like the brilliant color of spring into the interminable heat and procrastination of summer? The gradual cooling of fall led to death in winter, and the acceptance of that death. The heart would go dormant to see if spring came again.

Maybe the bags were at her hip to stave off the spring. Sometimes you got used to winter, metamorphosed into a plant that thrived in a frozen wasteland. The only thing you had to fear then was the touch of the sun.

Was Daniel's heat going to turn her into a spring seedling again? How could she grow new plumage to take the sustenance of the sun if her roots had rotted and drowned in her tears?

Who was he, anyway? Meg had been numb when all this started, numb enough not to question her dark angel, only her sanity. Now she wondered at all he seemed to know about her, all he'd anticipated and done. She felt…good, and he was responsible. She felt aroused by his presence and incredibly alive.

A pair of teenagers walked by. She delighted in them, the boy's young neck bent attentively over his girl's shy, smiling face, their fingers intertwined and him guiding her protectively through the mall. Their linked fingers were a symbol—mine. Mine to care for, mine to protect. Mine to learn about love with.

The fresh, edible scent of ice cream reached in and drew her out as Daniel took her into the food court and up to the ice cream counter. A rainbow of twenty-eight flavors lay behind the slanted glass.

"What would you like?" He stood behind her and linked each of her hands in one of his. She leaned automatically against his chest and his mouth bent to her ear. "Don't worry about your hands. Whatever you get, I'll feed it to you."

"Chocolate Decadence," she said, noting and approving the rich shades of color, the smooth inverted curves made by the silver scoop that had flaked the ice cream into a cresting brown ocean wave. "In a cake cone."

"A traditionalist," he chuckled.

The girl behind the counter was about fifteen. In the corner behind her was a worn pair of ice skates. They leaned against a book bag crushed under the weight of a large denim purse so frayed at the straps that it was in danger of becoming a clutch. The girl wore her ice cream store smock over a sweatshirt and jeans, and her limp blonde pony tail was the color of golden vanilla. She had a pin on her stained uniform that said, 'My name is Robin. We're glad you're our customer.'

"How long have you been skating?" Meg asked.

Robin took them in with pale blue eyes framed by lashes as golden as her hair. It was the color of blonde that usually grew darker as a child grew into womanhood. Meg suspected that Robin's baby pictures would look identical to the round face before her now, only she doubted the eyes of the baby would be dulled by tiredness, or that the cherub mouth would be drawn by disappointment in the corners.

"Since I was little." The girl put the cone of Chocolate Decadence into the rack by the cash register and handed Daniel his change. "Have a nice day," she monotoned and turned to the next customer.

"Daniel," Meg looked up at him. "Can I ask a favor? Oh— Was it okay that I talked to her?"

He considered, amusement playing around his mouth. "You should have asked first, but I'll punish you for that shortly. What's the favor?"

The provocative expression in his eyes and the sensual threat bumped up her heartbeat several notches. Meg concentrated with an effort. "My purse. It's back at the store. Can you loan me two hundred dollars and I'll pay you back later?"

"Do you need it now?"

She nodded. Meg knew he had it, and she felt no shame in asking for a temporary loan. Money was the one thing she didn't lack. Insurance and alimony had been kind to her and spending meant little, except as a means to keep from imposing financially on Deb and Jeremy. She hadn't even cared about the existence of her bank account until now. She suddenly, urgently, needed to spend this two hundred dollars.

"All right, then." He pulled two hundred dollar bills out of his wallet.

"Can you hand it to her for me?"

"I can do that." He folded it into his palm discreetly. "I didn't realize you liked ice cream that much."

She chuckled.

Robin noticed them waiting at the counter and came back. "Yes, ma'am? Was something wrong with the ice cream?"

"No, not at all." Meg smiled. "Have you seen that red skating dress in the window downstairs at the ice rink?"

The girl nodded. "Yes ma'am. The one with all the sequins."

"With the red gauze skirt that hangs down in points?" Meg prompted. "The sleeves hook over the thumbs like…"

"Like King Arthur times," the girl finished, a ghost of a smile wavering at the corners of her mouth.

"That's right." Meg glanced at Daniel, his cue, and he handed over the money.

Robin took it automatically, then looked down at the amount.

"I want you to buy it for yourself when you get off work," Meg answered her startled expression. "There's enough for a downpayment on a pair of new skates, too."

Confusion swept over the girl's face. Wariness warred with annoyance as she focused on Meg and met her gaze for the first time. "Why—why are you guys… Is this a joke or something?" She struggled for the preprogrammed response.

Meg shook her head. "It's a gift to me. There's a boy working over at Pizza by the Slice. I'll bet he gets off at the same time."

"About thirty minutes after I do…"

Meg noted Daniel's understanding smile from the corner of her eye. Robin caught it, too, and momentarily lost her focus. "So, Robin?"

The girl brought her attention back. "Yeah?"

"So maybe that boy will go hang over the rail of the rink before he goes home. What do you think he'd do if he saw you spinning on the ice like a fire and ice flame?

Robin snorted. "He'd think it was someone else." She handed the money across the counter. "Keep it, ma'am. It wouldn't work."

Meg nodded, ignored the money. "You're right, he'd think it was someone else. This…" She inclined her head at the ice cream counter. "This isn't you, is it? Don't you feel most like yourself when you're out on the rink, skimming over the ice, spinning and turning?"

The girl's brown furrowed and she looked at the money in her hand.

"Take my word for it, Robin. Sometimes, when you put on a dress, you're putting on your skin, rather than hiding it. Sometimes, by putting it on, you're stripping off what you're not. He'll look over that rail and see you for the first time and I'll bet he'll fall in love with you, just the same way you'll fall back in love with yourself and life. Just give yourself a chance to remember who you really want to be and don't let go of it, no matter what you have to go through to get there." Meg suddenly, fervently wished she could run her hand along the girl's tense jaw or put a kiss against that bewildered expression, but she settled for impressing a warm, caring look upon her. "Good luck to you, whatever you decide to do with the money."

* * * * *

"You don't have to pay me back for that," Daniel said. He held her cone and drew her to the low tile wall around the wishing well, where she'd first seen him. "I'll consider it an investment. How did you make the connection between them?"

Meg shrugged. "I was sitting in the food court earlier today. It was just something about them. They kept glancing at each other, when each one thought the other wasn't looking. They were so alike, both so quiet and serious. I watched them and kept thinking both of them have dreams, but life is beating them down, making them lose faith. Do you think one amazing, unexpected moment of decision can kick start your life when it seems like it's stuttering?"

He lifted her chin, met her gaze squarely. "I hope so, Meg. I think people have a hard time letting go of certain types of pain. They think they've got it all under control, but that pain has a way of resurfacing, drowning them in the container of self-preservation they've built for themselves."

She lifted a shoulder in a mute, neutral movement, but the madness squirmed, bringing nausea.

"I think," he continued, his rich voice flowing into the troubled lands of her mind, "people need each other, just as Robin needed you in that moment. People need someone in their life they know will be there when darkness comes, someone who'll help them back into the light, not just once, but every time the darkness of pain pulls them down and tries to suck them into despair."

"Every time?"

"Every time." He pinched her chin lightly. "We work too hard at 'curing' people's pain. The body doesn't like pain, nor does the mind. It'll take care of it when it's ready. A scarred person doesn't lose the scars, they learn to look at them, accept the changes that scar wrought and go on. Forgiving yourself and letting yourself start over each time is the hardest part."

Meg's eyes wandered back to the food court, where Robin was staring thoughtfully at Pizza By The Slice. "It's easier if you think you're with someone who cares unconditionally. Sometimes just knowing you have someone to share your dreams with can give you the courage to enjoy them."

"Speaking of enjoying." He gestured with the ice cream. "This is starting to melt."

"Oh, sorry—" She cut it off short at his expression. "No apologies. I forgot. Where do you want to eat it?"

"Here." He brought her to the tile wall and caught the back of the skirt as she lowered to the marble. The bare cheeks of her ass pressed to the cold surface and the spray of the fountain misted her skin. Daniel sat next to her and stretched his arm along the rail behind her, putting her in the shelter of his chest and arm. He held out the cone. "Eat."

Meg leaned forward to nip the top off the cone, but he drew it out of her reach and ran a finger up the stretched line of her throat. "I want you to lick it, Meg. Treat it like my cock."

She glanced around and gasped at the tug on her nipples. He frowned, holding the diamond pendant between his thumb and forefinger and the ice cream cone in his other curled fingers. "Do we have to go through this again, Meg? Whose opinion matters?"

"Yours."

His fingers twitched. "Who do you belong to?"

"You," she breathed, the marble not doing enough to cool her heated flesh.

"Then do as I tell you."

She had to brace herself on her palms and lean forward get to it. The posture made the dress gap, so Daniel could watch her whole breast sway with her movements, her nipple rubbing against the silk of the dress. She looked back at him and he cocked his head, waiting.

Meg wanted him to want her in the same way he was torturing her.

Extending her neck with the slow grace of a swan, she touched her lips to the ice cream. Her tongue made a short, curling lick at the base of the scoop, then another as she sculpted the overlap into a tubular shape that fit the opening of the cone. When she stroked her tongue toward the head, his eyes left her breast and focused on her mouth.

She used the tip to etch vertical grooves in the cream. Flattening her tongue into a spoon, she slid it horizontally over the chocolate curve, melting the grooves away. Drops rolled off the edge of the cone and Daniel rotated it so she could catch it. Increasing the strength of her strokes, she circled half the base with the grip of her tongue. Meg leaned further and covered the head of the ice cream with her mouth for a moment, pulling back slowly, sucking the dessert into her mouth.

She kept her eyes down, covering a smug smile when Daniel pressed the knob of ice cream inside her mouth again. She rocked toward it, meeting each thrust with a tiny sinuous movement of her body. Her tongue filled with sweet melting chocolate on each penetration. The marble grew warm and slick beneath her buttocks.

Meg took her time, but when the generous scoop of ice cream gave way to the soggy edge of the cone, she raised her head, meeting his eyes as she licked her sticky lips.

Daniel tossed the cone in the trash. "Put out your tongue," he said, in a hoarse tone that thrilled her. She obeyed and he put a corner of the napkin on it. She drew her tongue back in, but managed a short swipe along his knuckle.

He lifted his brow, amused. "Pretty pleased with yourself, aren't you?"

Before she could respond, he took her chin in one hand to hold her still and rubbed the damp towel over her lips. It didn't matter. Daniel's dark eyes sparked with fire, and his touch was a bit less steady than it had been before. She wondered if he was more hard and erect than he'd been in the shoe store.

He lifted her onto his lap and pulled her skirt from under her before he nestled her onto his groin, proving he was. Her bare bottom nestled onto tweed and iron hardness. The silk fabric settled over his right arm, while his left arm cradled her. It felt odd, not being able to lift her arms, but the strength of his grip made her feel secure.

"Part your legs."

Hard command had replaced his reassuring tenderness. Meg swallowed on a dry throat, then shifted her thighs apart. The hand hidden by the drape of skirt slid up the side of her thigh and released the ring holding her right arm to her side before his fingers cupped the curve of her ass and stroked it.

"You may touch me, Meg."

She lifted her arm to his shoulder and he pulled her closer, helping her hook it around his neck. She buried her fingers into his thick, soft hair there, and a half smile pulled at his sensual lips. Sliding her fingers to his face, she traced his cheek, the line of his jaw, his lips. His eyes gazed upon the changing expressions of her face and she passed her hand over them, closing them for a moment as she caressed his features.

"You're so quiet, Meg," he murmured. "You can talk to me, you know."

"I'm afraid to."

"Why is that?" He opened his dark eyes and tilted his head into her hand.

"I might say something wrong."

His fingers slipped from her hip to her open thighs. In one slight, easy movement, he put two fingers deep inside her wetness. Her legs shut in reaction, her eyes flying wide open and her wrist yanking reflexively against its binding. "Don't—"

"Don't what, Meg?" He lifted an eyebrow. "Do you belong to me or not?"

The necklace choked where her pulse and the heat of her face fused. Meg looked around, and the fingers still outside her body twisted in her pubic hair. "Meg, look at me."

"I can't." Tears glazed her vision. "Someone is going to see us, and... you're touching me... there." She didn't know why she wanted to cry. She wasn't helpless, she could end this now, but she wanted him to be in control, she wanted to trust him. She was so afraid she was losing her mind—

"Meg, look at me." His expression was stern. "Open your legs, now."

She jerked a nod, but it took her a moment to make her trembling knees fall apart.

"Kiss me." His arm drew her close and she opened her mouth as it met his. His hand left her waist and held her head as he stroked her tongue with his, traced her lips and turned her body to liquid.

He kept a hand on the back of her neck, stared into her face as he moved his fingers slowly, turning them inside her. Her fingers whitened on his shoulder. Daniel pushed his knuckles against her clit and she moaned, burying her head in his shoulder, biting him. He caught her hair and yanked her head back.

"I want to see what I'm doing to you, Meg. Don't hide your face."

Pressure built low in her stomach. She clutched him. "Please... don't," she panted. "This is crazy... I shouldn't let you do this."

"This is about more than sex or choices. You're afraid you'll say something wrong." His fingers continued their dance and she couldn't capture his words. Her senses were drowned in mind-paralyzing arousal.

"There's nothing you can do wrong with me, Meg." He tightened his grip in her hair, balancing pleasure with pain to get her attention. "You're mine, everything about you is mine. I'm touching what belongs to me, Meg. I'm fucking you with my fingers because I like the way you feel when you're wet. I want to make you even wetter. No, don't turn your face away. Look at me and don't take your eyes from mine. Understand?"

She blinked through falling tears. Her mouth worked uselessly, struggling for breath and control. His middle finger pushed deep. She bit her lip and tasted blood.

"No." His hand slipped from her neck and his thumb pried into the corner of her mouth, opening it. "You're never allowed to hurt yourself, Meg. I won't permit it." His eyes darkened with unholy fire and he cupped the back of her head again, bringing her toward his lips. "Don't think anymore. Come for me again. Now."

He plunged his tongue into her mouth. His thumb made small circles against her throbbing flesh outside while his fingers pumped her inside, stroking her sweet spot. Lights exploded in

Meg's head. She screamed into his mouth, fused to hers. Her fingers clawed him through his shirt, taking blood and skin.

Gathering her close, he held her shuddering body tightly against the warm, pulsing life of his. The mall vanished. It was just the two of them, and his relentless fingers offered her no salvation except submission.

Her climax climbed higher and higher, waves surging toward the heavens rather than cresting. She was swept in a tide that had no beginning or end, a sensual Charybdis that denied her any control. The stronger the current, the more rigid she became, paralyzed by pleasure that allowed her to cling to nothing but Daniel, her anchor in the storm he'd created.

The soft gurgle of the fountain and a fall of silver icicles in the sky finally penetrated the gray haze in her eyes. He didn't remove his fingers as she came down. Floating like a feather, she descended on a gently rocking crescent of air. Gentle touches and circles of his buried fingers kept her quivering with aftershocks. Meg became aware again of his other arm, holding her limp, shuddering body protectively.

Her lovely curling hair fell over the side of her face, curtaining both of their faces from prying eyes. His eyes raged with raw passion, so strong she could almost see herself, pushed back on the marble, her legs spread wide as he sheathed himself in her right then. She trembled in his arms and knew she'd let him. She'd let him do anything.

"You're beautiful," he whispered. He kissed her face and spoke against her skin. "You sucked so hard on my hand when you came...ah, darling, I want you so bad. Can you feel how much?"

Yes, she felt the engorged length of him tucked between the cheeks of her ass. During her climax, when her hips had rubbed hard against him, her two globes of flesh had parted as willingly as her legs. Now when she moved, the ridged length of him stroked the sensitive tissues around her opening, tissues she'd never known could be stimulated. Her muscles tightened over his fingers at the thought and Daniel smiled.

"Careful, Meg. I need that hand back."

Her heartbeat pounded like a rabbit's as he leaned forward and pressed a gentle, whispering kiss to the corner of her mouth. She turned her head to him and his kiss became longer, more tender, the gentle dance of lovers' tongues, the savor of the lightest brush of one another's lips. It disturbed the small corner of her mind that still huddled from his demands, fearing to be captured and conquered.

"I—I want to look around."

He smiled. "Because you asked, yes, you may."

Meg turned her head. A pair of older women on a bench across the courtyard looked scandalized by their kissing, but most of the wandering mall shoppers spared them no more than an amused glance. Daniel had told her the truth. He really wouldn't let her be humiliated. She'd been exposed to him and no one else.

At a distance, dominance had seemed to be about humiliation, degradation. When she'd agreed to belong to him for the day, perhaps that was why she'd agreed. She deserved the humiliation and punishment of this stranger. He was an angel of justice sent to make her pay for her crimes.

But Daniel's dominance was about cherishing and protecting, and submission to his will, not humiliation.

"I'd never embarrass you, Meg," he repeated, as if reading her mind. "Your pleasure is for me only. You're safe from prying eyes." His fingers came out of her, out from under her dress. "Open your mouth." She tasted her saltiness on his fingers. He trailed his hand down her neck and rested his fingers in the shallow valley between her breasts. "This is the perfume I like, the wet musk from between your thighs."

He turned his head and kissed her wrist. All the times before, he'd closed his eyes, or looked at her when he kissed it. This time, his eyes were open, looking at her wrist, and he stopped in mid-gesture. He lifted her wrist from his shoulder and held it away to examine it more closely. She watched his eyes so closely, she knew the moment he identified what he was seeing. The lights and colors of the carousel came to a discordant halt.

Meg bolted from his embrace, throwing him off balance, but she didn't stop to see if she'd knocked him into the wishing well. She dodged clumps of people, hoping they'd give her enough cover to lose him. Nausea and dizziness washed over her. Stumbling on the steps to the upper level, she freed her other wrist with a short jerk of her arm that burned as the yank reverberated to her nipple.

Patrice. She'd find Patrice. She could leave the necklace and jewels there. He'd get them back and be someone else's dark angel. She'd been right at the beginning. He was a punishment, a temptation to drag her into the hell she deserved, but she wasn't brave enough to face her punishment.

The brief period of confidence and happiness vanished, a smoke illusion, a flimsy door that exploded inward and let all the pain and fear come rushing back with guilt and inadequacy shoving them from behind. It was the forked tongue of the madness, lashing her, capturing her, dragging her back into its embrace, only this time it would use his eyes, his face, his smell, to inflict its punishment, because that was the kind of cruelty the madness enjoyed.

Meg thought of the girl at the ice cream counter and cursed her own stupidity. She'd pushed the girl to expose her inner self to the dangerous outer world, where the madness waited for prey. Souls were no more than weak rabbits against it, their only weapon the ability to run faster if they saw it coming.

There were tribes that gave their children hideous names, or no names at all, for the first years of their lives to deflect the interest of evil demons in the treasures of innocence. The boy at the pizza place was probably a cruel date rapist, and the girl would go through life hating the red dress, hating the lavender and blue agent of destruction who'd given her the means to buy it.

The madness shrieked and danced in her head. Meg spun about wildly at the top of the stairs, not sure where she was going. The double flight of stairs yawned before her as she turned, the gaping teeth of a savage monster, eager to crunch her bones into gristle. She swayed over its savage maw, beginning her descent, cries of passersby like distant bird cries in her ears. Just a trip, the monster's swallow, and then blessed darkness. No more madness, no more anything. She opened her arms and heart to it and fell.

She crashed into Daniel's body as he spun around the turn of the second flight, lunged up five stairs, and caught her in arms stronger than any fear she'd ever had.

He yanked her off her feet, scooping her struggling form roughly into his arms, and strode past hostile peering faces that paved the gateway of hell and seemed so colorless the brilliance of the fire held appeal. Just like that red skating dress, glittering with sequins, the girl's pale hair the center of the flame.

Meg scrabbled at the necklace, determined to rip it off and be rid of the obstruction of her dark angel, but it wouldn't unlatch.

Daniel let her to her feet in front of the dress shop, then hauled her into it, one hand manacled on her rigid arm.

"Patrice," he snapped. "We need a private area. Where?"

The exquisitely perfect mannequin had the grace to look somewhat surprised, but she recovered quickly. "The stock room, sir." She pointed behind her. "If the lady needs to make some private adjustments."

"Let me go," Meg hissed.

Daniel ignored her. "Yes, some adjustments need to be made."

The stock room silenced the sounds of the outside world almost immediately. One dim light shone on racks of dresses yet to be displayed, cartons of gift bags, and rows of shelves piled high with accessories. Daniel shoved her into the aisle, blocking her exit with a line of shelves and racks on either side of her and his body before her. Meg swung at him, snarling. He caught her wrist, twisted her arm behind her and pinioned her face first against the sliding ladder mounted on tracks that ran along the shelves of file boxes. Even though she struggled against the wooden slats that pressed against her chest, her stomach, her hips and thighs, his hold didn't hurt her or allow her to struggle enough to hurt herself. She was no match for his strength.

"Meg, calm down."

She shook her head. A sob broke from her throat. When he loosened his grip, she spun around and darted past him.

His fist snarled in her hair. He jerked her head back, his mouth clamping over hers. Pushing her back against the ladder, he wedged his hips between her legs, lifting her off her feet. His other hand pulled open the front of her dress and locked onto the short chain between her breasts. He yanked, pulling her nipples up, and Meg moaned. The kiss went on and on, until she gasped against his mouth and writhed mindlessly. She was pleading with noises that weren't words, but she didn't know what she asked from him. Her body ached, her mind screamed and at last she could do nothing but hold onto him with both hands clutching his arms.

Daniel lifted his head, his eyes hard on her face. "Who do you belong to, Meg? Who?" Another sharp tug sent painful shocks through her breasts. He was truly angry.

"You," Meg whispered.

Again, he tugged and she whimpered. "I know your body is mine," he snapped. "I could fuck you here and make you come as many times as I wanted to. Who does your mind belong to? Your heart?" She shook her head wordlessly and he jerked her chin up. "Me, Meg," he growled. "It all belongs to me. If you don't get that through your head, I'll—" He stopped, bit his lip and looked away, though he didn't release his hold.

He'd told her this wasn't a game, and it wasn't about sex. Her body was the easiest defense to breach. He was looking for more. Daniel thought he wanted all of her. But nobody wanted all of her.

When he looked back at her with eyes gone soft, it destroyed her. He dropped his hands to her sides and re-clipped the bracelets to her hips, pinioning her once again. She shuddered as his hands covered her breasts and he spread the neck of the dress open, framing them. Kneeling, his eyes upon her face, he took her left nipple into his mouth.

The breath trembled out of her and her back arched. Meg automatically tried to raise her hands to curl them in his hair, then convulsed as the ring of wire tightened on the nipple he was rolling slowly over his tongue. He took his time, making a wet sucking noise like a child nursing.

It was the sexual caress that made her the most vulnerable, which both excited her body and calmed her mind, and she wondered how the hell he'd known. When his rough cheek brushed her white curve, her skin blushed in response. Her body went limp against the ladder as he curled his arm around her waist, holding her still. The quiet darkness of the room enveloped them, and she felt disembodied, like she could dissolve into pieces and become part of the room, content to never leave, a mannequin like Patrice. But of course, Patrice wasn't a mannequin. She'd pulled off perfection in living flesh, curse her.

Meg's head dropped back onto a rung of the ladder. Daniel worked his way up her throat to her lips. He leaned into her, tenderly kissing and sucking on her mouth until her hips again moved in a slow rhythm against his arousal, a marriage of fire and water. He was a ray of sunlight, charging her liquid waves and white crests of salty foam with shimmers of brilliant fire.

He raised his head, touching his nose to hers. "Tell me about your wrists, Meg," he whispered.

His heart beat against her. In the stillness of the storage room, she could feel and hear the evidence of their existence; slow, shuddering breaths, the brush of clothes, the whisper of his touch against her flesh. A certain level of trust had to exist between the living when paper dolls populated the rest of the world, didn't it?

"Tommy." The word stuck in her throat and it took several moments before she could say anything else. His fingers stroked her back. "We were married six years. Tommy truly needed me, and I felt like no other man ever had. I loved him so much." His arms gathered her close and she leaned, tucking her head under his chin. She pressed her nose into his white starched shirt.

"He was shy and indecisive. I handled all the practical stuff — paying bills, running errands, doing the groceries. I pushed him, harder than I should have, to be the things I needed him to be, to grow in the ways I needed him to grow. He took care of me emotionally and kept me from the dark places I've always had in my head, but it wasn't an even trade. I didn't give him what he needed.

"My parents loved each other," she continued as Daniel remained silent, waiting. "But it was a difficult relationship. They didn't support each other's emotional needs. They fought a lot, but I never… I thought it was an honest fight, on one stage. Every blow hurt, but they were blows that you could see coming."

There were nuances to pain, fathomless depths like two mirrors reflected against each other, showing infinite images of the same person. "About the time Tommy and I were planning to get married, Mom discovered Dad had been cheating on her for years… with prostitutes. Mom needed to tear something apart, and Tommy and I were closest. She told me, over and over, how Tommy was going to be like Dad, that he'd cheat on me, that he'd turn out to be someone I couldn't depend on…. I told her no, no, no… over and over. I'd made the right choice. I knew I had."

She stared, glassy-eyed. "He had the sweetest smile. It always made my knees weak."

The lumps that formed in her throat during moments like this scared her — so large they seemed capable of blocking off oxygen. Daniel's fingers eased up her neck and sculpted this one down to a manageable size. Tears ran down her chin onto his fingers.

"I don't think Dad saw how he'd betrayed our whole family. I always thought… I *knew* he wasn't comfortable with us, but I thought, when he said he loved me, he knew what that meant. But he didn't know, so he hadn't loved us at all, whether he believed he had or not.

"Tommy knew," she whispered. "He knew that I was standing on the edge, and the one thing that could push me over was knowing everyone was the same… That Mom was right." Meg curled her lips under her teeth and shook with the effort to hold back the sob. She was so sick of crying. Daniel murmured softly to her and she buried her face in his warm scent, accessible from the open collar of his shirt.

"He left me for a woman he met at work," she managed against his skin. "Someone who didn't try to run his life, who let him be who he wanted to be, not who she needed him to be. He left me before he slept with her, though. He cared about me enough to respect that."

"So I was no better than my father. I thought I loved Tommy with my whole heart and soul, but how could I have loved him, really, when what I was calling love drove him away?" Her eyes filled with misery, empty of tears. "The chance to love someone completely, with everything I am, was what I had searched for my entire life. All of a sudden, I found out that I didn't know how to do it right."

Daniel's fingertips traced the drying tracks of her tears and Meg turned her cheek into his palm, shutting her eyes tightly, holding back the emotions threatening to overwhelm her.

"I suppose you want me to tell you how all this ties into my wrists," she swallowed.

He tapped a light finger on her cheek. "You're a woman. I figured you'd take the circuitous route to it."

"Sexist pig." She raised her head and managed a ghost smile. Daniel tugged her hair and she laid her head back on his chest.

The madness had always been with her. For the first time in her life, she went into it willingly. Accepting its embrace as the one reassuring, constant presence in her life. "I'd tried so hard," she murmured. "I was so tired. Those magazines, you know the self-help ones? They tell you that it's okay when you can't do it all. But no one forgives you for it, least of all yourself, and you can't run from that. But I tried."

She took a deep breath, the gears of her heart pumping erratically, processing blood laced with a heavy grit of pain and regret. "The first time, I ran off a bridge. That's how I hurt my back. Everyone thought I lost control of the car." She chuckled, a sick, bitter sound. "They were right. I'd lost control. Every time I'd try to hold onto sanity, my mind became a torture chamber, a voice piped in day and night, chanting 'never good enough, never good enough'. I couldn't take it anymore."

The blackness of the storage room wasn't dark enough. Meg closed her eyes again.

"I drove to Winfield Park one night after it closed. I parked my car at the bank across the street so it would be found, then I went to the lake." She remembered the movement of the water, had found it curious, a current inside a closed circle, movement with no destination.

"It was a full moon."

Her eyes snapped open and she jerked her head back to look up at him.

Daniel nodded. "You laid on the grass by the lake, cut your wrists with a razor and watched the stars until you lost consciousness."

"You—" Shock drained the lethargy from her body, and she wanted to move away, but he held her against the ladder.

"I was there, Meg," he said. "No, not at the beginning." His fingers dropped, releasing her wrists from their bondage and lifting them to his lips, kissing the two scars. "If I'd been there from the start, I wouldn't have let it happen."

"But why… How did you…"

"Winfield Park is behind my neighborhood. There are jogging trails from our townhouses into the park. My dog found you. He smelled the blood and left the trail. You'd tucked a note in your breast pocket, your friend Deb's phone number."

"I wanted her to be the one to tell my mother," Meg murmured.

"I called her after I got you to the hospital." His fingers locked on her wrists, but it was the knowledge in his eyes that held her prisoner. "I stayed to make sure you were going to be all right. I didn't want to intrude or add to your distress, so I asked your mother and Deb not to tell you about me, but I couldn't step back. I kept tabs through your recovery and I spent time with them, learning about you through their eyes."

How much had he seen? She'd lost awareness of her surroundings during that time, going into a deep catatonia they'd tried to treat with a myriad of drugs, drugs that had made her hysterical and hallucinate, cold in summer and hot in the winter. You couldn't sedate emotions or a broken spirit, but they'd tried.

Had he been there that day in the grocery store when the fog had descended? When she'd become aware of her surroundings, she'd been sitting in the frozen food case. The aisle was littered with the boxes and metal shelves she'd pulled out so she could climb in and close the glass door, to stare out at life. Her mother, a paragon of control, had broken down and cried in front of a store full of nameless, gaping faces.

"I call it the madness," she whispered, looking down. "I hurt my mother so much—her brother killed himself. I think having to be around her every day, knowing I was hurting her so much, killed the only part of me that wasn't dead. But I didn't know how to stop. People are just blanks to me. It's like I'm not here or they're not real, and I'm moving around in a world where I don't belong. She sent me away to Deb's."

Daniel cradled her face, pain for her transforming his dark eyes with a warm compassion she could hardly bear to face. He kept her eyes on his with gentle, unrelenting hands. "She didn't send you away, Meg. After the day in the grocery store, I spoke to Deborah. She *wanted* you to come stay with her. She was worried about the two of you. I think she sensed what you just said, that your mother's pain was driving you further into yourself. We had a hard time convincing your mother to let you go for awhile, but she agreed. After you…" He paused, thinking, and she looked up at him curiously. "After you settled in at Deborah's, you seemed to be making more progress. I arranged with her to drop you at the mall today. I thought it was time we met."

"Why?" Meg whispered. "Why did you do all this? Why did you keep checking on me?"

"Is it so hard for you to believe that you're worth saving?" He shook her gently. "Don't you know that, in all the magical realms, if you know someone's name, you bind that person to you? You knew my name, Meg."

"What?" She stared, confused.

"When I knelt beside you in the grass, I wasn't sure what was happening," he explained, straightening her hair. "It was dark and you were lying on the ground. I couldn't see the blood, but your face was so white, I knew you were ill. When I touched you, you spoke my name. 'Daniel.' You raised your hand toward me. That's when I saw the blood.

"It would have been appropriate to leave you in Deb's care at the hospital. But I found I couldn't. I had to know what demons had compelled a beautiful young woman to take her own life. I felt like you'd put your soul inside my heart when you spoke my name, and I felt connected to you in a way I've never felt with any woman. I couldn't shake the feeling that I was supposed to be a part of your life, and I couldn't stay away. The more I got to know you, the more I wanted to know." Ironic humor touched his lips. "You bound me to you when you spoke my name, Meg."

She frowned, her brow creasing. She went back to that night, remembered the prickle of grass against her shoulders, the smell of the lake and the pines behind her. She hadn't brought a towel because she didn't want anyone, a child especially, to come upon the horrifying sight of her lying on a blanket soaked with blood. Meg had placed the razor on her stomach because she hadn't wanted a med tech or police officer kneeling on it and getting hurt. She'd looked up at the stars and her palms had filled with blood. She'd dropped her arms in the grass, then repositioned them. She hadn't wanted to look messianic. As her vision had dimmed, she wondered if she would meet Daniel.

When she was little, she'd had an illustrated children's Bible, a beautiful, expensive book given to her by her grandmother. Since she couldn't read yet, she'd made up stories for the pictures. Her favorite had been the picture of the man sitting among the lions. His stern eyes, made appealing by the dignified strength of his face and the beautiful fall of curling dark hair down to his muscular shoulders, had made him look like a brother to the lions. Daniel's enemies had stood in the background, looking on in anger or amazement, but Daniel had looked into the lions' eyes and returned to himself. He'd been in truth a magnificent, wild creature, their brother, unhampered by anything except natural law. He could roar with them, 'I am lord of all I see'.

Meg had responded to that—to him—at age sixteen as much as at age six. She'd asked her mother his name, but she'd refused to ever learn the actual story of the biblical hero. She wanted to cast off every warped expectation of an unnatural world and run wild with the wind and sea, be bathed in the fire of the sun and have the earth curled beneath her bare toes. Then she could be kin to the wild beasts, as Daniel had been, and she could find peace.

"Daniel of the lions," she breathed. "It was a coincidence." Her fingers curled in his shirt, touching reassuring flesh and hard bone.

He winced as she caught chest hair and he put his hand over hers. "There are no coincidences when it comes to suicide," he said crisply. "Only angels tread those waters."

"So what was all this?" Meg whispered. She touched the necklace at her throat.

He traced the soft skin of her throat beneath the necklace. "That's a different story, and a strange one."

She choked on an unexpected laugh. "Well, everything else about this has been so ordinary. Go ahead and shock me."

He smiled. Daniel put his hands on her back, smoothed the dress down to her waist, over her bottom, his fingers probing between her cheeks. "Spread your legs, Meg."

"But—"

"Meg."

His knee pressed and she relented. His cock had softened as she'd told her story, but even the press of his limp flesh created a ripple through her body. He touched a kiss to her temple, her cheek, caught the corner of her mouth. "My sister reads romance novels. When I was at the beach with her and her family, I paged through one and it fell open at a certain spot, like it does when that section's read a lot. I picked up that the heroine's heart had been broken by the man she loved. As a result, she'd given up the will to live. The man who truly loved her then kidnaps her, locks her in his home and seduces her forcibly, again and again, possessing her body until she relinquishes her heart and mind to him, to love, and therefore life.

"It was more than a story." He rubbed against the soft, quivering skin between her legs. His chest touched her nipples and pressed their jewels into her skin. Her body trembled in response, but she couldn't enjoy it as much now. The game was over. He knew all that she was, and she wasn't someone Daniel would want.

"The women I've been with have always had different stories about why we weren't right for each other. I gave them too much space, trying not to crowd them, or pushed too hard. I tried too much, spending too much time trying to figure out what they wanted. So I sat there, trying to understand why my sister had marked that passage. She's an intelligent, independent woman… like you."

Meg grimaced, started to speak, but he caught her chin and gave her a stern glance. "Like you, Meg. Put your arms around my neck."

She obeyed, sliding her fingers into his hair, then rested them on his broad shoulders.

"Why would she like a story where the woman's will is subordinate to the man's, where he made love to her whether she was willing or not, where he took care of all her needs?"

He moved back to the limit of her arms, looked at her bare breasts with such possessive pleasure that her nipples tightened and the grip of the silver rings around them shot sweet sensation into her lower abdomen.

"I think men used to know how to love women," he continued. "Before society became obsessed with political correctness. When a man loved a woman, he loved her completely. She was a possession, but his most valued possession, in the original idea of the word, someone who consumed his soul and tangled all his senses, someone he'd trade everything for. She was his because she possessed him as much as he possessed her. A woman trusted and respected him because he loved her that way, and she submitted to his love, obeyed him. He didn't deny her voice, her intelligence, or her spirit. He cherished them."

His eyes flicked up, captured hers. "When I fell in love with you, I knew that's how I'd love you, so you'd never doubt me."

Her heart reversed direction, dropped into the pit of her stomach. "You've lost your mind," she whispered.

"To you, that would make us perfect for each other."

"Daniel, I don't know…" How could he possibly love her when he'd seen the worst, the essence of who she was? But his gaze was fierce and tender, and his cock bumped against the sensitive moisture between her legs, rising in response to her body again. Or maybe she was dreaming it all, and this was just another cruel game the madness played.

Daniel took her wrists from his neck, refastened them to the silver rings, then stepped back. He unbuckled his belt, slid it out of his trousers. Meg wet her lips. "Daniel—"

He shook his head and turned her with a hand on her shoulder so she faced the ladder. "Push your breasts onto the rung in front of you, Meg."

She obeyed while butterflies flapped against the walls of her stomach. He stepped to her side, reached around the ladder and clasped the nipple chain, holding her breasts on display on the ridged wooden platform. "Gather your skirt and let me see your ass."

"I don't understand—"

"Do it, Meg," he commanded, his eyes stern and unyielding. "Trust me."

She pulled up the silk slowly, her bound hands making the task an inch-by-inch proposition. He used the time to toy with the chain, twisting it back and forth, pleasurably tormenting her nipples. It unbalanced her, so her breasts pressed heavily over the slat. Her chin rested on the rung above.

"Spread your legs wide and lift your ass so I can see what's mine, between your legs."

Cool fingers of air whispered across her exposed backside. "I'm scared."

"I know." He tugged gently on her nipples, then his fingers brushed her bottom and she felt the touch of the belt. "You're as wet as sin for me. You'll never run from me again, Meg, or evade my questions. You'll always be open and honest to me, as open as your legs are now. You can expect the same from me. Do you understand?"

"Yes."

"This is your punishment for hurting those you love, and when that punishment is over, it's over. Do you understand?"

She closed her eyes, trying to hold back tears. He yanked the nipple chain, not gently this time. She yelped. "Yes," she whispered.

He dipped his head in front of her and took one of her nipples in his mouth. The feel of his tongue over her swollen peak, rubbing against her flesh and the wire, rocked her hips higher. The belt cracked against her buttocks, licking the warm wetness between her thighs. A terrifying combination of arousal and pain, want and need, and fear, gripped her. Meg moaned and he sucked harder. The belt struck again and again. She held her skirt in clenched, sweaty palms and throbbed. Everything left her mind but the raging hunger to please him, to be open to him, his body, his demands, everything.

The pleasure and pain built, two tidal waves of a fatal level of emotion, and she'd be crushed between them. Loss and guilt, regret and despair came together in the desolate emptiness inside her and melded into a jagged crystal of dead hopes and vanquished dreams. She choked on the pain and begged, but he wouldn't be denied. The tumor began to rise, inexorably drawn toward her heart by his dark sorcery. "No…" she wailed.

The belt cut, a hard slap, and his tongue kept stroking, suckling. Emotions pounded from her heart and flooded her body. She pulled against his hold on the nipple chain, gasping, but even the pain couldn't give her an anchor.

The first ripples rose, shivering from a warm pond of life between her legs. The belt strokes burned into pleasure. Meg squirmed against the ladder, unable to grab at anything other than the skin and silk in her fingers, and Daniel kept the chain binding her breasts tight. Her nipple pushed even further into his maddening, flicking tongue as her hips pumped, as she was driven by the lashes of the belt to her toes. Her face and body convulsed.

"Let it go, Meg." Daniel spoke against her skin. "Let it go, love."

She did. The shrapnel of her past sliced through her heart and erupted from her throat with the guttural moan of a climax. She sank her teeth into the wood of the ladder to keep the death cry from echoing into the mall. Her eyes rolled up into her head. She saw blue flame, cleansing, pure, and peaceful. The world went dark.

* * * * *

The touch of a cool cloth on her forehead returned her to consciousness. Daniel sat cross-legged on the storage room floor with her in his lap. She supposed Patrice had brought the wet paper towel. Her dress was arranged so all of her was covered again.

"That ice cream is all you've eaten today, isn't it?" He didn't look at her. He seemed focused on her forehead, stroking deliberately with the towel.

"I—" She tried to think. "I don't know. I think Deb gave me a bagel this morning, but I can't remember if I ate it or not." She had a habit of forgetting, putting her food down on coffee tables or bookshelves and leaving it like an absent-minded mouse.

He nodded as tension vibrated his body. Once, when she and Tommy had been first married, she'd let the shower get too hot and had fainted in the cloying steam. It had scared Tommy to death.

She lifted her hand and found all of her bindings were gone, except the necklace. She put her hand against his jaw and throat, leading his eyes back to her face. "You know, most men would be pretty pleased with themselves, making a woman faint like that."

Humor crept in and softened the intensity of his dark eyes. Meg smiled, glad she could make him feel better. She nodded at the pile of gold and jewels on the floor. "You took it off."

"Your circulation. I was afraid—" He swallowed. "Damn it, Meg, don't ever do that again."

She snorted against his shirt, feeling giddy and giggly. He pushed her back to see her grinning face.

A grudging smile pulled at his lips. She traced their contour. His eyes grew serious as he stroked her hair away from her cheek, then took her hand from his face and kissed it. He lifted her off his lap and brought them both to their feet, steadying her as the blood returned to its normal circulation from her head to her feet.

"Meg, it's time you were master."

Her hand automatically went to the necklace on her throat.

A warm, intent look came to his eyes at her protective gesture, and he shook his head. "No, leave that on." He looked down at their linked hands. "There's a big difference between having to be dependent on someone and wanting to be, Meg. You still belong to me, Meg, but I'm going to show you that I belong to you, too. I'm giving you control for awhile. From this moment on, I'll obey all your commands, serve your pleasure."

Anticipation stirred provocatively in her stomach at his quiet words, but she hesitated. "I don't even know how to start."

"You don't?" He cocked a rakish brow. "Remember servants carrying you in a lounge chair?" He caught the neckline of her dress and brought her close with his knee-weakening strength. He breathed on her lips. "*I belong to you.*"

Daniel was six feet plus, probably about 200 pounds of solid muscle, yet he wanted her to believe she could be his master. With his consent, she supposed she could be. Wasn't that what she'd done? She'd told herself she had no choice, but she had, and she'd chosen to belong to him. What would it be like to have a man like Daniel obey her every wish?

Meg slid a tentative hand behind his neck and brought his head down to hers. His lips were eager, but it was different now. He gave what she wanted and obeyed a hundred and ten percent. She put a shaking hand on his chest and pushed. He stepped back obediently, but with reluctance.

Wow.

A ridiculous smile fought to surface on her lips and Meg turned her back before he could see it. Her toes were curling with delight inside their slippers, for heaven's sake. She drew a deep breath. "Follow me," she said, almost starting at the imperious tone in her voice.

She emerged into the pleasant lighting of the dress shop and Patrice's speculative regard. "Patrice."

"Yes, madam?"

The shopkeeper snapped to attention as if she, too, immediately noted the change of reins. Meg was impressed. "I need your help."

She turned to a rack as Patrice came around the counter. The chic mannequin on top of the rack displayed a poet's shirt. Cotton, full-sleeved with a slit neckline, a shirt no pirate captain would have been without a hundred years ago, and no present day straight male would consent to wear without electric shock treatment. But Meg was no different from any other woman who went weak in the knees when Tyrone Power stood on the deck of the Black Swan.

"Put this on," she said, handing one of them to Daniel. When he would have turned toward the dressing room, she laid a hand on his arm. "Here."

His eyes swerved back to her, startled. She raised an eyebrow, a slight, expectant smile playing on her lips. She tapped his chest with a finger. "Who do you belong to, Daniel?" she murmured.

He cleared his throat, nodded, shrugged out of his coat, and laid it on the rack. Meg made a concerted effort to keep her expression casual, her breathing even, as he began to unbutton the white starched shirt, revealing a light mat of dark hair over a broad, muscled chest and abdomen. Out of the corner of her eye,

Meg noted they'd drawn the attention of the other patrons in Patrice's store, two women and a man.

Daniel shrugged out of his shirt and took the new one from her hand, sneaking in a light caress of fingers. She frowned and he gave her an insolent smile.

"Wait." She took his shirt from the rack and ran it over her cheek, smelling his cologne as she took a long, good look at his chest. Her hand outlined his bare shoulder, and she ran her palm over his muscular pectoral. She scraped his nipple lightly with her manicured nails. A shudder rippled across his chest.

She raised her gaze to his face and found him watching her every move like a dangerous animal. A restrained, yet still dangerous, animal. She wanted to cup him, see if she was making him hard again, but she wasn't that brave. Shocked murmurs floated from the two women, but a casual glance showed that the man didn't look shocked at all.

"Don't put the shirt on yet."

She turned her attention to the male shopper. He was muscular and tall, not quite as handsome as Daniel, but handsome enough for a second look. He was dressed well, in black jeans with a cotton black t-shirt tucked into them. He wore cowboy boots beneath the jeans, the toes tipped with a polished silver edge, and a sports jacket over his t-shirt.

He rested a hand on the rounder of clothes before him, and his other hand was casually hooked in his jeans pocket, but his eyes were riveted with more than casual interest.

Meg trailed her hand down the middle of Daniel's chest, stopping just above his slacks to trace the short line of hair that disappeared into his waistband. The man's hand tightened on the metal bar of the rounder. Meg physically felt the space in the store narrow to the area occupied by the three of them.

She lifted her free hand, beckoning to him. She felt Daniel's muscles tense under her palm.

"Meg—"

Her fingers tightened in the hairs on his stomach, and she shot him a sharp glance. "Do you belong to me, Daniel?"

He drew an uneven breath. His uneasiness raised peculiar emotions in her. She felt tenderness for his vulnerability, but an implacable certainty that he must do as he was told, that she knew what was best and he must trust that she'd care for him. She recognized the words as his own from not more than a few hours ago. It had taken her less than five minutes to assume full mastery over him. Perhaps he was right. A dominant personality did exist inside her.

She wanted to arouse him to an animal level of sexual hunger. That prospect was the most arousing aspect of dominating him. She wanted him, too, but she wanted him begging for the privilege. She grinned.

The man now stood before her, wary, but intensely interested in the situation.

"What's your name?" Meg asked.

"Ron."

"Ron," she dipped her head. "I'm picking out a shirt for Daniel. What color do you think? I thought the white might work."

Ron glanced at Daniel's naked chest in open appreciation. Meg felt a slight quiver run through the muscles under her fingers. Ron turned to the rack and selected a shirt similar to the one she'd chosen, only it was dark blue. Rather than the simple slit neckline, it was laced down the front, with the lacing open so a modest band of flesh and hair would be visible almost to the abdomen.

"I like it," Meg nodded. "What do you think, Patrice?"

"It's beautiful, ma'am. His dark coloring will look excellent in it."

"Ron, do you have the right size? If you need to hold it up to him or touch him to determine the best fit, please do. But don't speak to him. He only speaks with my permission."

The quiver was unmistakable this time. Daniel was actually trembling. Ron hesitated, and Meg glanced up at Daniel's forbidding expression.

"Daniel," Meg warned.

He swallowed, tightening his jaw to granite. "I'm at the mercy of my lady's wishes."

Ron looked between the two of them, then smiled. He understood. This was a game known to them all.

He circled the rounder, coming up behind Daniel. Meg kept her hand on his hard stomach, gently keeping him from turning like a cornered animal. Ron held the shirt to Daniel's shoulders, then lowered it. He touched Daniel with one fingertip, outlining his shoulder muscle. "Impressive. It explains why his clothing is specially tailored. The trouser cut is particularly well done." His hand went lower. He paused briefly, a glance at Meg. She inclined her head and Ron's hand smoothed the tweed fabric over Daniel's left buttock, dipped and ran up under the right before he slid his palm up Daniel's back. "You'll need an X-large for those shoulders."

Daniel was rigid, and a light sheen of sweat had appeared on his skin.

"Thank you, Ron." Meg took the shirt he extended with a mild smile. "You've been very helpful."

"The pleasure was all mine." He inclined his head, gave Daniel another long, slow perusal, then sauntered from the store.

Meg pressed herself against Daniel. His eyes had raged against Ron's attention, but his body hadn't. She resisted the carnal urge to rub against him. She put the shirt in between them.

"Put this on."

His gaze flicked to her and he took an unsteady breath, nodded. He pulled the shirt over his head, providing the visual delight of smooth muscle moving under furred skin before he tucked the soft cotton into his slacks.

The dark blue intensified the appealing danger in his gaze, strengthened the angles of his already-strong face. Patrice stood by her and, with a glance, Meg confirmed that even the icon of retail professionalism was doing her best to keep her mouth nonchalantly closed.

"All he needs is a cutlass," she murmured.

Meg smiled and stepped close to Daniel, put her hand against his face. "If you got any sexier," she breathed against his jaw, "Patrice and I would take you down together."

He turned his head and kissed her wrist, flicking his tongue over her skin. His dark eyes registered the rapid increase in her pulse with a spark of arrogance. Meg drew her hand away.

"We need some jeans for him."

"These would be perfect." Patrice went to another rack and came back with a black pair. "The belt he's wearing should match."

Meg took the jeans. Daniel unbuckled his belt, began to open his trousers.

"Wait—" She stopped him, a flush staining her cheeks.

He raised an eyebrow. "Don't you want me to put them on here?" An amused smile twisted his lips. "Or are you getting modest now?"

She composed her face, tightened her lips. "If you don't stop being so insolent," she warned, keeping her voice steady by speaking in slow, distinct syllables, "I'll call Ron back and have him put the jeans on you. How would you like that?" She sauntered close, pressing her breasts to his chest. "Perhaps we'd belt your hands above your head in the dressing room," she whispered, sliding her hand under his arm to stroke his back muscles with languorous fingers. "Ron could strip off your trousers and pull these up your legs, tugging tight over your... ass." The whisper covered her slight falter, because she saw no flicker of arrogance now. "When he tucks the shirt in, I'm sure he wouldn't be able to resist stroking you." Meg watched his eyes as she touched the tip of her tongue to her lip. "Eventually,

I'm sure he'd get around to zipping the fly. Maybe you'd like me to call him. I'm sure he's nearby."

A muscle twisted in his cheek. Daniel's eyes burned with a combination of desire and fury so hot she was afraid they might catch fire. She tested it, pushed the jeans against him. "Go put them on. Now."

He put his hand behind her neck and she slapped a restraining hand on his chest. "I didn't give you permission to touch me." She held her breath until his hand eased back to his side in a clenched fist. His eyes closed and his breath was a hot, exasperated sigh on her temple.

Meg smiled, rubbing against his wonderful pectorals. She liked how her nipples stiffened while he could do nothing but stare and feel their hard points pressing into his flesh. She stepped back, made a show of viewing herself in the mirrors placed outside the dressing room, cupping the underside of her breasts to examine how aroused she'd become. He stood next to her in silent, vibrating frustration.

"Go, now. Shoo." She grinned at his reaction, a sardonic twist to his lips.

When he disappeared into the dressing room, she dropped her hands and sank on trembling knees into a chair conveniently left next to the mirrors. She felt like a lion tamer. Daniel of the lions. How far would his control last? Why did she have such a reckless desire to know?

Patrice came over, quiet, solicitous, and astonishingly impassive of expression again.

"How did you know his size, Patrice?"

The woman lifted an elegant shoulder. "It's part of my job, madam. You should like the fit. That particular style—it's not tight, but it is snug. It'll hold him...in a pleasing way."

"Thank you."

Patrice left her to attend the needs of the other two patrons, needs Meg suspected were certainly a little more mundane than hers and Daniel's. She gazed at the dresses with her eyes, but her focus was inward, grasping for control of the overwhelming urge to follow him into the dressing room and attack him, have carnal knowledge of him in every way possible. She was in control of him, but she was losing control of herself, discovering a pure, wanton side she hadn't known existed. Rather than being appalled, she was gazing back on her subconscious with a feral grin etched on her lips.

She heard his footsteps and felt him approach, much as she knew she'd feel the presence of a wild animal loose in her room in the middle of the night, even if she were sound asleep. She shifted and faced him.

The jeans fit perfectly. Patrice was definitely the fairy godmother of bondage fashion. The material hugged his hips and cradled his testicles and cock in an obvious but not blatant way, a way that would draw women's eyes.

Meg lifted a finger as he approached, indicating he should turn. Daniel glanced around self-consciously, but obeyed. With a hot gaze and wet, slightly parted lips, she openly admired the way the muscles of his backside shifted beneath the denim. She wondered what it would be like to take him back into the dressing room, make him stand before her like this, while she sat on the crushed velvet of the Victorian chair and brought herself to climax with her own fingers. She imagined the crotch of his jeans growing tighter and tighter, trying to contain his erection, as he was allowed to do nothing but watch, forbidden to touch himself or her.

God, she was sweating, and he was watching her with a knowing, aroused look in his beautiful eyes. She rose and motioned that he should turn away. When his back was to her, she took his duster from the rounder and guided it onto his arms, helping him shrug it on.

"We have to find a pay phone. It's almost six o'clock, and Deb said she'd pick me up at seven." She took his arm and led him from the store.

"There's some." He nodded at a rotunda of phones in the middle of the mall.

"I don't want those." She kept walking, enjoying the looks women cast over Daniel, even enjoying some of the looks men gave her. They were a pair surrounded by sensuality and everyone they passed absorbed it, responded to it. Daniel glared at a man eyeing her too appreciatively in her sheer dress, and Meg felt a tightening in her chest. The sweet craving of being possessed, the tortuous pleasure of possessing.

Outside Belk's, a short hallway led to a single pay phone and a fire exit. The sign over the exit illuminated the hall with a dim red glow.

She drew him into the shadowed hall and retrieved the quarter she'd asked Patrice to place in his duster. She made sure she took her time, stroking her fingers along his hard thigh. "You have an incredible body," she murmured, and savored his slight flush of embarrassment. She was certain Daniel knew he was an attractive man, but she also knew that having someone admire you when you were at their mercy was unnerving because you couldn't protect yourself with a denial. No walls were allowed. He had to keep himself vulnerable to her, which meant he couldn't retreat from any of her desires, even the desire to stroke him verbally.

"I want you to call Deb." She pressed the quarter into his palm. "Tell her I'm fine. Tell her you'll bring me home. Later."

He nodded, reached for the phone. Meg stopped him with a hand on his forearm. "No matter what I do, you'll keep talking to her and you'll keep your free hand on the shelf below the phone. You understand?"

He nodded, his sensual mouth tight. She softened, tracing his lips with her fingers. "Are you all right?"

"I've..." He cleared his throat. "This is new for me. I'm off balance."

She nodded, then dropped the leash, so to speak, and put her arms around him, hugging him. She laid her head on his chest, nestling, letting him feel strong again. "We can stop if you want."

He shook his head. "I'm yours to command, Meg. Get tougher or you won't learn anything." He shrugged her off and stepped back.

She didn't take offense at his abruptness because she saw him swallow, had felt the tremor run through him before he backed away. He was a powerful man, used to being in charge. He probably couldn't remember the last time he'd lost control of a situation. She couldn't remember the last time she had had it.

She straightened, stared him straight in the eye, and slapped his face, hard. She liked it. She did it again to his other cheek. He stood obediently, taking it.

"Make the call. I don't want to see anything but pleasure from my commands again."

He turned, put the coin in and began to dial. Meg's stomach lurched. *He knew the number by heart.* She slipped her hand inside the duster and went straight for his ass. She fondled and squeezed as the phone rang. She heard a man's voice answer, Jeremy.

"Yes, may I speak to Deborah? This is Daniel."

She slid down the front of his body and knelt beneath the phone, her actions curtained by his coat.

Daniel looked down, startled. "Meg, what— Deborah, hello. Yes, I—"

Meg unbuckled his belt and unfastened his jeans, working the zipper over what lay so temptingly beneath. A quick glance showed he was obeying her, his palm flat on the metal shelf, but his knuckles were white on the phone.

"We met just as planned—"

She peeled back cotton black underwear and his erection stretched before her.

"Ron, you don't know what impressive is," she murmured. She rubbed her cheek against him and slid her hands around his hips. She pulled his pants down far enough so she could grip his bare cheeks in both hands. He was hard everywhere.

His voice was suddenly gruff. "We had dinner," he lied.

Meg opened her mouth and took in as much of him as she could. He was enormous, like the rest of him. His hand touched her hair and she sank her teeth in lightly. His hand returned to the shelf and she made a noise of satisfaction. She began to slide up and down his shaft, sucking as hard as she wanted, which was as hard as she could manage.

Daniel pressed the phone into his shoulder. "Jesus, God, Meg," he groaned.

She slapped his ass.

"Yes, Deborah, I'm here. Meg is fine. We bought her a new dress and..." His breathing shuddered. "Some jewelry... Yes, she seems to like being with me—"

Meg chuckled against his cock and took more, pumping harder.

"Aaannd, yes, she said I could drop her off later, if that's all right. We'll probably catch a movie..." His hips were beginning to move and she sensed the imminent explosion building in his loins. She felt her own wetness on her calves, beneath her bottom.

"She wants to talk to you," Daniel rasped.

She pulled her mouth free, slowly, tasting every inch, savoring his shaft like chocolate. His eyes were closed. Daniel held the phone in a grip so tight, she was surprised the hard plastic didn't crush in his palm. Meg took the phone from his hand and turned her back to him. She drew her skirt to the side like a horse's tail and rubbed her bare bottom against the tip of his erection.

"Hello, Deb. I just found this wonderful thing I want Daniel to see, so we'd better go."

He was as still as hot air behind her, and twice as palpable.

"Are you sure things are going okay, Meg? I wasn't sure that letting Daniel meet you like this was such a good idea. I just..."

"It's all right. Things are fine—"

"No, I know. I just… if you're mad about anything, I don't want you to be mad at him. Be mad at me."

"I couldn't be mad at you, Deb."

Daniel moved against her. He bent his knees slightly, ran his hands up her legs beneath the skirt to her hips. Before she could turn a commanding glance on him, to bid him behave, he lifted her in one effortless motion. He took her from behind, plunging his cock into her to the hilt.

Meg needed no words to know that Daniel had taken back the reins of control. She caught at the metal housing of the phone and sucked in her breath at the fullness. Pulling her back against his chest, he held her secure with an arm around her waist, his large hand collaring her throat. Her head fell to his shoulder, her breasts thrusting upward. Sliding his arm from her waist, he cupped one of them in his palm, toyed with her nipple. Her hips jolted against him. She couldn't tell where she stopped and he began, save for an explosion of sensation, a sensation so strong it was like a point of origin, not just a joining. It was the creation of a new being.

"Deb, I…" she whispered.

"When he called me, he was just this stranger who'd found you at the park," Deb continued over her. "When I got to the hospital, I barely looked at him. It didn't occur to me he'd even stay. Then I found out he'd already handled the police. He even gave me the doctor's preliminary report. I didn't know if you had any medical insurance, so he got the number of your office from me and called your workplace. I didn't know you'd quit three weeks prior, of course. Daniel told me not to worry about it. He gave them some kind of bank number and said he'd take care of your bills. He wouldn't let Jeremy or me or anyone else argue, even your mom."

He pressed deeper inside her. His lips traced the pulse along her neck.

"When you woke the first time, you were cuffed to the bed. Do you remember that?"

Meg shook her head. "No, I don't."

"You went ballistic. I was there and told Daniel we needed to call someone. He said no. He released you and pulled you into his lap. Meg, you calmed right down. You were like a baby curled in his arms. The doctor had to pry your fingers from his collar to get you back into bed."

His hand left her breast, slid down the front of her body and scraped the satin moisture between her legs. Sensation spiraled, an ascent toward an unbearable climax woven by his touch and Deb's words.

"I don't remember him..." she said faintly.

"You were so out of it that first night. Then there was that awful catatonia where you weren't aware of anything for weeks. God, Meg, I wanted to kill Tommy or make him come down and see what he'd done to you. Daniel said no, that you were deep in your head by your own choosing and it was up to you to come back. It's so incredible, now that I think about it, how we all took his words as gospel. He had this way about him. I've been going crazy this afternoon, thinking how little I really know about him and wondering about you."

"I'm...fine." She tried to push him, but his hand tightened on her throat and he thrust deeply into her. Meg bit her lip, strangling a moan.

"We spent a lot of time in that room together, watching you," Deb continued. "He made me talk about Tommy. It was so strange. He seemed to figure out all sorts of things that I hadn't, but the moment he said them, I thought, yeah, that's Meg all over."

"Like what?" she rasped.

"He said that loving someone is more important to you than anything—your job, your goals, your identity. You wrap your whole heart and soul into it. He said he thought you needed someone stronger than you, someone who could take control, take possession of you so you'd never doubt that person's love. Anything less and you'd be afraid, always thinking you'd have to stay in control of a relationship to hold onto it."

His teeth sank into her neck, a stallion demanding submission to his mounting. It was a menage-a-trois with Deb an unwitting participant in an act that was driving Meg to a perilous height of pleasure. When she went over the edge, she was going to smash on the raw edges of her emotions.

Daniel withdrew and thrust into her again, harder and slower this time. When he reached his full length, he stopped, holding her tight against him. His cock pressed deep, resting against the spot that made her knees weak. Searing pleasure rippled out and Meg struggled, wanting to let loose, ride him wildly to relieve the pleasure and block the pain before the roller coaster reached the top where the two opposite forces would rip her apart. His powerful hands dug into her hips, holding her body motionless.

"Your mom spent time with him, too," Deb said. "It helped her, Meg. She thought it was her fault you were there."

She closed her eyes, not wanting to hear the words that had hammered against the inside of her skull every time she'd looked into her mother's pain-filled, confused eyes. She pressed the mouthpiece of the phone into her neck. "Please stop, Daniel," she begged.

He shook his head against the side of hers. "No, Meg."

It was like she must experience it together, his mastery, his desire, her pain and regret, her return to life. She was being reborn, only this time she was fully cognizant of the crushing pressure of the birth canal.

"She even took him to your apartment," Deb said. "I've never seen her talk so easily to anyone. She showed him your baby pictures, told him a thousand stories about you. I know we probably shouldn't have done that, Meg, but we were desperate."

His fingers dipped, pattering a gentle tattoo against her clitoris like rain drops. "Spread your legs wider for me, Meg," he breathed against her ear.

The ache in her chest expanded, but her legs obeyed, her body supported by the strength of his arms.

"We trusted him, Meg. He brought you out of that first really bad funk you fell into. He visited you one morning and, the next thing I knew, he was calling to say you were awake. And it didn't stop there. When you slipped back the second time, your mom called Daniel before she even called the doctor. He told us to take you to a children's piano recital at Thalian Hall that day. Do you remember?"

She shook her head and felt the first tear touch the corner of her mouth. "No," she lied.

"You didn't respond at first and I was sitting next to you, thinking he was nuts. Then this little girl sat down and played 'Pop, goes the Weasel.' You snapped out of it halfway through the song, and started crying."

The image of a white dress, red velvet sash, pink ribbon in fine black hair went through her mind. Short fingers hurrying along the keys, too fast, nervous, wanting to finish it.

"The next time you went under, he told us to take you to the butterfly gardens. Another time he told me to put a seashell to your ear, then another time, Jeremy and I were just supposed to sit with you on the porch and hold your hands while the sun set. It all worked, every time. It was like he could get into your head when you'd locked out everyone else. Your mom said the doctors were treating your head, but Daniel was treating your heart."

A thin stream of tears tracked down her cheek, tears as vibrant as the fluid making her slippery for him. The knot in her throat had become a goose egg under his hand. Meg swallowed and it started to crack, the flood of anguish and arousal too powerful to be contained by its fragile, pale wall. Her body shuddered, the tremor before a quake.

"Deb, I've got to — "

"Oh, I know, I didn't mean to babble. You just sound...different. Like you're really there. I was so worried, Meg." Deb's voice trembled slightly and the agony compressed like a vise around Meg's heart. "I guess I should have known he'd take care of you, just like he did that very first time he brought you out of the funk."

"What..." She closed her eyes as the hand at her throat loosened so his fingertip could outline her breast. His other hand continued to hold her pinioned fast on him. "What did he do?"

"I had a hard time getting that out of him. But, not too long ago, I asked again. He just said he told you a story about a tree house."

The world stilled, and the sun disappeared behind a cloud. She stiffened. "Deborah, I have to go."

"But — "

"I'm fine, but I have to go." She hung up the phone and tried to pull herself away from him. It was futile, of course. Daniel simply tightened his grip and held her still with his hand collared around her throat again. "Let me go." She jerked her head to the right, trying to stay out of range of his lips. "What did you tell me about tree houses?"

He nuzzled her ear. "Why does it upset you?"

"You invade my life, you pry into my memories, you take advantage of me — " Her voice rose shrilly. She choked against his hold and coughed. *This is what she should have done from the beginning, she should have walked away from him, that damn dress...*

"Meg..." His hold loosened, but he didn't release her. "Calm down."

"I will not, you bast — "

He took her by the shoulders and pulled out of her. Meg gasped as he forced her against the cinder block wall in the shadows beside the phone housing. He held her with just the weight of his body and she heard the crinkle of a wrapper as he withdrew something from his coat.

"Daniel, no—"

His hands manacled her wrists, crucifying her to the cold, hard surface. He parted her knees with one leg like an experienced cop and entered her backside with one thrust, the lubricated condom making it a smooth, irresistible entry.

"Daniel—" She bucked, frightened.

"Behave, Meg."

"You can't—"

"I just did. Every part of you is mine, Meg. You'll deny me nothing. Your ass grips me just as tightly as every other part of you. Your whole body knows what your mind keeps resisting—you're mine. Feel that." He withdrew, then slid back into her. "Relax and feel it, Meg."

It was an odd sensation, not the immediate, pleasurable gratification that came from the friction on her clitoris, but she rubbed her quivering cheeks against him despite herself.

"Please," she whispered. "Please don't do this to me."

"Do what to you, Meg?" He pressed against her back, driving deeper, opening her legs wider to accommodate him. He laced his fingers into hers. When he spoke, she heard his voice through her chest, resonating like they shared the same heart.

"It was in your diary. The way your father betrayed your mother, your pain for her. Your pain for yourself. In the middle of your thoughts, you wrote memories of your father. You wrote about being in the woods, tagging along with your brother and his friend when you were little. He teased you, called you a baby, and to prove you weren't, you climbed into his tree house. But you were afraid and couldn't climb down, and you wouldn't let your brother help you. You screamed and cried when he tried to climb up and get you. So they went for help."

"Stop." She shut her eyes, pressed her forehead into the rough concrete.

"No. Your father and one of your neighbors came into the woods, riding their bikes. You couldn't remember if it was your father who got you down. Your father was afraid of heights. You wanted to remember that it was him who rescued you, but you couldn't remember if it had been him or not."

"I didn't write that."

"No, you didn't." He released her hands, left them curled helplessly against the cement, and cupped her breasts in his massive hands. He squeezed, then pumped slow, even strokes into her that wrung a moan from her throat. "But it was there to put together. You wanted to believe that he loved you enough to overcome his fears for you. You wanted to believe that, no matter the strength of the storm, when the time came, your father's love would be stronger. He'd stand and prove that his feelings for you and your family were stronger than the sum total of his weaknesses. You wanted to be sure of that, but you never will be, because he died soon after you and Tommy got married. You couldn't remember if it had ever been true, even for that one instant in the tree house.

"I was looking for the password, Meg. You'd locked out the world and buried the key somewhere in your life. When I read about the tree house, I knew. That was it. The safety, the security, the foundation of unconditional love. It was the only gift large enough, tempting enough, to turn you away from the promise of death."

Her body convulsed on a sob, and he wrapped his arms around her, holding her inside his strength. "All I had to do was convince you that I had it, Meg. I came to your room that morning. I knelt by your bed, took your hand…"

It flashed before her, the tall, dark-eyed man, kneeling at her side, so strong his presence had filled her mind. The hospital room had slipped away.

"You told me you were going to carry me out of the tree house." She wept against the press of his palm against her cheek. "All I had to do was reach for you."

He nodded against her hair. "You did. My sweet, brave Meg. You didn't believe any man could ever love you enough, but I will. It's trust that turns control into freedom. I've brought you down from the tree house, and I'll bring you down every time you get trapped up there, every time you're afraid to come down alone. Your father and everyone else be damned. I love you, and I'll keep you through better or worse as long as we live, no matter what you do or say."

She'd waited for the promise of love to give her back the sense of safety she'd lost. She thought she'd found it with Tommy, but then she'd found herself back in that tree house. No, it had been worse than that; she'd found she had never left it, as if her whole relationship with him had been a pointless soap opera dream sequence. It had taken her to the edge of madness.

Somehow, she'd found the courage to reach out toward the promise of a stranger. He'd clasped her to him in her darkest moment in a white room flooded with a sunrise, and now he told her to believe with all of her fragile, healing heart that he'd never let her fall. Maybe he would or maybe he wouldn't, but suddenly she didn't want the safe pain of the darkness anymore. She wanted the chance that the dream might be true.

"Daniel." Words barely made it past the thick emotion in her voice. "Please, please let me see your face."

He went rigid. For a long moment, they stood still, his body pressed against hers, his cock penetrating her, his breath hot on her neck. Then he pulled out of her. He bade her keep her cheek to the wall a moment longer, and she listened to the soft rustling as he removed the condom he'd donned and arranged his clothes before he turned her to face him, taking a firm hold on her shoulders.

Harsh lines cut deep around his eyes. The command and possessiveness hadn't slipped, but now she also saw the absolute love, and the raw anguish of need.

"Why would you want me, Daniel?" she said. "I've lost my heart."

"I have your heart." He cradled her face in his two large hands, gently kissing her nose. "I picked it up off the ground at

Winfield and I've never let it go. You've still got only one choice to make, Meg. Wear the necklace or not."

She closed her eyes and her lashes pressed into more hot tears. He put his hand beneath her chin, demanded she meet his gaze as she made her choice. He'd shelter her from all harm, but he'd never let her hide from herself. He'd planted a delicate seed of trust inside her, nurtured it and brought it into bloom.

He'd taken her heart, her body. Her mind was the one thing she must offer freely. Entering the lion's den, rescuing her from the tree house, he'd saved her life and declared his love for her. It was an oath bound in her own blood.

Stepping away, she lifted her arms and found the catch to the necklace. She released it, pulling the braided strands from her throat. Lifting his hand in the cup of her trembling one, she folded the jewel into his palm, closed his fingers over it. Tension shimmered and fear struggled in his eyes. His jaw tightened, preparing for a battle he might not win.

She raised her free hand to his lips. "I don't have to wear it, Daniel," she said. "You've put it here, around my heart, around my soul. Make love to me, Daniel. Please."

His arms banded around her and he yanked her to him, crushing his lips to hers. She opened his jeans with trembling fingers, then wrapped her arms around his neck. His hands slid to her waist and he lifted her onto him, pressing them both against the wall. Locking her legs around his hips, she moaned fiercely as his cock sank into her.

"Are you all mine, Meg?" He buried one hand in her hair, thrust hard into her, pressing her thighs wide to accommodate him. Her breasts strained against the blue shirt and the man beneath.

"I belong to you, Daniel," she gasped. "Heart—"

He withdrew and slid slowly back into her canal.

"Body—" Her breath hissed as he did it again.

"Mind—oh God!" He was torturing her, each stroke igniting fire in her sensitive tissues. She gripped his back, dug in her nails. "Oh, Daniel."

"You're mine, Meg. All mine."

"Yes, Daniel. Please, let me come for you. Please."

"Not yet. I love you, Meg."

She groaned, begged.

"Tell me what's mine, Meg."

"I am, I am. Oh God…" The world turned orange and she spasmed, clawed, bit his shoulder and screamed against his flesh. "I love you, Daniel. I love you…"

His body trembled with control, and he kept the strokes even, slow, pressing her hard against the wall so she couldn't pump and shorten the experience. The carousel whirled faster and faster, she spun higher and higher, and she was sure lightning flashed before her eyes. His powerful hands slid under her thighs, pulled them up high so she couldn't shy from the full crash of the tidal wave. Her legs snapped out straight like wings and she took flight.

"Daaaaannnnieeellll……"

Her cry pierced the air like the yearning of a mourning dove, a low, passionate cry that whispered along the air currents of the mall and touched each person it passed like the sensual memory of a cherished lover.

When the carousel came to a slow, musical halt, Meg collapsed weakly back against the wall, his grip still strong on her waist. He was still hard inside her and her body shuddered at every tiny movement against her blood-filled flesh. He was speaking to her. Again. Again.

The world came into focus and she heard her name. "Meg." He pushed her hair from her face and kissed her lips, her eyes, her cheeks. "I love you, Meg. Who do *I* belong to?"

She looked into his proud, relentless face, a face filled with love and barely-restrained passion. Against the laws of medical science, she was able to hook her hand behind his neck and haul her body up his, sinking further down his hard length again. "You belong to me," she managed. "Forever."

Inside her body, inside her heart, inside her mind, he shuddered and gave control to her at last. The warm current of his seed took hold of her and she gave herself to him completely, making the gift a circle.

* * * * *

They picked up her things at Patrice's store. Meg went very still when she looked at the logo on the silver foil bag. She walked outside and studied the store name with a trace of a smile playing on her face. So many things had escaped her notice lately. That was going to change.

"A long time ago, when we believed in fairy tales…" Warm breath and a familiar, timbered voice filled her ear. "A fairy princess found the courage to assume mortal form and take back her dress. She refused to let the pain of mortality destroy her."

She'd been that fairy princess and the touch of mortality had driven her mad, stripped away her faith and left her isolated, alone. Deep within her was still that connection to pure life, to the sense of what was wild and true, and Daniel of the lions had found it. He'd heal her broken soul with love and an unconditional acceptance of every part of her.

"She wasn't as strong as she thought she had to be." Meg raised a hand to his jaw. "So a protector came, devoted to her, body and soul, and brought her magic back to her. He was the magic."

Daniel took her elbow, caressing it with strong fingers. She switched the bag so she could put her arm around him and they walked away from the dress shop known as *Make Her Dreams Come True*.

Enjoy this excerpt from

Natural Law

© Copyright Joey W. Hill, 2004

Natural Law

ဢ

"I've got a meeting with the captain at ten, Mac." Sergeant Darla Rowe took a seat behind her desk and lifted a brow as one of her top people closed her door before taking a seat before her. She straightened, put her hands on her desk, one folded over the other. "What's on your mind, Detective?"

"We found a second body last night," Mac said, forcing himself to sit back in the chair and ignore the painful knot low in his belly. The dead kid he'd just stood over had had a much worse day than he was having, no matter how bad his sergeant's reaction was going to be.

He'd been working in her squad over two years, and he trusted her. She had a level head, an unfathomable patience for bureaucrats, but no tolerance for bullshit, and she was loyal and fair to her people. He was counting heavily on fair, but he was venturing into territory where fair was often drowned by moral reaction.

"Same MO. Mid to late twenties male. Worked as a stockbroker. Good WASP background, church-goer. He was dressed in a leather thong, dog collar, cuffed spread-eagle to his four poster bed, dildo up his ass, begging your pardon. Bullet in the base of his skull."

"Detective Ramsey said she thought that the murderer may resent the victims' social standing, may be trying to humiliate them." Rowe nodded. "Have we been able to keep a lid on the press?"

"No leaks on the way the vic was found. We've told them it appears to be a sex crime, bullet to the head, but that's all." Mac lifted a shoulder. "Connie has good instincts, but we're still waiting for the official psych profile, and it doesn't mesh to me. If the perp was trying to humiliate them publicly, I'd think she'd have sent pictures to the paper by now."

"She?"

"Nail gouges on the victim's back suggest it, but they were done with gloves on. We're doing DNA checks. In both cases a caller has contacted one of the parents, told them that they have to come right away because there's an emergency at the victim's home. I think she's revealing the truth about the victim, perhaps reenacting a similar trauma that happened to her, or something she wants to reveal about herself but never has gotten the chance or the guts to do it. Just amateur analysis, granted, but it smells right."

Darla's eyes narrowed. "'Revealing the truth'?"

"Yes, ma'am. Both men frequented a fetish club called The Zone in Tampa. I had a uniform go down there today, talk to the manager, confirm their memberships with a warrant to pull their specific records. They were very cooperative as soon as they understood their members could be in danger. They'll be a helpful ally. I think our murderess is a practicing sexual Dominant, a Mistress, and she's choosing her victims from The Zone, even if she's not playing with them there. Granted, two victims doesn't establish a definite pattern—"

Rowe sat back, her brows lifted. "But it does give us some lead on her preferred trawling grounds. Excellent work, Detective. Who called the families?"

"A man, both times. Called from a pay phone, but it's suspected from the speech patterns described by the parents that the caller was a drifter or homeless person the perp paid to make the call. Different men, based on the voices described. We're casing the local liquor and convenience stores near the booths to which we traced the calls to see if the store employees remember a homeless person coming in and dropping an unusual amount of money for a bottle of booze in the past forty-eight hours. However, both calls were made from the worst areas of Tampa, so it's likely they've rabbited and we can take our pick of a few thousand drifters."

"So how did you make The Zone connection? Business card for The Zone in their wallets?"

Mac hesitated. "No, ma'am. Both victims were extremely circumspect about their lifestyles. That gels with the reputation of The Zone. The club even provides lockers there for members to keep their paraphernalia, so it's not kept in the home. They don't give out member ID cards. They put your social security on file and when you come, you enter it into the entry key pad. That's how you get in." He shifted. "I've done a little research."

Sergeant Darla Rowe had seen Mac Nighthorse come out of situations that would give nightmares to the most grizzled veteran. He'd started his career in undercover work, proving himself so adept at deep cover and maintaining the integrity of his personality in that high stress area, that they'd kept him in it for over five years. When he'd advanced into public field work, he quickly obtained his Detective rating, working cases 24/7 to solve murders, armed robberies, kidnappings. She'd listened to wire taps of him breaking up volatile drug deals. A few months ago, he had taken down a Tampa serial killer one-on-one in the cramped quarters of the sewer system when the killer had gone to ground there with an AK47. Mac had been disarmed, his arm broken during the fight, and had brought the killer down with nothing but determination and a healthy dose of fury. He didn't freeze, and he wasn't cocky. He was so steady the other guys called him The Oak, not just because of his size, but because of that unflappable demeanor, no matter the circumstances.

At the moment, she was watching the wooden arm of her visitor chair grow slick with nervous sweat from his palm.

"What's on your mind here, Mac?" she asked, pointedly glancing at the damp surface.

He stared at it, then lifted his hand, leaned forward and clasped both hands loosely between his splayed knees. It emphasized his broad shoulders, the long columns of his thighs. As usual, Darla sternly forced her gaze off the nice shape of his groin outlined by the dress slacks. Since she was happily married, it was aesthetic appreciation only, but it wasn't exactly professional to be caught eyeing the crotch of one of her detectives. She had often wondered why Mac didn't have a woman in his life, but suddenly she got the feeling she was about to find out why.

"To find her, we're going to need to send someone undercover in The Zone. She's picking up submissives, that's the terminology, winning their trust, so she's likely already working her next target."

"So we pull in an undercover team."

He shook his head. "That won't work, Sarge. This isn't a seedy adult club where the criminals mix with the thrill seekers. The activity at The Zone is legal, and the clientele is high dollar. This is about sexual gratification, not perversion." He raked a hand through his hair. "It's not the same as the criminal side. To most people in the vanilla world it looks that way, but it's the difference between a murder and a natural death. One is forced coercion. The other one's about natural law. A cop who doesn't understand that would stand out so clearly he might as well wear his badge pinned on his chest."

Darla sat back. "I'm going to repeat my question, Mac. Why don't you tell me what's going on between the lines here?"

He nodded, looked down at his big hands, laced them together, then he raised his face so he met her expression square on with those silver eyes that could freeze a criminal in his tracks or pry the truth out of the most devious snitch. Right now, they looked like they were facing the prospect of a prostate exam with Andre the Giant donning the latex gloves.

"I know those types of clubs, Sarge. I've been part of the D/s scene since I was in my late twenties. I know the language and the people. The Zone isn't my usual haunt. It's out of my income bracket." A light smile touched his lips. "But every club has a certain percentage of new blood running through it, guests of members, prospective members, people who try it out for a couple months."

"I see." She tapped two fingers on the desk, a meditative gesture that the men and women of her squad recognized as a sign she was mulling things over in her head. "And if you're made as a cop? You're a little well-established to be doing undercover work again."

"It might not rouse suspicion, particularly if it's obvious I'm part of the scene. A cop who plays in those waters would have as much interest in concealing his or her profession as any of the well-heeled clientele. On the floor, most use assumed or first names only. The rule is, if you happen to see someone you know on the street, you either pretend you don't know them, or that you met them at a mainstream place, like a bar. That's how I made the connection. I recognized the second victim. He's been at my usual club before, several times, but I knew The Zone was his preferred digs."

He sat back, sliding back on the familiar ground of the case, trying to ignore that his sergeant's gaze was as intense as a dentist's drill on him.

"Robert Myers was a submissive. High-powered, but amiable. Enjoyed having a woman dominate him with soft bondage techniques, but he could accommodate a higher level. I don't know if that figures into the MO or if there's some other aspect of the two men that was the attraction. The psych profile may help me figure that part out. I'm expecting that in a couple of days. Neither of them would have let his dick overrule good sense. Again, begging your pardon, ma'am. They would have spent some time with the murderess before taking her into their home, or they would have already known her in the scene."

"Do you have someone on the inside you can use as your initial connection to the place?"

"Not at this point, but I should be able to pick up someone. It's not unusual to connect with someone there for play. Sometimes it sticks for a few days, sometimes just for the night, but by then you get to be a known face."

"How will you bring in your backup?"

He shook his head. "I won't be able to do that in this scenario. Unless they're part of the lifestyle, they would be made as fast as a cop trying to pass himself off as a dope addict. I figure I could keep Consuela – Detective Ramsey – informed of my itinerary and whereabouts through the usual call-in set up."

"You going in as a Dominant or a submissive?"

Mac blinked. "A sub. Makes more sense that way."

"I'm not seeing anyone buying you as someone's whipping boy, Mac. Not with your size and presence."

She watched him lace, unlace his fingers again, lean forward, and felt the shock run down to her toes at the truth she saw in his pained expression.

"It's best I go in under my own preference."

"Well, I'll be damned," she said at last.

About the Author

ຂາ

Joey W. Hill is published in mainstream, paranormal and erotic romance, as well as epic fantasy. Most of her erotic romance falls into the BDSM genre. She has won the Dream Realms Award for Fantasy and the EPPIE award for Erotic Romance. Nominated for the CAPA award and the PEARL, she also has received many gold star reviews from Just Erotic Romance Reviews, multiple Blue Ribbon reviews from Romance Junkies, and a Reviewer's Choice award from Road to Romance. She regularly garners five star reviews from erotic romance review sites. In 1999, she won the Grand Prize in the annual short story contest sponsored by Romance & Beyond magazine.

Following the dictates of a very capricious muse, she often brings in unexpected elements to a storyline – spirituality into erotic romance, paranormal aspects to a contemporary storyline, an alpha male who may believably perform as a submissive… all with intriguing and absorbing results for the reader. As one reviewer put it: "I should know by now that Ms. Hill doesn't write like anyone else." All of her erotic works emphasize strong, emotional characterization and the healing power of love through sexual expression.

Joey welcomes mail from readers. You can write to her c/o Ellora's Cave Publishing at 1056 Home Avenue, Akron OH 44310-3502.

Why an electronic book?

We live in the Information Age—an exciting time in the history of human civilization in which technology rules supreme and continues to progress in leaps and bounds every minute of every hour of every day. For a multitude of reasons, more and more avid literary fans are opting to purchase e-books instead of paperbacks. The question to those not yet initiated to the world of electronic reading is simply: *why?*

1. *Price.* An electronic title at Ellora's Cave Publishing and Cerridwen Press runs anywhere from 40-75% less than the cover price of the <u>exact same title</u> in paperback format. Why? Cold mathematics. It is less expensive to publish an e-book than it is to publish a paperback, so the savings are passed along to the consumer.

2. *Space.* Running out of room to house your paperback books? That is one worry you will never have with electronic novels. For a low one-time cost, you can purchase a handheld computer designed specifically for e-reading purposes. Many e-readers are larger than the average handheld, giving you plenty of screen room. Better yet, hundreds of titles can be stored within your new library—a single microchip. (Please note that Ellora's Cave and Cerridwen Press does not endorse any specific brands. You can check our website at www.ellorascave.com or

www.cerridwenpress.com for customer recommendations we make available to new consumers.)

3. *Mobility.* Because your new library now consists of only a microchip, your entire cache of books can be taken with you wherever you go.

4. *Personal preferences are accounted for.* Are the words you are currently reading too small? Too large? Too...**ANNOYING**? Paperback books cannot be modified according to personal preferences, but e-books can.

5. *Instant gratification.* Is it the middle of the night and all the bookstores are closed? Are you tired of waiting days—sometimes weeks—for online and offline bookstores to ship the novels you bought? Ellora's Cave Publishing sells instantaneous downloads 24 hours a day, 7 days a week, 365 days a year. Our e-book delivery system is 100% automated, meaning your order is filled as soon as you pay for it.

Those are a few of the top reasons why electronic novels are displacing paperbacks for many an avid reader. As always, Ellora's Cave and Cerridwen Press welcomes your questions and comments. We invite you to email us at service@ellorascave.com, service@cerridwenpress.com or write to us directly at: 1056 Home Ave. Akron OH 44310-3502.

THE
⚥ ELLORA'S CAVE ⚥
LIBRARY

Stay up to date with Ellora's Cave Titles in
Print with our Quarterly Catalog.

TO RECIEVE A CATALOG,
SEND AN EMAIL WITH YOUR NAME
AND MAILING ADDRESS TO:

CATALOG@ELLORASCAVE.COM

OR SEND A LETTER OR POSTCARD
WITH YOUR MAILING ADDRESS TO:

CATALOG REQUEST
c/o ELLORA'S CAVE PUBLISHING, INC.
1056 HOME AVENUE
AKRON, OHIO 44310-3502

erridwen, the Celtic Goddess of wisdom, was the muse who brought inspiration to storytellers and those in the creative arts. Cerridwen Press encompasses the best and most innovative stories in all genres of today's fiction. Visit our site and discover the newest titles by talented authors who still get inspired - much like the ancient storytellers did, once upon a time.

Cerridwen Press

www.cerridwenpress.com